FRAT WARS

MASTER OF MAYHEM

SAXON JAMES

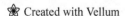 Created with Vellum

DEDICATION

This one is for Chet
Always hilarious, ridiculous and unexpected

1

_____

ROBBIE

THE SECOND BAILEY PRINCE WALKS IN THAT FRONT DOOR, I know there's gonna be a whole hell of a lot of sex noises happening this afternoon.

Too bad I'm not the one who'll be making them.

I tilt my head back from where I'm lazing on the couch, in the middle of kicking Brandon's ass at Tekken, and watch Bailey close the front door behind him. The blast of cold December air cuts off instantly, and Bailey throws an unsure smile our way.

"Hey, Chad upstairs?"

It's only been a few weeks since I found out my frat brother was dating a dude from our rival frat, and I'm still not sure how to feel about it. Having a Rho Kappa Tau member in the house is fucking weird, given the majority of my college years have been spent targeting the brothers in that house with pranks.

"Bedroom," Brandon answers.

"KO" blasts from the speakers, pulling my attention back to the TV to find the asshole kept playing while I was distracted. That little shit.

By the time I glance back toward the front door, Bailey is gone.

"I don't get how you're so chill about him always being here," I say.

Brandon shrugs, focus still on the game. "He's Doomsen's boy."

"He's also part of the frat that put you in the hospital." Because while our house might be shitheads when it comes to pranks, the Kappas took it way too far a few weeks ago, and Brandon ended up having a massive asthma attack because of their stupidity. And all in the name of King of Thieves, something that is supposed to be a friendly competition between the two houses.

"One of our pledges was the main problem, which you know," Brandon says. "Plus, they gave us back everything they stealth stole, they paid for my ambulance, and *I'm fine* for the hundredth time. As far as I'm concerned, things are back to normal."

Normal. I know they're supposed to be, but I still can't look at him without seeing him gasping for air.

I prod his thigh with my foot. "Go again."

"Urg, keep those things away from me."

"What, this?" I lift my foot to poke his ear, and he bats it away.

"You have issues."

"Me?" I snort. "I once hooked up with a chick who liked to suck on my toes. *She* had issues, brother."

Brandon cringes.

The game restarts, and we have a few blissful moments to

zone out as we beat the shit out of each other.

"Fuck, *fuck*." Brandon grunts as his character is flattened. He tosses the controller on the coffee table and drags a hand through his blond hair. "I guess I better head out."

"Going to see Jenny?"

"Some sorority tea party shit."

I laugh at the clear pain in his voice. "That's what you get for doing the relationship thing. We're in college. Most of the chicks on the row want you, and instead of taking advantage of that, you've gone and got yourself a girlfriend." Brandon is one of those guys who can get by on looks alone. Not pretty, more … *Hollywood*. Symmetrical face. Blond hair that does that perfect wave thing. The most unusual thing about his face is his vampire teeth. Girls go crazy over that shit.

"I don't have time to take advantage of anything. I'm too busy herding you idiots every weekend."

"*Hey*. I'm fucking delightful."

"You and Doomsen are going to give me a heart attack one of these days."

I frown at the throwaway phrase. Normally shit like that doesn't bother me, but after the asthma attack, I'm getting way too sensitive to it. Is it *my* fault I thought he was going to die?

As if right on cue, the telltale sounds of rhythmic thumping and moans come from overhead, and we both glance toward the sound.

"That's me out," Brandon says. "What are you doing?"

"I'll hang here."

"You don't wanna come and eat too-small sandwiches and drink out of itty-bitty cups?"

I send a grin his way because he knows what I think of tiny food. I'm a big guy at six foot four and two hundred and sixty pounds, and there's nothing I find more fun than eating shit that makes me feel like a giant.

"I'll pass." Not that I don't want to go, but because there's something I've been thinking about doing for a few days, and it isn't going to leave my brain until I balls up and do it.

He leaves, and I head for the stairs.

The sex noises are louder up here.

Usually it's not too bad because the house is full of people and the noise is canceled out, but Sunday afternoons are when most people are working or studying or nursing hangovers.

By the time I reach the hall, I have a front-row seat to a full-blown porn soundtrack … and I don't hate it.

Instead, my pulse jumps at the husky sighs and deep grunts.

When you live in a frat house, hearing your brothers have sex becomes a standard weekend, but hearing one have sex with a dude is new. There are frats with queer members all up and down the row, but until Chad came out, there were none in *this* frat. So until the last few weeks, I had no idea how hot overhearing gay sex could be.

My curiosity is running riot.

I tried watching some gay porn, but that evidence is incon-fucking-clusive, because it was sex, and *all* sex can get me off. There was also that one time, freshman year, when I hooked up with a dude by mistake. I was blind drunk, he was pretty, and I didn't put the pieces together until he whipped out his cock and told me to suck it.

So I did what any champion would do and got on my knees.

If only I could remember more than a lot of choking followed by projectile spraying his cum all over him.

I grin at Chad's closed bedroom door. Good times.

The noise inside has died down, so I give them a minute to catch their breaths before I knock.

"We're busy, asshole," Chad says.

"Sounds like you just finished up."

There's a muffled curse, and after cracking the door and giving them a second, I walk right on in.

Chad quickly throws the sheets over him and Bailey, and I eye where Bailey is lying boneless on the bed, curls plastered to his forehead, and cheeks redder than they were when he got inside out of the chilly wind.

"You guys look like you've been having fun." I pump my eyebrows as I grab Chad's desk chair and straddle it backward.

"Tell me you weren't listening at the door," he says.

"Door. Living room. A street away. It wouldn't have made any difference."

Bailey sits up, leaning back into his hands as Chad tucks his behind his head. He's got one hairy thigh not covered by the sheet, and my gaze snags on it, hovers. It's not like I've never seen Chad naked in the locker room before, but I've never actually paid attention.

"I have a favor," I say before I can get sidetracked.

"I won't hide the body with you, but I'm happy to provide an alibi," Chad says.

"Is murder a frequent occurrence?" Bailey asks. "Because manual labor isn't my thing either."

"Nope," Chad says. "But I figure if I always reply like that, the odds are in my favor."

"You'd have more chance with Brandon," I point out.

"This is cute, but I'd like to clean up once you're done, so want to get to it?" Bailey says.

"Ah, right. Yeah. Look, I'm glad I caught you two—"

"In my bedroom? After sex? What a coincidence," Chad says.

I flip him off and turn to Bailey. "You're the most reasonable one in here—"

"I'm really not."

I huff. "Can I ask what I wanna ask without you guys interrupting?"

"Not sure." Bailey tilts his head. "Can you?"

I turn to Chad. "I've changed my mind. Back to you. This is important."

Concern immediately crosses his face. "What's wrong?"

"Nothing's *wrong*. Specifically."

"So why the hell couldn't it wait until after I'd spooned Bailey for a bit?"

"I've been thinking about this all week!"

"All week?" Bailey smirks. "Sounds painful."

"Bro my god, fuck you both. I'm feeling the love here."

Chad laughs. "Tell me. You're all thinky and quiet, I don't like it."

"Fine. But I'm invoking the Chet Protocol first."

My buddy immediately sits up, all teasing gone. "I'm here for you, man."

"Chet Protocol?" Bailey asks, eyeing Chad's sudden change.

"Named after a brother in the seventies who accidentally fucked his cousin," Chad explained. "It's a judgment-free pass."

"And we really want to give that to *Robbie*, who barged in here after listening to us have sex and now is looking … shifty?"

Chad kisses his head. "Sorry, princess, we don't have a choice."

"Frat boys, I swear."

Bailey can act as exasperated as he likes; I already know he'd do anything for Chad. It's the reason I decided to like him, even though I hate Kappas as a rule.

"Go." Chad nods at me.

"I want to touch your dick."

Silence follows my words.

A really. Long. Silence.

I point at Chad. "You're judging."

"No judgment. No, no. I'm ... confused."

"You are aware we're dating." Bailey's voice has a hard edge to it. *"No judgment."*

"I know. I don't wanna mess with that, but Chad's my best bro, and I can't think of anyone else to help me out with this."

"With what?"

"Well, I'm sort of curious what dick is like."

"Haven't you already done the experimenting thing?" Chad asks. He lifts a hand. "No judgment."

"Technically, I guess, but I was trashed. I didn't know my ass from my face that night."

"There are apps, you know," Bailey says. He still looks kinda shitty with me, but not like he's about to lunge at me.

Though, he *is* naked, so I suppose I'd inadvertently cop a feel that way.

"And the apps are a thing I could do. I'm not picky about who I'm sleeping with, but first, I think I should probably be sure I'm comfortable with snake wrangling before I jump into the viper's pit."

Chad starts to laugh. "No judgment," he chokes out. "But fuck no."

I scowl and turn to Bailey. "What about you? A couple of pumps and I'll know."

Before Bailey can reply, Chad flops onto his back and tucks his hands behind his head again. "No judgment, brother, but you touch him and you won't need to know your ass from your face because I'll rearrange them both."

Bailey pats Chad's exposed thigh, and my gaze returns to the beefy strip of skin. "Uh-huh. *You're* the tough one."

"Come on," I whine. "I'm not fussy who. A dick's a dick."

"New rule," Chad says. "One bro does not ask another bro's ho to see his dick. It's so not frat."

I snigger.

"Call me a ho again," Bailey challenges until Chad gives him a sheepish smile, and then Bailey turns to me. "Why don't you find someone who's actually available?"

"Because the only guys I know are straight, and I don't want to be going up to random gay guys and asking to fondle their junk."

"Why?" Bailey asks. "They'd love it."

I scowl. "Because I don't want to look like an idiot if I chicken out."

"Well, you're shit out of luck here," Chad says. "We know a great gay club down in New York if you ever want to go though."

"You're missing the point," I grumble as I stand and push the chair back under his desk. I go to leave when Chad calls me back.

"I just want to say that even though I don't want a piece of all that"—he waves his hand toward me—"I'm happy for you to be figuring yourself out. And I'm always here to talk."

"Naked?" I grin.

"Get the fuck out."

BRANDON

THIS PARTY BLOWS.

It's not the party itself—it never is because Robbie knows what he's doing when he's planning a fun time—but being risk manager of a house like Sigma Beta Psi means being on all the damn time.

It's rare I get to drink and let loose, and since my brothers are all behaving themselves tonight, I maybe could have indulged, but instead, all I've done is pose for photos and charm Jenny's friends.

Neither one of those things is remotely close to being a good time.

My relationship with Jenny is running dry, but since she's from one of the top sororities on the row, I have to be careful how I go about ending it. If I make her mad and get her house off side, we can kiss the high head count at our parties good-bye, because as epic as they are, without hot chicks to hook up with, no guys will come. And there goes the money we need to put toward our dues.

The last thing I want is to sell the hashtag relationship goals bullshit, and I cringe every time I'm pulled into the spotlight.

Being one of the Sigma dudes means it's a lot though.

We've always been the party house, the cool one, but with Robbie and Chad tearing up Greek Row for the last year, we're in the spotlight more than ever. The Sigma executives are like currency.

Zeke, our president, is the trophy, even if he's rarely interested in hooking up. Chad being VP was the next hottest commodity, but now he's locked up, the rest of us are in demand. Especially Robbie. All the chicks want Robbie, because he's so unapologetically himself. He doesn't have a stylish bone in his body, he's crude, he's loud, and doesn't do strings ever, but he's also got a big heart and a big … other things.

He has a reputation for being well proportioned, and for some reason, chicks wanna tame the beast.

Good luck to them.

I've been trying to control him all year.

"There you are," Jenny says, entering the room in a flurry of lace and taking the place beside me on the couch. Her brown hair is up in some kind of complicated twist thing, and her makeup look tonight is "natural," whatever that means. "You look tired."

"Yeah, I'm beat. Between our game yesterday and traveling back last night, I'm not in a hugely social mood."

She gives me an indulgent smile as she brushes my hair back, and I feel like a shithead for wanting to jerk back from her touch. "Thank goodness the season is over. We can go to that Gamma mixer together next week."

I will streak the quad before I'm caught dead at a Gamma party. "Hmm … maybe."

She huffs. "I swear it's like you don't want to do anything with me."

Because everything we do is high-maintenance. Robbie's right. Getting myself into a relationship—especially one where she wants to play young Kennedys or Vanderbilts or whatever—was a dumbass move. "Maybe it will be different now the season is over." Though that was the one reason I had to get out of things, now it's over and I'm one of the few guys in the house who doesn't need to work, my excuses are going to be slim.

I kiss her cheek and stand. "I'll be back. I need to do a quick lap."

Which isn't a total lie—fuck knows I need to check up on things—but I make straight for the front door anyway. As I step out of the house where we have the heat pumping, the cold air hits me like a solid wall, and my balls immediately try to climb inside my body. I huddle into my Henley, only planning to be out here for a few minutes to clear my head.

I breathe in a lungful of chilly air and remind myself that once senior year is done, that's it. Chad is always talking about how we need to make the most of this time, but I get so bogged down in details, I forget to have fun.

I want to have fun again.

I want to be a complete dickhead with my brothers and fuck the consequences.

But while my brothers are careful about getting on the dean's radar, they're also not the smartest guys around, and frat guys have a bad habit of making dumb choices.

Even the high-and-mighty Kappas aren't immune.

The door creaks, and a moment later, Raymond follows me out. "You okay?"

He's huddled in a coat and wool hat, but he's still shivering. After his part in covering up the Kappas prank, he's lucky to have been initiated into the house, rather than kicked out with the scum pledge who sold us out. Since then, he's kept his mouth closed and worked every party to earn back his place here.

And even though he's officially initiated, he's still considered a pledge and has pledge duties, until fresh blood rushes the fraternity.

"I'm good." I eye him. "You?"

"Yeah, man, just cold working the door."

"So … you came outside?"

He chuckles, and a puff of cold air unfurls before him. "Yeah, I …"

I know he's about to apologize again, so I hold up my hand. "We've been over this. It's done. And I gotta say, it'd be nice if everybody stopped acting like I was on my deathbed."

"Robbie?"

"Fucking Robbie." He's gotten better since everything calmed down, but I still catch him looking at me sometimes like he can't make me out. In all the years we've been friends, he's never paid me so much attention.

"He was worried. We all were."

I'd believe that a bit more if Raymond hadn't tried to cover up what happened.

The door behind us cracks open again, and Bailey sticks his head outside. "Brandon, Chad needs you."

What was that I said about my brothers behaving themselves? I pat Raymond on the shoulder as I make my way back inside and follow Bailey to where Chad and Robbie are in the kitchen.

"Brandon," Chad says as soon as he sees me. "Can you please tell Robbie he can't go around asking to see our cocks?"

I stumble to a stop and narrow my eyes at them. "Why do I get the impression I'm walking into something?"

"If it feels like an uncomfortable conversation, you'd be right." Chad looks pointedly at Robbie, and the big man huffs.

"You suck. You all suck. If I can't count on my brothers, who can I count on?"

I glance from one to the next. "I'm starting to think you're serious."

"Because I am," Robbie says.

"You wanna see a dude's dick?"

"Yes."

"What if I told you that you're surrounded by cock in the locker rooms?"

He gives me a look like *I'm* the idiot. "I'm not gonna go around perving on my team."

I guess now isn't the time to mention I've checked out his dick countless times. Though, that thing is hard to miss.

"Besides, I don't only want to look. I want to touch. It's like pre-drinks. Get the first part out of the way, find out what I like, then drown myself with it."

I turn to Chad. "I have no clue what is going on."

"He's curious. And he's now hit up me, Bailey, Miles, and Zeke. You're the risk manager—get him in line before he asks the wrong brother and they smash his face."

Robbie chuckles. "I'd like to see them try."

"Just saying, man. I think it's awesome that you're not beating around the bush—"

"Beating." Robbie grins.

"—about this. And while no one in the house is giving off fuckwit vibes, you still have to be careful. There's a line. Most dudes are okay with their brother liking dick, but they're not okay with being hit on."

"I'm not hitting on anyone. Like I'd actually want to hook up with anyone in this house anyway."

"Do I need to remind you you're offering hand jobs?"

He splutters. "I so am not. All I want is a quick rub, then I'm out."

I groan and massage my forehead.

Chad laughs. "I think you broke Brandon."

"I'm not *broken*. I'm wondering how much more I'll have to endure this year."

"I'm not being unreasonable," Robbie says. "All it would take is one dude to flop it out, let me check I'm not going to be scared away, and then it's done."

"And excuse me." Chad raises his hand. "I'd also like to point out that I've laid off the pranks lately."

"Yeah, because you're too busy fucking your boyfriend," I point out.

"Lucky bastard," Robbie mutters, and Bailey steps forward and wraps his arms around Chad's waist.

I'm more than a bit confused by this conversation. "Where has all this come from? The whole time I've known you, all you've cared about is chasing skirts, and now you suddenly want dick."

"I'm curious. Sue me."

"Well, is there a rush? Is it something you need to do right this second?"

"Nah, but I want to get it over with. It's stuck in my head, and I hate focusing on one thing for so long."

True. Robbie isn't the kind of guy who stews on things. His

gaze suddenly flicks to me, and I hold my breath, waiting for the inevitable proposition. When he reaches up to rub his jaw, my gaze tracks the movement, and I'm so sure the next words out of his mouth will have something to do with my dick that I'm caught off guard when they're not.

"Fine. I'll shut up about it," he says instead.

My gut twists unexpectedly, but I nod. "Good."

"For tonight."

"Of course." I shake my head and leave them behind, but Robbie is hot on my heels.

"Could your clothes get any tighter?" he taunts.

Like he can talk when he knows shit all about what looks good. He's wearing utility pants covered in pockets, a fanny pack, and knit sweater. "At least I bothered to look in a mirror before I left my room."

"What the hell is wrong with what I'm wearing?"

"We do *not* have enough time for that conversation." I find Jenny exactly where I left her, playing on her phone and looking way too overdressed for a kegger. I drop down beside her, assuming Robbie will get the message that I'm done talking to him, but he follows me onto the couch and almost traps me under his bulk.

"Fucking asshole," I grunt, shoving where he's sitting half in my lap and move closer to Jenny so I end up squashed between them both.

Robbie chuckles and sets his beer aside. "How you doing, Jen?"

"Jenny," she corrects as she turns to face him. Her fingers trail down my neck, and I have to fight from shrugging her off. "And I'm good. Just waiting for Brandy to be done."

"I told you, I can't be done until this thing wraps up."

She purses her lips and ignores me. "Anything new with you?" she asks Robbie.

I quickly point at him. "Don't answer that." Because I know the first words out of his mouth will have something to do with his newfound love of dicks—in the most crass way possible.

"What?" he asks innocently.

"Nuh-uh, man."

Jenny leans forward, smelling gossip. "What is it?"

"Can't say." Robbie mimes locking his lips, stare trained mockingly on me.

Fuck it. She wants to know. I wave at him to go right ahead.

"None of my brothers will let me touch their cock."

And there it is. I cringe. "Dude, considering you have actual brothers, you probably shouldn't say shit like that too loud."

They both ignore me.

"You're into that?" Jenny asks.

"Dunno. No one will take one for the team."

"It's not for the team when it's literally only you who has an endgame," I point out.

They both ignore me *again*.

"Good for you," Jenny says.

"What?"

"*What?*" Robbie's laugh is so loud it travels over the music. "You're cool with it?"

"We're in college," she says like it should be obvious. "I think everyone should figure out what they like."

"Exactly. I think I could be into it, but it's not like I can test my theory out solo."

"So you're experimenting?"

"Nope. I *wanna* be experimenting."

She tilts her head, thinking. "You know … I think you're jumping ahead."

"What do you mean?"

"Well, you're assuming you need to touch a dick, but doesn't kissing come first?"

"Yeah, but I can do that shit in my sleep."

"With a girl, maybe. I've kissed some of my sorority sisters, and it's a whole different experience."

"Huh." Robbie cocks his head like he's actually thinking about it. Then his eyes flick to me. "What do you say?"

Oh, fuck. "About?"

"Kissing?"

"With … you?"

"Duh." He exchanges a look with Jenny like *I'm* the one not making sense.

And just as I'm about to tell him to fuck right off out of here, Jenny leans forward and squeezes my arm.

"Come on, Brandy, live a little."

It's not her words that pull me up short but the way she says them. Like it's something I'd actually consider. Kissing. With Robbie.

No way … but my gaze drops to his lips and the way they're stretched tauntingly. He doesn't think I will. He doesn't think I'll even stop to think about it, and he'd be right, but … what was I saying about wanting to have fun?

I cringe. "I don't know …"

Robbie latches onto my hesitation, and suddenly, he doesn't look so smug. "Shit, really? Come on. Just a quick one."

"I …"

"She's right. You need to live a little, Brando. It's college —everyone experiments."

"No, they fucking don't." But now it's in my head, I *am* curious. I know I'm straight, and I doubt I'll enjoy it, but hell, this could be my only chance to actually kiss a guy to know what it feels like. Something for the bucket list, I guess.

I finally pull my attention away from Robbie and back to my girlfriend. "You don't care?"

"No way. I'm a cool girlfriend. It's fine."

And clearly for her, me doing this has something to do with her image … somehow. I don't get it.

"It's fine," she says again. "Stop overthinking and do it."

Do it. Just … do it.

How's this for living?

I close a hand around the back of Robbie's neck and tug him into a kiss. It's … awkward. His mouth feels harder somehow, and even slamming my eyes closed doesn't help me forget it's him when his stubble is scraping my skin. I give it a second, then two. I'm about to write the whole experience off as a fail when Robbie's large hand cups my jaw and tilts my head back before he pushes his tongue past my lips.

It's so unexpected I immediately gasp, breathing in hot air and warmth. His tongue strokes mine, slowly, cautiously at first, and as though figuring out he likes it, he lets go.

He surges forward, pressing me into the couch and kissing me with purpose. I can barely keep up with his mouth and the force he's kissing me with, but I do my best to hold my ground. He makes it almost impossible though, and I'm quickly being swept up in how good his mouth feels on mine. My hands are balled in his stupid knit sweater, one of his thighs is half over mine, and he towers over me, big hand holding my jaw as he controls the kiss completely.

And I submit. Give in. Let him take what he wants. The power in his body is new and different, and the unwanted sound that leaves me makes me think … I don't hate it.

"Wow."

Jenny's voice is like a bucket of cold water, and Robbie jerks away.

The party snaps back into focus, and I'm struggling to catch my breath and work out what the hell just happened. I glance around like I'm lost, but even though it feels like the entire world has been rearranged out of comprehension, no one is paying us any attention.

"Huh, right, well," Robbie says, not meeting my eyes. "Good talk." Then he stands abruptly and walks away, but not before I catch sight of the hard outline of his cock.

And mine is in exactly the same state.

I can't pin down a thought in my mind, and by the time the party wraps up, my head is still spinning. When Jenny and I go upstairs to my room and she ducks into the bathroom down the hall, I do something I've never done before.

I roll onto my side and fake sleep.

3

ROBBIE

I POWER THROUGH MY POLI-SCI NOTES, SITTING UP AT THE front of the class to make sure I'm following everything. A group of us has a shared notes section going, and I flag a few things I'm not sure about so one of them can come back and answer it for me. My dumb jock reputation is spot-on, but what I lack in brains, I make up for with dogged grit.

People can say a lot of things about me, but one thing they can never say is I didn't *try*.

As soon as this class is done, I've got frat duties, and training key pledges in our way of mayhem is something I've looked forward to ever since becoming social chair.

The more I focus on schoolwork and my fraternity responsibilities, the less time I have to think about other things.

Other things like the very hard, very masculine tongue I had in my mouth last weekend. The thing is, I'm all for experimenting and having a good time. I'm so not having some kind of queer freak-out, because a mouth is a mouth, right? So what that dick can probably do it for me as much as pussy does? Though the evidence is still out on that one.

Nah, the thing that I'm avoiding thinking about is *who* that tongue belonged to.

Brandon and I have always been close but in a weird way. Chad's my best bro, and I can tell him anything, but our relationship is all about the fun. We have our serious moments, sure, and I know I can go to him with anything, but when it comes to Brandon, I've always had a sort of wariness there.

Some kind of instinct to keep him at arm's length.

It helps that we never see eye to eye on things. Ever. We bicker like old dudes in a nursing home, and if that's where we end up together one day, I wouldn't be surprised, because as much as we might get into it, we always seem to be together through some unspoken agreement.

Having breakfast? He's there.

Chapter meeting? He's by my side.

We even drive or walk to campus together most days, even if we're arguing for a good part of the way there.

Even when I actively *try* to stay away from him, it never ends up that way.

But last weekend, I think we both found something we can finally agree on. Our kiss was goddamn hot.

And in the three days since, I haven't seen him once. At least him avoiding me means I haven't had to avoid him.

I cringe as class winds up, and I stuff my laptop into my backpack, then pull it on.

This is too much thinking for me.

I have prank wisdom to bestow upon the shitkickers in our house, and I plan to make that my full focus for the rest of the day. With Zeke, Chad, and some of the Bigs in the house joining us, it'll put up a sorely needed buffer between me and

Brandon. I'm glad it was so dark at the party and no one was paying us attention, because all I'd need is for one of those assholes to get ahold of this information and have it become the butt of all jokes from now until eternity.

A constant reminder is not what I need when I'm trying to forget.

The second I step foot out of the social sciences building, the cold slaps me in the face. Fucking New England weather. Growing up in Arizona did not prepare me for this.

I'm walking so fast I'd be jogging if I wasn't worried about going ass over tits in the snow when I hear my name being called and turn to see Chad and Brandon hurrying to catch up with me.

"Dude, we got a ride in with Bailey this morning, but screw walking back. You have your car, right?" Chad asks.

"Yeah, because I'm not a dumbass." I nod toward the parking lot. "Come on, I'm freezing."

We're all silent until we get to the car, where I immediately turn it on and pump the heat. My face stings as it thaws, and it's only when my hands work properly again that I finally get moving.

On the way back, Chad runs through how we should structure the meeting this afternoon with my occasional input, but Brandon stays silent. Every time I glance at him in my rearview mirror, he's staring out the window, blond hair perfectly windswept and nose still a bit pink. I swallow and look away before he can sense me looking at him.

Chad suddenly spins in his seat. "You're quiet," he says to Brandon. "I thought for sure you would have vetoed *something* by now."

I can't stop myself from glancing back, and Brandon's

stare flicks to mine for a quick second before he redirects to Chad.

Talk about some awkward tension.

This is driving me nuts. Since when do I give a shit about feelings and avoiding issues? It was a goddamn kiss. If I freaked out every time I kissed someone, I'd never get laid, and that would be a catastrophe. Time for typical Robbie to break the ice.

Only, when I open my mouth to—I dunno, thank him for the kiss, maybe—nothing comes out.

My hands grip the steering wheel tighter as I navigate onto Greek Row and pull up down from the house.

"Ride's over, bitches." I snap open my seat belt, grab my bag, and am out of the car before either of them can follow me. My shoulders feel so tense, I carry my bag instead of trying to put it on.

"Dude, you okay?" Chad calls, followed by the sound of two doors closing.

"I'm getting my freezing ass inside."

They catch up with me when I'm kicking my boots off in the doorway, and as though he can't help himself, Brandon finally speaks.

"I've told you not to wear T-shirts under your coat."

"Like I need a lecture on fashion right now."

"It's not about fashion. If you want to be warm, you need to wear wool."

"I *do* wear wool," I say, plucking at my sweater.

"As a *base* layer." Brandon rolls his eyes, and the prickling urge to fight back starts to rise.

"Sure, I'll run out and grab some with all of that money I have lying around."

I don't see how it makes a difference anyway. I'm not used to this weather, plain and simple.

"As much as I love the married couple routine you guys do, we need to get set up." Chad pushes me toward the hall, and I lead the way down to the room at the back of the house. It's the second biggest and will have more than enough space for our four pledges, their big brothers, and the four of us. This room is where the pledges are taken through mastering mayhem every year, which is why we call it the war room. We're basically preparing our troops for battle.

Zeke's already here, typing on his laptop. The line through his eyebrow is freshly shaven—his way of trying to give his baby face more of an edge to it—and he sends an upnod our way.

"I assume you guys have this handled?"

"Please." Chad lifts his hands. "Who are you talking to?"

I high-five him, because when it comes to pranks, he's got the balance between fun and safe down to an art form. I've learned from the best.

"If there's any good thing to come out of the Kappas prank," Brandon says, "it's that these new guys should know how easily things can go wrong."

Hmph. I'd prefer we weren't all a cautionary tale, to be honest. I could do without thinking one of my brothers is going to die.

Apparently, I don't keep my grumbling to myself because Brandon nudges me on his way past to rearrange the furniture.

"Man, you've gotta get past it."

"I don't have to do anything."

"What, you're going to hold a grudge for the rest of the year?"

I shrug. "What's it to you what I do?"

"It's making you look at me weird. Stop it. I'm not about to drop dead."

"That's not funny."

"Wasn't trying to be."

I grunt and move away, helping sort things into a half circle so once everyone is here, they have a view of up the front. I'm being a killjoy, and I need to cut it out. The Kappas tried to make amends, and Brandon is *fine,* but my brain refuses to let it go. It's frustrating as hell.

First that, and now the kiss.

Yep, I *really* shouldn't have tried it with him.

I'm too in my head.

And the last thing I want to concentrate on is how much I wanna do it again.

I arrange the last couch into place, then go and join Chad and Zeke. Chad'll do most of the talking, and Zeke is here for presence and to make sure the two of us don't say anything dumb—which would maybe offend me if that wasn't the kind of thing I'm known for. As risk manager, Brandon will try to drill into these guys the importance of safety, but like every brother in his role before him, he's fighting a losing battle.

Once everyone files in and gets seated, Zeke stands and clears his throat. We've invited the four pledges that had the most promise for being pains in the ass on Greek Row. Raymond is here even though I'm still not sure about that dude, plus three others called Shifley, Dean, and Lance.

"As you all know, you're here to learn the art of mayhem making," Zeke says. "Chad and Robbie will be your teachers, and Brandon is the guy you run all your plans past. Over the next few months, you guys need to write up mock pranks and have them rated for effectiveness *and* safety, and in the mean-while"—he points his thumb over his shoulder at us—"you need to vote which of these two should be crowned this year's Master of Mayhem. Take all past and present pranks into account, as well as parties, Greek games, and any general tomfoolery. Got it?"

The pledges agree, and their Bigs nod at Zeke even though they already know what's going on. Once he's satisfied, Zeke motions for Chad to get started.

Chad takes the front of the room like a king in his spotlight. He claps his hands and rubs them together, and a trickle of excitement for getting to be a part of all this leaks into me.

Sexual confusion and near death aside, this is the shit dreams are made of. Brotherhood, fun, and pranks to get the blood pumping. When it came to moving across the country on a football scholarship, or staying near the West Coast like my brother did, I'm glad I took the jump, because no frat in the country has what we have here. There might be eighty of us all up, but I'd put my life on the line for any of my brothers, and I know they feel the same.

Even the douchey ones.

I turn on the projector, and Chad and I walk the guys through some of our more notable pranks. We've got planning diagrams and photo evidence, videos of some of the really spectacular ones, and I remember sitting here as a new initiate and being talked through the kind of fun I could have as a Sigma brother. It was like the world opened up to me.

So I also remember that when the risk manager at the time got up and started talking about guidelines and hazard logs, filling in incident reports, and checking on allergies, I immediately checked out.

It happens with this lot too.

Brandon jumps up and tries to hold attention, but I can see

their eyes glazing over—some of the Bigs have that faraway stare going on too.

Fuck that shit.

"Listen up, kids," I say, getting to my feet. And one good thing about being so large is that when I'm talking, people pay attention. "You better memorize every word out of Brando's mouth because there'll be a quiz at the end, and any of you fuckers who don't pass it will be banned from pranking people until you do. He might be boring as batshit, but this stuff is important, and if you can't get that through your thick skulls, you can go play Frisbee on campus with the rest of the geeds."

And like that, all eyes are up front.

I pat Brandon's shoulder. "Take it away, man."

"Thanks," he says dryly.

I catch Chad's questioning look as Brandon gets started. *Important?* he mouths.

I shrug it off, acting like it was no big deal, but fuck if someone is getting hurt on my watch. Ah … *again.*

I've heard a lot that the social chair and risk manager need to work together, and I got it on some level, but that didn't stop the pissing match between me and Brandon as I tried to plan big, and he tried to rein me in.

Maybe I kinda sorta have a new respect for his position now.

Because I never want to be the cause of someone going through what he did.

An idea forms in my brain, and I rub the scruff on my chin as I eye him. To his credit, he's engaging when he talks. And even when he's running over the difference between a hazard and an incident, he makes you *want* to pay attention.

He might not love this shit, but he's good at it.

Like I'm good at what I do.

And if people want us to work together, maybe I could lean into that more. Get his buy-in for the next party, run my ideas by him, maybe try to find a way he can let go for once since that obviously annoyed him last weekend.

Because the more time we spend together, the faster we'll get past this weird awkwardness, and then I can move on with my experimenting.

What did Jenny say? First kissing, then dick?

Well, as it turns out, I think I want to try the kissing thing again.

For research.

After all, I'm probably hung up on this whole thing because it was new and different. Anything that's a shock to the system is bound to stay with you.

So if I do it again, and *maybe* again, it'll become normal. Boring. Just a thing that I could do.

But for some reason, I can't concentrate on kissing another guy until things are straight with Brandon.

So I'll work on that first.

Kissing second.

With anyone other than him.

4

BRANDON

I'm woken rudely by a large body hitting my mattress and almost launching me into the ceiling.

"Motherfucker." I grunt and swing my pillow blindly, clocking someone in the face, and the familiar laugh that answers lets me know exactly who it is.

I steal my pillow back and bury my head under it.

"Is that any way to greet your brother?" Robbie mocks.

"I'd push you out of bed if I had the energy, so think yourself lucky."

My pillow disappears, and I hiss as sunlight assaults my eyelids.

"What time is it?" I ask.

"Past eight."

I crack an eye open. Robbie's lying beside me, propped up on one elbow, shit-green knit sweater stretched across his massive chest.

"Geez." My voice comes out sleep drenched and husky. "Where did you even get a sweater that ugly?"

"I made it."

In that case, it isn't as bad as I originally thought. "Huh. Sorry."

"I don't care." To his credit, he doesn't sound like he's mortally offended. "I've been waiting for you downstairs."

"Why were you waiting for me?" He's been all set on avoiding me since our kiss, and I haven't called him on it because I was okay with how things were.

In a way.

I needed the distance, but also, not having him around constantly has been weird. Our verbal sparring and shooting the shit with video games is the way I wind down. Sure, I have other friends, but Robbie is … I don't know, really, but I do know he's someone I want to be around, even when I don't.

Now, if that isn't confusing as hell, what is?

"I want your opinion," he says.

That wakes me up. "What did you do?"

"Wow. My heart is breaking that you immediately think the worst of me."

"Can you blame me?"

"Not at all, but ouch, man. We're brothers. Where's the trust?"

I give him a flat look, willing him to get the fuck on with it.

"K. We're having a party."

I half groan and half sob. "Again? We only had one last weekend."

"I know, but this is a pre-break one. The night before the last day of classes, I want to have a big one where people can go all out and get loose before heading home."

There is so, so much about that plan that doesn't excite me. "Two parties three weeks apart is insane."

"I'll easily be able to pull it off, and we all need that fun memory to get us through Christmas with family."

"Except me, apparently."

"Why not you?"

"Because I'm the only one who doesn't get to have fun at these things."

To my surprise, Robbie's grin widens. "That's the thing. I figured since it's the last party of the year and I'll be the one here cleaning up the next day, I'll stay sober so you can drink."

What? I stare at him, not fully understanding his words. Robbie plus party equals drunk off his ass. I don't think I've ever seen him get through one sober, and I have no idea what's bringing this on now, but … "I don't believe you."

"I swear on the house." He even goes so far as resting his hand over his heart.

I roll onto my side to mirror him, kicking the blankets down to stop them tangling around my legs. "Why?"

"You should have some fun before you head home too."

"And you shouldn't?"

He lifts the shoulder he's not leaning on. "Can't afford the flight, so I'm staying here again. I'm sure there'll be plenty of fun I can get up to while everyone is away."

Yeah, I've heard the stories of how Robbie fucked a girl in every room of the house while we were all gone last year, but I also know those rumors are completely untrue. He was bored out of his brains, and he spread that around so people wouldn't feel sorry for him.

Him being prepared to stay sober right before two weeks of nothing has me doubly suspicious.

"Here." He flips the tablet and shows me the list he's put

together. "I figured the theme could be date night. Usually when people show up together, there's less drama."

"Or more if someone wants to leave with someone else."

He chuckles. "Truth, but you'll have me and the pledges all there to contain the trouble. I'll play risk manager for the night."

I scoff. "You wouldn't know the first thing about being risk manager."

"Sure I do. I've just gotta put on my big-boy panties, shove a stick up my ass, and ruin everyone's fun. Piece of cake."

"Technically, you should shove the stick up there *before* you put on panties. Geez, you wanna be with a guy and know nothing about butt stuff."

"Since you're so knowledgeable, are you offering?"

Fucking Robbie. I flop onto my back again. "Why are you such a pain in the ass?"

"I can *be* a pain in the ass."

I spare him a small smile. "You wish."

His tablet is resting between us so I pick it up and scroll through his plans. There're lists for what we need, how and what to set up, possible risks involved, and job allocations for the brothers he knows will be there. "When did you work on all this?"

"Last night?"

"Lucky you. I was going over the pledges' prank ideas."

"Any good ones?"

I screw up my face. "One that held promise, but most of them are a mess of college movies and hazing. It's like they didn't even listen at the presentation."

Something dark crosses Robbie's face. "Pass them on to me, and I'll go over your notes with them."

"Yeah, thanks, but I can do it. This isn't going to be like the meeting on Wednesday."

"What was wrong with the meeting?"

"You stepping in like I needed saving. I'm a big boy. I can speak for myself."

He scowls. "That's so not what I was doing, and you know it."

"Do I though? Because it kinda sounded like you were standing up for your side piece, and hello, that's not me."

His mouth drops, and I can't blame him. That last part wasn't supposed to slip out—especially because I hadn't given it conscious thought in my brain—but apparently avoiding a topic makes me blurt it out, and there I go referencing something I never wanted to talk about.

Ever.

"Is this about the kiss?" Robbie asks.

I throw a look at my closed bedroom door, almost as though I expect to see people crowded around outside it. "No?"

He lifts his eyebrows.

"Fine. I'm not sure. But it was … weird. Or something."

"That's the aftereffects of the Rob-dog. I'm like an aphrodisiac."

"I don't know what's worse, you talking about yourself in third person, the terrible nickname, or you thinking you somehow turned me on."

"I don't think, I know." He looks pointedly at my crotch, and I hurry to tuck a hand under the blankets to rearrange myself.

"To be clear, this is morning wood."

"Right. Nothing to do with Rob-dog."

"Talk about yourself in the third person again. I don't think you've met your douche quota for today."

"Don't worry, it's still early. It's sweet you're concerned though. I think kissing me gave you feelings. It's only natural."

"Fuck off. Don't act like you're all cool about having your tongue down my throat. This is basically the first conversation we've had since."

"Fine. It was awkward as shit."

"Exactly."

"Because it was so goddamn hot."

My gaze flies to his. "What?"

"Are you surprised? I mauled you."

"I …" A small laugh slips out to hide the way something flutters through me. "Yeah, I noticed. But I didn't expect you to admit it."

"Want me to be a dick about it? Pretend it was the shittiest kiss I've ever had? Act like you were the only one who got hard over it?"

And suddenly, my morning wood is becoming something else. "Got … hard?"

"You going to deny it?" His words hold a challenge, like he knows that's exactly what I was going to do and he's daring me to even try. "You going to pretend you didn't like how it felt? Weren't clinging to my shirt and kissing me back?"

I swallow.

"Weren't picturing what my stubble would feel like scraping against your thighs?"

I shove him. "Fuck off." Because I can truthfully say I wasn't thinking about that … until now.

He drops the teasing and flops onto his back. "Don't worry, I don't want anywhere near your dick anyway."

I hesitate, the question on the tip of my tongue. I can't look at him as I ask, "You think you want that though? Dick?"

He hums, deep and gravelly. "Maybe. I think I want to try kissing again first though."

"Does that mean I get to claim turning you gay?"

"Not gay. And I'm pretty sure you don't want people to know about us, which is lucky, because neither do I."

"Yeah, true."

"Tell me though. After kissing me, was the sex wild?"

Sex … I'm about to remind him we definitely didn't fucking do that when he continues.

"With Jenny. You know, because I got you all worked up? Tell her I'll accept beer and chocolate as a thank-you."

Right. My girlfriend. And because I have no clue how to explain—even to myself—why I pretended to be asleep, I nod and commit to a half-truth. "You have no idea."

"What are your plans this weekend?" he asks.

"Some Gamma thing Jenny and her sisters are going to that I'll probably be dragged along for."

"A Gamma party?" Robbie looks horrified. "No, ditch that and come out. We'll go to a club or something."

"A club? Wow, you know me so well."

"I added *or something*. You choose. Anything. You can't be caught dead with a bunch of Gammas. They'll probably try to recruit you into a cult."

"What the fuck do you think they do in their house?"

Robbie snorts. "Why do you hang out with those losers?"

"I don't. Jenny does." And until I end things with her, I have to play nice with the white and rich crowd. Kappas have a bad rap for having money, but they're legitimately decent. They don't bubble wrap themselves in privilege and act like anyone without money is beneath them.

Not like those Gammas.

They fuck around because there are zero consequences. People—and houses—like that are still low-key hazing people and risking all of Greek life purely because they're Teflon. Someone overdoses on a dare? Their money reminds people it was an accident. Third-degree burns? Oops, stupid pledge set his own pants on fire.

Assholes.

They're on the other Greek street, and since we prefer to hang out on our side, we rarely have much to do with them. Until the last few weeks … months … while I've been dating Jenny. Even though I don't have the money they do, I'm still reasonably cashed up, and that, plus being a Sigma, buys me status with them that none of my other brothers have.

"Why do you look like you need to take a dump?" Robbie asks.

"It just hit me how much I'm dreading this party."

"So don't go."

"Jenny would kill me."

He scoffs. "So, end things with her already."

"Sure, and then Jenny gets the shits and convinces all the sisters at her house to blow off our next parties, then when we need to raise the dues, who will be the one our brothers blame?"

Robbie's pulling a face. "You can't risk manage your own relationship."

"Feels like I need to sometimes."

"I have a rule that fun should always outweigh obligation in a relationship. As soon as the scales tip too far the other way, it's over."

I smirk at him, wishing it was that easy. "And that, my friend, is why you've never had a relationship."

"Judging by this conversation, I never will either."

He rolls out of bed, cracks his neck to the side, then grabs me and hauls my ass out too. My cock gives this weird twitch at how easily he manhandles me, and I remind it to settle the hell down.

Things are confusing right now, and I don't need my dick thinking it has a say in any of this.

"I'll come to the party with you," he says.

"What?"

He nods. "And I'll intercept douchebag Gammas and keep them away."

"Okay, but … why?"

"Quid pro quo, brother. You helped me with my problem, I'll help you with yours. Then we're even, and shit can go back to normal."

I doubt that will ever be possible, but might as well give it a try. "Sure. You're on."

"What are brothers for?"

5

ROBBIE

FUCKING BRANDON. I'M DISGUSTED WITH MYSELF FOR EVEN contemplating a Gamma party, and yet here I am, pulling on my best cargo pants, filling up the pockets with cans of beer, and grabbing a knit hat I made with a large wool ball on top. I'll only wear the hat until we get there, but chicks are obsessed with it, so I'm hoping it works that way with dudes too.

People *love* to squeeze the pompom.

When I go to grab Brandon from his room, the first word that pops into my head is *hot*, and I immediately go to push it down when I pause. If I'm attracted to dudes, I'm allowed to think that way. And, come on, Brandon is better-looking than most dudes.

He's wearing dark pants, a gray sweater, scarf, and coat, and the whole thing should look boring as fuck, but it makes my mouth dry.

"Bro, you need to think this girlfriend thing through. You

could literally score with anyone you wanted, looking like that."

His stare snaps to mine, and he doesn't immediately answer. Then slowly, a smile forms, showing off those vamp fangs, which surprisingly make him look hotter.

"What, like you?"

And I know he's only teasing, so it makes it easy to play along. "I'm into dudes now, remember? I can tell a guy he's hot."

"You going to be my gay best friend?"

"As long as you don't expect fashion advice."

He drops my gaze, hazel eyes roaming over my body. I puff myself up a bit, not sure what I'm hoping to achieve because he's one hundred percent guaranteed to hate what I'm wearing.

"A flannel shirt?" he says on a sigh. "If you want to hook up, you need to put in *some* effort."

"I've never had a problem before."

"Yeah, but you've never been trying to hook up with dudes before."

"There's no way a guy cares more about what I'm wearing than chicks do."

"Sure. Because that's not exactly what we're talking about right now."

I sneer at him. "I'd like to see you fit a single can of beer in those pants." They're practically fucking sprayed on. "Actually, I'd like to see you even fit a credit card in there. I wouldn't worry about needing to hook up—by the time you get those bad boys off, it'll be February, and your dick will have fallen off from lack of circulation."

He gapes at me. "Stop talking."

"But it's my best quality."

"I promise it isn't." He leads the way from his room, and I fall into step with him. "Besides, there'll be beer there. I don't need to take my own."

"Yeah, enjoy drinking the piss they supply. What's the bet they're half-strength seltzers?"

"You mean, what I've been trying to get you to supply for our parties?"

"Sure, you can't break up with Jenny because of our dues, but you can push me to serve people what's basically soda. Great plan."

He looks like he wants to argue, so I bat my lashes at him like the innocent fucker I am.

And when Brandon laughs, I can't help grinning.

"There's no way you can tell me that your beer won't be shaken to shit by the time we get to the party."

We leave the house and walk around the block to the next street over. It's already dark and so goddamn cold, but it won't take long to warm up once we're there.

"Some of them will be," I say. "But that's part of the fun. Like a lucky dip. Which ones are good to go, and which ones will start an impromptu wet T-shirt contest?"

"Don't you ever …"

There's something in his tone that makes me glance over. "Yeah?"

"You're always so *on*. Isn't it exhausting?"

Surprisingly, I've never thought of it that way. "Well … I don't think of myself as *on*. I just … am." I frown because that sounds like some kinda douchey self-help shit. "Do you think I'm too much?" It panics me that I actually care about his answer.

"I think when you're dancing on a table and end up landing on me, you could maybe tone it down a notch." He flashes those teeth with a quick smile. "But, nah. Don't change. Especially not for a party pooper like me."

I know he's joking. I know it was a throwaway comment, and I *know* I'm the one always calling him that in the first place, but I'm someone who loves people. Loves them exactly the way they are. Even the geeds, though maybe not so much the asshole Gammas we're going to be partying with tonight.

But loving people the way they are includes Brandon and all his uptight, planning ways. I nudge him.

"You shouldn't change either. Especially not for a loose cannon like me."

He laughs, a little puff of white leaving his parted lips. "Let's see if you still think that the next time you suggest auctioning off people to have sex with."

"It was *for charity*."

"It was basically prostitution."

"I was trying to meet my philanthropy quota," I argue.

"Dude, you would have been the only one involved."

"Still would have made an easy hundred bucks, surely."

Brandon cuffs my shoulder as we reach the Gamma house and start up the stairs. "You're selling yourself short, big guy. I bet you could have even made one hundred and *one*."

I blow him a kiss as we step inside and pay our entry.

The party is decent, I guess. There are a lot of people, every room filled with alcohol and music, but it doesn't have shit on a Sigma party. It's lacking the finesse of something I would have planned, which makes it exactly the same as every other fucker throwing a house party, and yet they still have the balls to charge twenty a head.

What do these guys even put the money toward?

"Where's your girl?" I ask Brandon, following him through the party.

"No clue. Let's get drinks before we go and find them."

"Fine by me." One drink turns into two, and then I have a third, while Brandon still makes no indication he wants to move on.

"You avoiding Jenny?" I finally ask.

"Nah, nothing like that."

"Sort of seems like it."

He waves a hand toward the people dancing. "See any guys who look interesting?"

I don't take my eyes off his face. He's deflecting, which means there's definitely something up there. If he's only staying with her to protect our parties or some dumbass move like that, he needs to quit being a martyr. I'm the party king. If I can't deal with a little blowback like his relationship ending, I don't deserve to be social chair. "Dude, if you need to—"

"There you are!"

Before I can finish my sentence, Jenny appears, throwing her arms around Brandon and drawing him into a deep kiss. I try not to sneer at the way she's trying to eat his face, and maybe sensing me watching—or maybe he really is over her—Brandon cuts it off.

Jenny glances my way. "You brought Robbie?"

"Yeah, is that cool?"

I love being spoken about like I'm not here. "Last I heard it was an open party. Did I need to get y'alls opinion?"

Jenny bats at my hand with a giggle. "Of course not, but Brandy didn't mention you were coming." She leans in. "I'm glad you're here, actually. Some of the girls heard about your queer quest and want to help."

My jaw tenses. Do I give a shit people know? Of course not. I haven't tried to keep it quiet. But people talking about it, calling it some kind of queer quest like it's all a fucking joke, has me on edge.

Also, *Brandy*? When is she going to quit it with that name?

Brandon glares at her. "Did you tell them?"

"It's fine. None of them care."

"Yeah, but it wasn't your thing to tell."

She eyes him curiously, and there's something about that look, about the way she can't understand him sticking up for a friend without getting suspicious, that pushes me to be reckless. "It kinda was," I cut in. "After all, I'd probably feel threatened if my boyfriend got off on kissing someone else too."

And like I expected, they're both shocked silent.

Then, they start talking at the same time.

"I did *not* get off on it—"

"I wasn't *threatened*—"

I grin at them. "Did I make things awkward?"

"Of course not," Jenny says, and Brandon shakes his head at me.

"You guys have nothing to worry about. It's not like I want to kiss him again." And my mouth is out of control because it definitely sounds like I'm issuing a challenge. Why? Who the hell knows? Kissing Brandon again would be a terrible goddamn idea, and yet here I am, taunting him into doing it again.

"If anyone got off over it, it was you," he says.

I nudge Jenny. "Think he'll float away with a head that inflated?"

"Please. I saw the kiss, remember?" she says. "You were totally into it."

I raise my hands like I'm surrendering. "Sure. Fine. Whatever. You both seem *super* sensitive about this."

"Sensitive? Why would I be sensitive?" Jenny asks.

"You just really want me to have liked kissing him. You don't have to worry though. I'm not going to tell people he's a bad kisser."

"He's *not* a bad kisser."

"I didn't say he was." I mime locking my lips. "But either way, he's basically the last person I want to kiss tonight."

Brandon's eyes narrow. "I know what you're doing."

"Scouting for a guy to hook up with? I already told you."

"Are you ready to progress to dick?" Jenny asks.

"Nah, still kissing. I want to kick ass at that first, then I'll move on to the complicated stuff."

"So why don't you practice with Brandy?"

Bingo.

I lift my hand and tilt it side to side. "Eh."

"Fuck you." Brandon laughs.

"He's a great kisser," Jenny says.

"Look, I don't want to cause issues here. It's fine."

"Why would you cause issues?"

"Some chicks get jealous, is all …"

She rolls her eyes and pushes Brandon my way. "I didn't get jealous last week, did I? I'm cool. Do it."

"I don't want you freaking out."

"Please, you can kiss as much as you want, I don't care. Kissing doesn't mean anything, and you guys are friends."

That's what I always thought, and yet the idea of kissing Brandon again is getting me excited. Way excited. So excited I'm going to be disappointed as fuck if he says no.

"So you won't care if I kiss him when you're not around?" I ask.

She pauses. "Not when I'm not around. But if I'm here, go nuts."

"Do I get a say?" Brandon asks.

"Of course. If I'm too much man for you, I understand. Masculinity is a fragile thing ..."

He steps closer. "You are such a dick."

"Why's that?"

"Because you're trying to taunt me into kissing you. Wasn't once enough?"

"Hey, I promised I'd keep the douche canoes away from you, and it just so happens they're allergic to the gay. You're welcome."

His eyes drop to my lips and flick back up again. "Why do you wanna kiss me so bad?"

"I don't."

"Uh-huh." His mouth pulls up on one side. "You're practically begging me."

"Maybe you're the safe option."

His voice drops to a whisper. "Or maybe you liked it."

"You're a dude, and I'm experimenting. Of course I liked it. It has nothing to do with you."

His eyes narrow.

"You gonna kiss me or not?"

His attention shoots to Jenny, and for some reason, that pisses me off. "You sure this is okay with you?"

"Everyone experiments in college, Brandy, and the girls all think it's cool that you're not threatened by toxic masculinity and will do this for your friend." She strokes his neck. "And hey, if you guys want to try a threesome, I'm game."

He frowns. "No threesomes."

And thank fuck, because I have no interest in touching Jenny. Brandon though ... huh. Maybe I *could* picture touching him. Possibly.

"You ready, *Brando*?"

He grabs my flannel shirt, curling his fingers into fists. "What are frat brothers for?"

His smile is the last thing I see before his lips are on me, and I'm hit with that same all-consuming high as last week. I don't need to warm up to the kiss this time around; I'm immediately drawn into it. His mouth, his tongue, the way he nips my bottom lip. I'd say he's kissing me like he has something to prove, but it's every bit as good as I remember.

My dick has thickened behind my fly, and I tug Brandon's body against me, slotting a thigh between his legs and almost groaning at the feel of him hard too.

Well aware that we're in the middle of a party, standing in front of his girlfriend, I reluctantly pull away. Then kiss him again, then pull away for real this time.

His lips are puffy, and his hair is a mess from my hands, but he's smiling.

"Still think I'm a shit kisser?"

I shove him with a laugh. "Fine. *Maybe* I'll concede that wasn't half bad."

And as we're following Jenny back to her friends, he leans in to whisper, "Half bad, huh? I'd say that monster in your pants thinks otherwise."

Then the smart-ass pumps his eyebrows at me, and it's all I can do not to grab him and maul him again.

6

BRANDON

By an unspoken agreement, Robbie and I don't talk about the kiss. Or the, umm, ones that came after. Or the way they made us both hard and I definitely sort of want to try it again.

Which is terrifying.

I've never considered being with a man, and then here comes Robbie acting like the whole thing is so easy, it's gotten into my head.

Because I think I believe it.

None of our friends are homophobic asswipes—Chad did the hard work there—and sure, my parents might be taken by surprise, but they're not the type to make a huge deal out of it, and—wait.

Whoa.

Those thoughts took a detour.

How did I get from experimenting with my pain-in-the-ass frat brother to, what, coming out? What would I even say?

Mom, Dad, there's a guy in my frat who could probably bench-press me, and when we kiss, I get confused. My girlfriend? Oh, don't worry about her, she's totally fine with it.

Even in my head, the whole mess sounds idiotic.

Instead of focusing on what's going on with me, I throw myself into my risk manager duties and finalizing my last assignment of the year. With only six months left of college, you'd assume I'd be more prepared for it to end than I am, but I keep being hit with these melancholy moods. Grad school is on the cards for me, but do I want to hang around here when nothing will be the same? The brothers I've had by my side since the start, who I rushed with, partied with, helped out with coursework, and listened to their problems, all of them will be gone.

Some of the junior guys are cool, but it's not the same. We have a bond, but it's not airtight. Not the way I am with Chad, Zeke, Robbie, and some of the others.

"Blakely, there you are."

I glance up from where I've been hiding and find a dude from Gamma house called Martin approaching. He's one of Jenny's friends who I can't stand. I might have managed to avoid him at the party last weekend, but he's got me now. We're two of only four guys whipped enough to have come to yet another sorority tea party. Most guys get wind and make sure they pick up shifts these days as a way to get out of it, but I don't work, and with football season over, all my excuses are weak.

"Heard you got up to some fun last weekend?"

Great. Yes. This is *exactly* what I want to be talking to Martin about. His lips are pulled into a sneer, showing off his chemically whitened teeth that look horrible with his spray tan. Even in winter, he's wearing a polo shirt with a popped collar.

I joke about Robbie being a douche, but his stems from obliviousness and the want to have fun. Martin and his friends are manufactured douchery, which makes them the actual worst thing to happen to Greek life.

"No more fun than anyone else," I answer as dryly as I'm able.

He chuckles in a practiced, cringy way. "My father says everyone experiments in college, so no judgment from me. It's definitely not my taste, but to each their own."

This must be the seventh circle of hell. Small talk on a topic you're trying not to think about with someone who you have to pretend to like even when they get on your last nerve.

WWRD. *What would Robbie do?*

If flipping him off and leaving isn't an option, he'd make things as uncomfortable for the other person as possible, so *they* leave.

I wink at Martin. "You're missing out."

"My girl has everything I need."

"Oh, yeah, mine too," I hurry to say because I don't want shit to get back to Jenny. "But kissing a guy … you haven't lived until you've tried it."

Instead of getting uncomfortable and leaving though, Martin takes a step closer and ducks his head. "Oh yeah? What's so different?"

"Everything and nothing. If you want to find out, you'll have to try it for yourself."

He thinks for a moment. "Let's go ask the girls."

"What?"

"Well, Jenny lets you hook up if she's there, right? I bet Jodie will be the same."

I take a step back. "I thought that *wasn't your taste?*"

"You've convinced me." He gives me a smug smile like I should be proud of that or some shit.

I shake my head. "Yeah, I'll pass."

"Why? You have no issues sticking your tongue down the throat of that loudmouthed barbarian."

"He also happens to be one of my best friends."

Martin's face bunches up. "I thought you two hated each other."

That's news to me. "Who the hell said that?"

"You're always fighting."

"They're discussions." I scowl. Sure, we argue a lot, but it's how we communicate. That doesn't mean we hate each other. I mean, who could hate Robbie? He has the biggest heart of anyone I know. Except maybe Chad.

"So, what? You two exclusive on the weekends, and you bang Jenny through the week? Is that how it works?"

"Fuck you."

"Is it the whole if you're drinking when you do it, it doesn't make it gay?"

"I wasn't drinking the first time, and I was barely buzzed the second. Are you seriously annoyed I won't hook up with you? Get the fuck out of here with that shit."

He gives me a nasty look. "Maybe it's more than an experiment. Maybe you two are fucking around behind Jenny's back."

"I dare you to start shit."

He holds up his hands. "Nah, Blakely, we're good here. Just making sure, brother."

I'm about to tell him he's not my goddamn brother when a group of sorority girls enters, and Jenny is with them.

"Hey, baby, why are you hiding away in here?"

Martin tilts his head, but I ignore him.

"Stomach's playing up."

She freezes, hand halfway to my arm, and steps back instead. "Do you need to leave?"

I hate how disappointed she looks, and it's all on me for making her that way. This thing needs to end, and soon. It's not fair on her for me to string her along.

"Yeah, I should."

"Photo first?" She looks so hopeful, but I can't do it. I can't keep playing this part with her.

"I better go before I shit my pants."

And ignoring the scandalized looks from her sisters, I swing by the food table, pile up a plate, and head home.

The walk is freezing, and it's quieter out with us so close to break. Even in winter, there are usually people all over the row, but I make my way up onto our front porch without seeing a soul.

I open the front door to the sound of video games coming from the front room to my right, friendly arguments are coming from my left, and someone has their music on upstairs that's mixing with the sounds of either someone having sex or working out.

It's busy and overwhelming at times, but I love it.

I pass the plate from one hand to the other as I strip out of my coat, then go in search of Robbie. Since it's lunchtime, the kitchen is a safe bet, and as I reach the hall outside, I hear his booming voice singing along badly to the music.

"I can't tell if someone is singing in here or murdering a chicken."

Robbie throws a look over his shoulder but keeps belting out the lyrics.

"Make him stop," Chad complains from where he's sitting on the counter drinking his protein shake.

"Maybe this will help." I hold up the plate as Robbie finishes making his own shake, and he grabs it on his way past to the small table we keep in here.

And when he pulls the napkin off the plate and notes the small square sandwiches, mini quiches, and bite-sized tarts, his whole face lights up.

"Fuck yes." He meets my hand with a high five before dropping his bulk into one of the chairs.

I'll never understand what he finds so amusing, but I watch as he chuckles while he makes his way through the plate.

"You are one weird dude," Chad says. "I have closing shift, so I'll see you guys later."

I nod as he leaves and move to sit opposite Robbie. He tilts the plate in invitation, but I shake my head. I've already eaten enough miniature food for one day, and instead of finding it fun like he does, I just find it frustrating. That shit isn't filling anyone up.

"You know you can buy almost any food in small sizes," I say.

"Yeah, it's freaking awesome."

"So why don't you?"

He snorts and takes a small bite of the quiche. "No fun if I'm buying it myself. I like to be surprised. Like this." He waves a hand at the plate.

"Chad's right. You are weird."

"If weird means fun, then I'll be weird all day long." He moves the plate into the middle of the table. "Come on, pretend to be a giant with me."

"Except you're not pretending. You're enormous." In size but also in attitude, which only makes him seem bigger.

"And this is itty-bitty." His large fingers daintily pick up a raspberry tart. "Come on … it's adorable."

"Sure."

He shakes it side to side and makes screaming noises before popping the whole thing in his mouth. He grins at me as he chews, and I can't help smile back.

"I think this is another thing we're going to have to disagree on. I don't get it."

"You're more tense this year," he says when he finishes chewing.

"Maybe I'm growing up." I lean in as he cringes. "Or *maybe* I'm too busy cleaning up after you fools to have any fun of my own."

"Next weekend. We're going to make sure you have fun."

"Right, yeah, this party," I say, nervous over how little we've discussed it. "How low-key are we going to make it?"

He makes a dying noise, because *intimate* gatherings so aren't the Sigma way. "Well, since this isn't a scheduled event, we only need to cover the party costs. The cheaper we go with shit, the fewer people we need there. That said, I have a contingency budget that I usually blow on Sigma-only parties, so we can dip into that as well."

"I think if I'm going to have fun at this thing, we need to make sure there are no dumbass freshmen who can't handle their alcohol and no strange sorority chicks we don't know. The bigger the pool of people, the higher chance of shit getting out of hand."

"Then why don't we make this thing brothers-only?"

I'm surprised he'd even make that offer. "I think somewhere in the middle is fine. Maybe invites-only?"

"Exclusive. Yeah, man, chicks dig that shit. I think we can invite the Beta brothers, a handful of the guys from next door, no Kappas, duh."

"What about Bailey?" I point out.

"Dammit, I forgot about him."

"There's no way Doomsen won't bring him."

He sighs. "Fine. But only him. The rest are a bunch of twatknuckles."

"You've a way with words, my man."

"You can hit up Jenny and her girls, right?" Robbie asks, pulling out his phone to make notes.

"Ah …" Now probably isn't the time to tell him my plan to bail from the relationship. Maybe this party can be our last one together, then I'll end things over break so she has time to move on before next semester. "Well, obviously."

"Sweet. I'll sort out the alcohol—"

"A keg and seltzers only."

"No." He shakes his head dramatically. "No way, man."

"Safest options."

"Are we planning a party or a fucking Sunday school meeting?"

"You said we could work together."

"Yeah, on something *fun*. Remember? The whole point of this is for you to let your balls loose."

"My balls are doing perfectly fine." I pin him with a look. "You *said* we'd plan it together."

"Yeah. Together. I didn't say I was giving you free rein. You might as well head down to Kappa house and start a circle jerk at this rate."

"*Wow*, you have dicks on the brain. I didn't realize being a cockhead was a literal thing."

He slumps back in the chair and runs a hand over his face. "Pretty sure Dooms and Bailey infected me."

"Dude, that's not a literal actual thing that can happen. Maybe you've always been bi, but you're more into chicks, so you never gave it much thought."

"Who said I'm bi?"

"Aren't you?"

"I don't fucking know. That's literally the point. That is *literally* the whole, entire point, and none of our goddamn house, the dudes who are supposed to have my back, will help a brother out."

"I *kissed* you. More than once."

"Yeah, and now I'm ready to move on to advanced lessons, and all you peanuts are bailing on me."

I stiffen at the thought of us doing *advanced* stuff, because there's a part of me that's curious.

He laughs. "Relax, you don't need to look so shit scared. You've helped me enough. There's nothing hot about stroking off a floppy cock while you stand there and judge me."

Except, floppy wouldn't be a problem. I clear my throat. "So. Party."

"We have to make sure there are some cool guys there, because I don't want anyone being a dick to Dooms and Bailey or dropping words if I find a guy to hook up with."

"That's fair." I hesitate. "Think you will?"

"Who the fuck knows. I'll wait until the night and see who's around. But I swear to god if you cockblock me with the guest list, I'll cover your bed in lube."

"Again," I mutter.

"You've thought twice about stealing my hookup since then though, haven't you?"

"Not my fault she thought I was hotter."

He splutters. "You told her I wanted to piss on her."

"Oh yeah." I grin. "Good times."

"How about we make a deal."

That doesn't sound good. "I'm listening."

"We'll do this whole thing your way if—"

"You're not touching my dick."

He blinks in surprise. "I was going to say *if* ..." He nudges the plate toward me. "You play giant. Just once."

I'm not sure why that response disappoints me. Robbie touching my dick should be the last thing I want, but the bastard isn't even giving me the satisfaction of saying no. I shake away the confusing thoughts and focus on the plate instead. "Why?"

"It's fun. You know. That thing you wanna have."

Fun. To eat mini pastries. "Fine," I say, holding back from rolling my eyes. I swipe a sandwich off the plate and go to toss it in my mouth when Robbie grabs my hand.

"You're doing it wrong. Scream a little. Put on a giant voice. Give it something."

"You've got to be kidding me."

He takes the sandwich, folds it in half, and mimics a train. "Choo choo! *Oh no, here comes a tunnel.*"

"Why? What did I do to deserve this?"

"Open uuup!"

"Please no."

"*We're gonna craaash.*"

All I can do is thank fuck there's no one around to see us, and ... open my mouth.

He shoves the food in, and before I have a second to react, he presses a massive palm to my face and pushes me from my seat.

I land on the ground with a thud.

"Dick!" I get out around the food.

Robbie's booming laugh fills the room. "I was right. That *was* fun."

He leaves before I can go after him.

7

ROBBIE

THE LAST WEEK BEFORE BREAK GOES ACHINGLY SLOW. I'M pumped for the Sigma party, and our brothers responded to the idea of invites only better than I thought they would. I guess there have been so many holiday parties going on already, and it's easy to forget that not everyone has the stamina for going all out that I do.

I still haven't found a date though, which is a massive hell no for the social chair, but it's not like I've put in much effort. I have a name on campus and could ask out any of the chicks I'm friends with, but I wasn't lying when I told Brandon I want to find a guy to hook up with. A guy who isn't him.

It's not a fun thought, if I'm honest. I almost feel like because I started this with him that we should be continuing on as we are. It's working, we have chemistry when we mouth fuck, so why wouldn't we have chemistry with every other kind of fucking?

But while I was playing with him and Jenny last weekend, I really don't want to come between anyone. There are more than enough people out there who I can fool around with, I don't need to focus on someone who's already attached.

If only goddamn Chad had let me touch his dick, I probably never would have gotten into this mess.

"You ready?" Chad asks.

I come out of whatever trance I was in and blink the others at our mastering mayhem meeting into focus. Almost the whole room is watching me, and while I'd normally brush it off as Brandon putting me to sleep, that would be hypocritical considering the lecture I already gave these guys about paying attention.

I bounce to my feet. "Just giving our prank one more think over. It's very important to make sure you consider every option."

Even though I'm not looking at him, I catch Brandon watching me out of the corner of my eye. Yeah, yeah, Robbie's changing his tune. Truthfully, whenever Chad comes to me with a prank idea, my first response is "Yes" followed closely with "How?" Safety doesn't make the list, and I know that's dumb of us, but we've also been doing this for a long time, so most of that stuff is instinctual.

"I've checked it," Brandon says. "You're all good. I've also emailed it to everyone here, along with notes on the pranks you all submitted. Compare the two, and try again."

There's some whispered conversation that quickly shuts the fuck up when Chad picks up the GoPro and straps it to his head. I do the same, since we're going to be leading the two different teams into the house.

To watch the action unfold, Zeke has the projector set up on the wall, streaming everything in real time. Chad turns to face me, and I give his camera the finger guns, watching the image show up overhead.

Rick sticks his head inside. "They've left for their meeting."

And we're on.

Once a week, Kappa house heads to campus for their fraternity meeting since their house isn't big enough for all their members to be in the one room. They used to only leave a pledge behind, but after getting sick of us hitting their house so frequently, a handful of guys—usually one from each year—stays at the house and watches the meeting on a video call.

But four guys are no match for the ten of us.

Kappas will never learn.

We do though, and we know that if the guys on campus see their house being hit, they'll head straight back, which gives us roughly five or so minutes to do the most damage we can. And because everyone here will be watching, I'm sure they'll be keeping track of who to vote for in Master of Mayhem based on how this prank goes.

Champers has a backpack full of dishwashing detergent, I've got a trash bag full of shredded paper from the office I work part-time at, and Miles has a bag of sand.

They're going to be pissed.

Because of the tight time frame, we've got two stages. First, we grab the Kappas and zip-tie them to the nearest object; second, half of us cover the house in detergent while the other half stealth steal whatever they can get their hands on. Once it's off the Kappas' land, they can't do shit about it.

These mastering mayhem classes are too easy to build into King of Thieves.

"Ready?" Chad asks.

I fist-bump him, and then we're off.

We leave the house as one group and make for the road that's been cleared of ice and snow before breaking into a run. It would have been easy enough to sneak through the back-yards and take the Kappas by surprise, but first, I wasn't inter-ested in freezing my ass off, and second, they can see us coming all they like, it isn't going to stop shit.

We fly across Greek Row and thunder up the stairs at Kappa, and Chad lets us in with the key he swiped from Bailey earlier. I have to admit that them getting together does have *some* advantages here.

The Kappas inside clearly aren't expecting us because they glance up from where they're huddled around the computer in surprise.

"*Chad?*"

"Bailey?" Chad immediately comes to a stop. "I thought you were going to the meeting?"

Bailey blinks big eyes at Chad, bottom lip drooped. "You wouldn't get me into trouble, would you?"

"Ah …"

I slap Chad's head. "Stop thinking with your dick."

"Right. Yes. Sorry, sweetheart."

The innocent look drops off Bailey's face. "You have to catch me first."

He takes off, and the other three Kappas scatter.

Fuck. This wasn't part of the plan.

Chad and I tear after Bailey.

"You think you can outrun us?" I ask.

"I don't have to," he calls back. "I only have to keep you distracted long enough for everyone to get back here."

He ducks into the hall, and Chad and I pause.

"I'll go that way," I mouth, pointing straight ahead. "You loop around."

He nods and disappears back through to the living area while I creep along the way Bailey went.

"Oh, little Bailey …" I call.

There's the sound of scuffling in the rest of the house that almost drowns out his reply.

"Fuck off, big Robbi—*oomph*!"

I round the corner to where Chad is trying to contain Bailey, but he's putting up a fight. I quickly grab a chair and help wrestle Bailey into it before Chad zip-ties his wrists to the arm rests.

"Are you for real?" Bailey hisses.

"I don't have a choice."

"I'll remember that, dick."

Despite the venom in Bailey's tone, Chad doesn't seem worried. He drops a kiss on his boyfriend's nose. "What if I let you tie me up later?"

Bailey stills. "Naked?"

"Duh."

"Fine," he grumbles. "But if you do anything to my room, there's no sex for a month."

"I really don't need to hear this," I say, checking to make sure Bailey is secure.

Chad smirks. "Sure, listening at my door to us having sex is one thing, but listening to us plan to have sex is where you draw the line."

"You got it." I tap the camera over my forehead. "And I think they'd agree with me. Now, let's move. Your fucking boyfriend put us behind."

"You're welcome," Bailey sings as we go check on the others.

The three remaining Kappas are all secure, and Miles has already rolled up the rugs in the main rooms and the hall. Time to get to it.

Champers pours detergent over the floors, while Rick follows with a broom to smear it into every crevice, then Miles and Larken cover it in sand for grip and shredded paper to make the cleanup even harder.

Classic prank. Low effort, minimal cost, big cleanup.

We leave them to it, very aware of the ticking clock over our heads, and stuff the bags we brought with as many items as possible. This is what the Kappas had been trying to do a few weeks back when they hit our house, and if Brandon hadn't ended up in hospital because of it, they would have managed a clean sweep with the game. Being locked in that room for possibly hours would have given them all the time they needed to clear us out.

But unlike those dickheads, we know what we're doing.

While some of the guys make work of things downstairs, Chad and I head for the second floor. We raid as many rooms as we can, taking shit like pens and desk clocks and family photos. I snort, picking one up.

Like, damn, I love my family, but I don't have photos of them on my nightstand.

"Come on," Chad says, appearing in the doorway. "I want to find Lucas's room so I can rub my balls on his pillow."

"Gross, man." But fair considering what a fuckstain that guy is. "I'll go second."

But before we can make it to the stairs, there's a shout from one of our brothers. "They're back, run!"

Shit. I look at Chad, and he stares right back.

The front door slams open.

"It appears we're fucked," he whispers.

We can hear their heavy footsteps in the hall, and then … someone thunders up the stairs.

Not today, Kappas. I grab his shirt and haul him into a bedroom, heartbeat pounding in my ears.

"Robbie, brother, I love you, but I told you you're not touching my dick."

I hold back from flipping him off and head for the window. There's an awning over the back deck that we can climb out onto, but the thing doesn't look trustworthy. What's a little life endangerment when we have a competition to win?

I take a deep breath and force confidence. "We're going out here."

Chad laughs. "So we can die?"

"So we can get this shit back to the house. I'll go first, you throw that crap out, then you follow."

"And if they catch me?"

"You're on your own." I shrug and say, "King of Thieves," like that explains everything. Which it totally does.

"Fine." He yanks up the window. "But hurry."

I climb my fat ass out and pray the roof holds beneath my weight. My adrenaline is pumping, nerves pulled tight as I wait for my footing to give out at any second. A door slamming inside makes me jump, and I almost slip but catch myself in time. It's only a few feet and then a drop-off to the ground, but I hold my breath as I creep across and try not to slip on any ice.

It is so. Fucking. Cold.

Somehow, I manage it without dropping a Robbie-shaped hole through their back deck, and the second I hit the ground, I hold up my hands to catch the bags Chad tosses to me, wincing as they hit my frozen fingers.

If he doesn't hurry up, I'm bailing and leaving him here. My Arizona ass isn't built for this shit.

Luckily, he hits the ground, grabs one of the bags, and

bolts for the side fence. I follow him over, creep around the front, and then we're home clear. We reach the road and make the run back. I'm breathing hard, amped up on adrenaline, and pumped that the whole thing was caught on camera.

Shouts follow us, and I glance back to see Lucas try and tackle Miles, but Miles slips through his fingers. People from the other houses have stepped outside to see what's going on as yet more Kappas tear into the street.

But there's nothing they can do. Our items are off their property, therefore they're property of Sigma house until Harmony Week—unless they steal them back.

Good luck with that.

And that, folks, is what you call a stealth steal for the books.

I have no idea how many guys got away, but when we enter the war room, the waiting Bigs and Littles cheer as we enter.

"That was awesome," someone says.

Chad takes a bow, and I'm about to join him when Brandon punches me in the arm. *Hard.*

"What the fuck was that?" he asks.

I cringe and rub my shoulder. "Abuse?"

"Back at the house. Did you really *jump off a roof?*"

"Aww, Brando, you do care."

He scowls and points at himself. "Risk manager. I'm the risk manager—of course I care. Do you have any idea how much paperwork that would have been if you fell and broke your neck?"

"What I'm hearing is …" I say as I loop an arm around his neck. "You were scared I'd come to bodily harm, and you were worried for me. So sweet."

He bats me off him and stalks back over to where Zeke is sitting.

"Sure, he didn't punch *you*," I mutter to Chad as we join them.

Zeke holds up his phone. "Five missed calls from Charles. Well done."

"Hear that?" Chad addresses the room. "Their prez is shitting hotcakes over this prank. Ten bucks says he tries to meet with Zeke to discuss"—he holds up his hands for air quotes—"parameters."

I could lose my shit laughing. Charles is so uptight that he makes Brandon look relaxed.

It looks like out of all of us, only two guys aren't back yet, so either they're hiding out, or the Kappas got them. Such is the way of this life. Don't bother trying to prank people if you're going to be a baby about being caught.

As long as no one reports us to the dean, we're all good on the row.

Zeke holds up his phone and calls Charles, the loud ringtone coming through on speaker. He answers a moment later.

"*Again*, Zeke?"

"What can I do for you on this fine winter's day?" Zeke's voice couldn't be more bored. He likes Charles about as much as the rest of us, which is not at all.

"Look, we're going to have to go over the parameters for—"

I can't help the sounds that burst from me as Zeke ends the call. Could the guy be any more predictable?

And as the room devolves into conversation around what we did and place bets on how many points we'll end up with, I catch Brandon watching me, so I blow a kiss his way.

He responds with an expected eye roll, but then something

I'm *not* expecting happens. His cheeks flush a ridiculously bright red.

I didn't even know Brandon could blush.

And he is.

Over me.

Oh, this has just gotten interesting.

8

BRANDON

I DON'T DRINK AT FIRST, WATCHING ROBBIE TO SEE IF HE follows through on his promise, but the only thing I see him pull out of his pockets is cans of soda, and his fanny pack only appears to be holding snacks and gum. A few hours into the party, I relax enough to throw back a few shots.

As much as I don't want to admit it, Robbie has things covered. He's doing a constant loop of the party, checking in with our pledges stationed at the doors to make sure only the guest list has been let inside, and he's thrown off any potential trouble before it's had a chance to get started.

It's pissing me off that everyone is on their best behavior for him. It almost makes me want to drunkenly jump on a table to give him a taste of his own medicine.

And maybe there's a tiny part of me that wants to do it for his attention too.

He's barely glanced my way all night, and the more buzzed I get, the more it's getting to me. He said he was going to find someone to hook up with, and cockblocking a brother isn't the frat way … unless they've done something to earn it. For once, I can't even make that claim. He's left me and Jenny alone all night—and I hate it.

The thought of him kissing another guy turns my stomach. It's *our* thing.

Which is hypocritical as fuck, seeing as how I have a girlfriend.

I burp loudly and push away from the wall I'm leaning against, tipsier than I thought I was.

"Brandy, where are you going?"

"Away from …" I almost say her friends but catch myself in time. Insulting sorority chicks would be a disaster, and I'm not interested in having the Sigmas blacklisted. "Going to check in on Robbie."

"O … kay?"

I stumble away from them and approach the big guy. He's watching the people dancing in our living room with an intensity I don't like.

"Hey, risk manager." I slap his ass. "How does the stick feel up there?"

"It fits good. Why didn't you ever tell me what a power trip this is?"

Power trip? He's got to be kidding. "Yeah, go a few parties without drinking, and it loses the fun fast."

He's still watching the dance floor as he lifts a can of Coke to his mouth and downs the rest. I greedily watch his neck working with each swallow, caught off guard by how fucking hot it looks.

I rock where I stand, mind filled with images of leaning forward and running my tongue over his throat.

"What?" he asks.

"What?"

Robbie bursts out laughing. "You just said you want to taste my neck."

"The hell I did." Did I? Goddamn, how drunk am I?

"It's the Rob-dog effect."

"Thank you."

Confusion crosses his face. "For?"

"Calling yourself Rob-dog again. Like that, all urges have miraculously disappeared."

There's definite curiosity on his face as he eyes me. "How much have you had to drink?"

"I didn't think much at all, but apparently my brain-to-mouth filter is defunctive—"

"Defective?"

"Uh-huh. So maybe a big more than drunk. Big—*bit*." I frown and flex my jaw.

He chuckles and gives my shoulder a squeeze. "Better pace yourself, or this party will be a fast one."

I watch as he turns his attention back to the dance floor, and annoyance sparks in my gut. I step in front of him, which does sweet fuck all because he looks right over the top of my head. "What's so interesting out there?"

Robbie shifts, rubbing at his arm like he's … nervous? "See that guy?"

I follow his line of sight to a blond twink. I'm not proud of the aggressive snort that leaves me. "You'll break the poor kid in half."

"Maybe, but he's made it clear he's interested, and I'm starting to think I should … do it."

"Right."

"What's that tone?"

I shrug. "I've never known you to settle for the first piece of ass to walk by."

"That's literally all you've ever known of me. I'm not picky."

I narrow my eyes at the guy and turn back to Robbie. Before I can think it through, I grab his T-shirt and tug, forcing him to meet my eye. "If you're looking for someone to kiss, you know Jenny's rules. I can go get her."

His eyes immediately drop to my lips, but then ... he shakes his head. "Nah, if we keep doing that, things are going to get weird. I'm not interested in drama."

"No drama." I push onto my toes, bringing our faces close. "I'm just trying to be a good guy and help you out here."

"Right. And you get nothing out of it, do you?" The flirty tone matches the spark of interest in his eyes. I've known Robbie so long, and he's such an open person, that it's too easy to read him.

"Well, maybe I think it's pretty hot too."

A corner of his lips lifts in an evil smile. "I think I've moved on from kissing now though. I'm ready to get some dick."

Heat flares below the belt, and like it's been summoned, my cock starts to take interest.

"I wanna touch one ... suck one ... maybe replace that stick up my ass with one ..."

Now there's an image.

"So, Brando, still want to be a good guy and help me out?"

"I ... I ..." Holy shit, I think I might.

But there's one very big thing stopping that from happening. I'm not a cheater. Kissing him with Jenny's permission is one thing; wanting to take it further than that is another.

I step back. "I've got to go."

"Wait, I was kidding."

"We both know you weren't."

He opens his mouth to say something, but I leave before he can.

I find Jenny where I left her, and when she tries to pull me back into their conversation, I step away and shake my head. "Come with me."

Thankfully, she follows, because the last thing I want is to break up with her in front of people. She might annoy me sometimes, but she doesn't deserve that.

"Where are we going, Brandy?"

"To talk."

"Talk …"

I lead her upstairs to my room, and when I close the door behind us, it muffles the music from downstairs.

"What are you …"

"We need to break up."

Her mouth drops, and she watches me for a long moment. "What?"

"Sorry." I watch her cross my room and drop onto the side of my bed. "I wanted tonight to be fun, and I was going to wait to do this in the morning, but …"

"You want to break up?"

"Ah, yeah …"

"*Right* before the holiday?"

I don't have a reply to that. It's shitty timing, but it would have been no matter when I did it.

"You were going to meet my parents," she says.

"*What*? When did I agree to that?"

"It was going to be a surprise."

"We've been together … a month?"

"Ten weeks, actually. And all you've done in that time is treat me like shit."

Okay, *now* I'm offended. "What do you mean? I do everything you ask. I show up to your little get-together things, I play nice with your friends, I pose for all your couple photos that get plastered all over social media."

"You don't like or comment or anything."

"Am I supposed to?"

"You do when it's your brothers. Whenever it's someone from your house or your football team, you always at least drop an emoji, but I get nothing."

"Fuck, sorry. I didn't realize that giving you everything in real life wasn't enough."

"It would be if you were present."

"Present?" I begin to pace. Any thoughts of this being an amicable split are going down the drain. "I'm *always* present. I do more with you than my friends."

"Yes, but you always make it very clear who comes first."

"We've been together *a month*, maybe two. They've been my friends for *years*."

She glares. "I don't ask for much, but you whine about coming to a little Gamma mixer with me, yet you have no issues with letting Robbie use you as his flavor of the week."

Anger ripples along my spine. "Excuse me?"

"You were a throwaway bit of fun for him, but I know you. I know you liked it."

"You're the one who pushed me into kissing him in the first place. You."

"Yeah, but I didn't realize my boyfriend was going to suddenly like dick."

That's rich. A hollow laugh comes from me. "Let me get this straight. It's okay for me to kiss guys when it's all for show? When you can use it as evidence of what a cool girl-friend you are, but if I actually enjoy it, then *I'm* the bad guy?"

"You have a *girlfriend*."

"Who taunted me into doing it in the first place. Surely you knew there was a chance that maybe I'd like it."

"I thought you were straight."

"And the fact that I might not be makes you uncomfortable?"

"Obviously."

"You do know that I can be interested in guys *and* girls but still be committed, right?" If I had feelings for Jenny, it wouldn't matter how many people I kissed, she'd be the only one I wanted. But we never had that moment where we clicked. Everything has been superficial—on both sides.

What started as hooking up led to sleepovers, and then everyone assumed we were dating and exclusive, and I went along … until now. Even with her obsession with status, she's mostly harmless. But I don't like the way she's implying if I'm anything less than straight that I'm not who she thought I was, and I *really* don't like that she was okay with me kissing Robbie as long as I didn't like what I was doing.

What kind of girlfriend pushes her boyfriend into a situation she *expects* him to be uncomfortable with?

"I think that's the problem," she says. "You're confused. Everything with Robbie has twisted you up. The kissing was a mistake. You need to stop, and then we can talk again when we're back from break. You're drunk, and you're not thinking clearly."

"This has nothing to do with Robbie."

"Doesn't it?"

"No." And I mean that. Sure, I might want to experiment with him at some point, but my relationship with Jenny was over long before I ever kissed him, and if I hadn't been so worried about her reaction and the blowback on our house, I would have ended things way before now.

"I don't believe you."

"What do you want from me?"

"The truth."

I shake my head. "Trust me, you don't."

"Of course I do." She crosses her arms, not planning on leaving.

And apparently I'm drunk enough to give it to her because I start talking. "Fine, but don't say I didn't warn you. The truth is, I'm not even sure when we started dating, but you were suddenly introducing me as your boyfriend to everyone. I thought we were just hooking up. Having a good time. Meanwhile, you're trying to create this fairy-tale romance that's complete bullshit. You're a cool chick, but you get so caught up in image that nothing is real. Right now, I'm willing to bet that you're not upset about us ending, you're upset about having to tell people about it."

She opens her mouth, but nothing comes out.

I fall back next to her. "I know I was a shitty boyfriend too."

"You were."

I have to clench my teeth against her fast agreement, because I never signed up for the boyfriend thing in the first place. "If it's easier, you can tell everyone you broke up with me."

"Fine. But I'll be telling them it's because I knew I deserved better."

"Sure." It's not like I'm worried about my boyfriend material status. I don't want a relationship, and with the end of college not too far away, I'm going to use that time to figure some things out about myself.

"Well, I guess that's it, then."

I nod.

She doesn't leave for a full minute, and then as though she's realized there's nothing else to discuss, she gets up and walks out.

Thank fuck we got through that with no tears.

I flop back onto my bed, planning on waiting out enough time for her to hopefully leave the party, but instead, I pass the hell out.

9

ROBBIE

AFTER BRANDON DISAPPEARED ON ME, I DIDN'T SEE HIM AGAIN that night or all the next day. I trudge through the final classes of the semester, my mood getting lower and lower at the prospect of two weeks alone.

Chad's taking Bailey to visit his family in Georgia, and Zeke is flying home, along with every other brother in the house. Because my position as office bitch is an unpaid internship, Mom and Dad have agreed to pay my fraternity dues and food each week, and once those things are covered, it doesn't leave a lot of money for things like flights across the country.

My scholarship is good but not a full ride. I might be a decent left tackle and could maybe aim for the NFL, but the lifestyle is too unstable for me. Best I could hope for is riding the bench. I'll never be one of the greats. I'm no Shane Miller.

It's hard, but I'm hoping this internship will be worth it once college ends.

I've just finished saying goodbye to the final guy walking

out the door, and regretting not catching Brandon before he left, when my phone lights up in my hand and my little brother's name fills the screen.

"Yo, marshmallow!" I say.

"Fuck off, *Robert*."

"Ohh, first-naming me. Someone's feeling snarky."

He sighs. "I can't believe you're not coming home again this year."

"Yeah, me too."

I can tell by his silence he's sulking. We're so similar and yet complete opposites. Marshall and I look a lot alike, except he wears glasses, and where I'm always unshaven, he keeps his face smooth. Our resemblance is all surface-level. He never got into football like I did, and I never got into …. whatever nerdy-ass shit he's into.

"If the family get to be too much, head back to school," I tell him. "At least it isn't far for you."

"Still five hours' drive."

"Better than a five-hour flight."

"True." He pauses.

I'm used to Marshall being quiet, but this is something else. "Everything okay?"

He puffs out a breath. "I miss you."

"Yeah, you too." He's two years younger than me, so we've always been close, which is good, because our parents don't *get* Marshall. He's funny and sarcastic, but the studious, quiet side doesn't fit in with our loud family. I've always joked that we never let him get a word in, so it's not like it's his fault. "Oh, hey, you wanna hear something fun?"

"Always." The down tone he had going on disappears.

"I kissed one of my frat brothers."

There's silence and then … quiet laughter. "You what?"

"Yeah. Turns out I'm bi. Wild."

"I'm not even surprised."

"You're not?" For some reason, that makes me ridiculously happy. "What, I set off gaydar or something?"

"No." He sounds close to laughing again. "Probably the opposite, but what would I know? I meant the way you said it like it was the most normal thing ever."

"Well, it is."

"Yeah, but not everyone thinks like that. Can I … how did you know?"

The curiosity gets my attention. "One of my other brothers is bi, it sounded fun, so I wanted to try it … why?"

"No reason."

Ah, yeah, there's definitely a reason. Interesting. Could we be even more alike than I thought? Even if he's going through something similar to me, I'm not going to push it. If he wants to tell me, he will, and in the meantime, I'll trust him with my shit so he knows he can trust me with his. "I dunno what to do about it though."

"About what?"

"My frat brother."

"Who was it? One of the ones I know?"

I hesitate over telling him, but hey, he's across the country, and he's my *actual* brother. He's not going to message Brandon and spill all my secrets. "It was Brando."

"Holy fuck."

"Yep."

"So …"

"So, what?" I ask.

"Well, I've always thought you two were close. Is there … do you want more, or was it some stupid frat thing?"

"Stupid frat thing," I hurry to say.

"Right."

"And also, *maybe* if he didn't have a girlfriend, I'd want to get him naked."

"A *girlfriend*?" He sounds scandalized.

"Relax, the kissing was all her idea."

Marshall lets out the same booming laugh I have. "I don't know what to tell you, other than I know you, and you always get what you want."

Not always. I didn't hook up with that twink last night. I didn't get my tongue down Brandon's throat. I didn't even get to say goodbye to him today … "I think it'd be smarter to cross anything to do with him off my list."

"Yeah, but you're not the smart one, remember?"

He's got me there. "So you're saying I should go for it?"

"Not if he has a girlfriend."

"Well, obviously."

"But … if he's interested and they break up, or she wants a threesome or whatever, then yeah. Go for it. Don't worry about the details."

"Now that I can do."

He gives a distracted hum.

"You sure you're okay?"

"Huh? Oh, yeah, one of my housemates just walked in."

"Which one?"

"The one who hates me," he says, not bothering to keep his voice down. "I better go before I, you know, breathe wrong or something."

"Love you. Give Mom a kiss for me."

"Love you too."

We hang up, and I slump back on the couch, letting the silence engulf me … for a whole second before a taunting voice makes me jump.

"*Give Mom a kiss for me.*"

"Shit." I whirl around to find Brandon leaning against the doorframe. He's wearing flannel pajama pants and a hoodie.

"You bastard, I thought everyone was gone."

He chuckles, tucking his hands in his hoodie pockets and crossing to drop beside me on the couch. "Sorry to disappoint." Brandon relaxes back into the couch, blond hair a sleep-rumpled mess.

"What time are you leaving?" I ask.

"I'm not."

I struggle for words for a moment. "You're not heading home?"

"Nah, it's my last college Christmas, so I thought, what the hell?"

"And this has nothing to do with me staying?"

"Well, yeah, a bit." His lips twitch. "What kind of risk manager would I be to leave the biggest hazard on campus here solo?"

I shove him, and he shoves me back. My smile is huge as it sinks in. I'm not going to be spending the break alone. Even better, I'm going to be spending it with him.

"You're not going home at all? Not even for Christmas?"

"Nope."

"Wow. Exactly how pathetic do you think I am?" There's no bite to my words, because I'm too happy.

Sure, last year was boring, and I wasn't looking forward to it this year, but I'm not the type to sit around feeling sorry for myself, and yet, Brandon canceled on *his family* to spend the break with me. He can feed me all the crap he likes about this being our last Christmas in the house, I know there's no way he would have stayed behind if he was going to be here alone.

I drop the teasing. "Thanks."

"Careful, man. That sounds a lot like gratitude."

"Gratitude this." I flip him off, but he grabs my hand and sinks his teeth into my finger. Instead of hurting, it draws my attention to his lips, and those teeth that are quickly becoming a massive turn-on of mine.

Nope, bad Robbie!

While Brandon has a girlfriend, this thing is done between us. No flirting, no kissing, no nothing. Because dammit, he always leaves me wanting more.

So against all urges, I extract my hand from his grip and push him into the other side of the couch.

"What are we going to do, then?" I ask.

"What do you normally do at home? Big feast, gifts, that kind of thing?"

"Yeah. Usually a Christmas movie and lots of eggnog."

"Eggnog?" He pulls a face. "How does anyone stomach that?"

"You've got to make it yourself. None of that store-bought shit."

"And *you* know how?" The skepticism in his voice makes me determined to show off.

"Damn right. I can cook too."

"No way."

"Way." I wink at him. "Man of many talents."

"Okay, then first thing's first. We go shopping."

Hmm … didn't think that through. I mentally tally the amount in my bank account plus what I'll get for groceries next week.

Brandon lightly kicks my calf. "I've got it."

"I can't let you—"

"Dude, I want to. My parents gave me some money for Christmas, so I'm all cashed up."

I know Brandon is better off than most of us, but he's still far from being able to afford a whole Christmas feast. "Go halves?"

"You're on."

When we get to the supermarket, we throw any and everything that's on sale into our cart.

"Hey, wait." Brandon pauses beside some discounted Christmas lights.

"You wanna decorate?" I ask.

"I was thinking … the Kappas are gone, aren't they?"

"Yeah, but King of Thieves is paused over break."

"Not what I'm thinking." He holds up a crushed reindeer box. "Let's grab some of this, then go along the row collecting all the decorations and load up Kappa house with it all."

The excitement in Brandon's voice makes it impossible to say no. "Only if we can set everything up in porny poses."

"Was there any other option?"

And that's how, three hours later, Rudolph is giving Dasher head on Kappa house's front lawn. I'm frozen solid, but I take a minute to look around at our handiwork. Santa is jerking off instead of waving, there's a reindeer orgy, and Brandon's sex doll, Sally, is on top of a Christmas tree in a toilet paper dress. Every time the Christmas tree star lights up, so does she.

Plus, we've scraped a giant dick into the snow and lined it with twinkle lights, right beside a Frost-She the snowgal who's boobs are kinda lopsided.

And as much as I wanna stand out here, admiring the art we've created all night, my balls have turned to ice cubes, and I'm worried about them snapping off.

I walk backward. "We did a great j—"

My heel hits a string of lights, and I'm too cold for my

reflexes to be working. I go ass over tit in the snow. Even in ski pants, I freeze instantly.

Brandon thinks it's hilarious.

"Hey, fuck you."

He keeps laughing.

So I grab a fistful of snow and fling it in his direction.

"Dick." Brandon ducks and scoops up a handful of snow, and all I see is him packing it into a snowball before I scramble to my feet and start running. I scoop up snow and toss it back blindly, Brandon's answering taunts making me think I missed.

"You wait for—" My head snaps forward when he hits me. "*Now* who's the dick?"

Fuck this. I duck down and grab a handful, then rub it into his face as he goes to run by me. It's less of a snowball fight and more of a scuffle where we try to flick as much ice at each other as possible without losing our footing. I'm breathless from laughing and losing feeling in my limbs when Brandon pours a fistful of snow down my shirt.

My entire body goes tense. "*Fuck!*" I choke out. "Fuck, fuck. D-dead man."

He bolts for the house as I grab as much snow as I can manage, and karma gets him good when he slips on ice and hits the ground. All the snow I've gathered ends up over his head, but when I go to run off, Brandon grabs my ankle, and I face-plant.

"Screw you, man!" But I'm not sure he hears me because my teeth are knocking together so hard, and he's already halfway back to the house.

I'm stiff, my legs don't want to work properly, but I finally get up and stagger back home. Brandon's clothes have been dumped unceremoniously in the front hall, and I can hear the shower going upstairs. I shrug out of my coat and sweaters, kick off my boots, and drop my ski pants with Brandon's gear, then head upstairs.

I pound on the bathroom door. "I can't believe you left me out there. What if I froze to death?"

"Then it'd be peaceful around here," he shouts over the spray of the water.

I try the door, finding it unlocked, and walk in. The shower has steamed up, so I can't see any of the good stuff, and it's immediately a thousand times warmer in here than it was outside the room. I quickly close the door behind me to trap the heat.

"You have two minutes, then I'm coming in."

"Go use Zeke's shower."

"And have him murder me? No, thanks."

"As if he'd know," Brandon says.

"You want to risk it?"

There's a pause, and then the shower cuts off. "Fine. I was enjoying that, asshole."

"I didn't say you had to get out, only that I was coming in."

The glass door swings open, and Brandon steps out and grabs a towel. I'm very, very good in that I don't check out his dick while he's naked, but once the towel is around his waist? Fuuuck, he looks good. Perfectly cut muscle, smooth skin, blond hair dark from the water and slicked back off his face. He grins at the way I'm watching him, and the sight of those teeth makes me tent my boxer briefs.

"I had to get out." He nods at my dick. "For my own safety."

I pretend like I'm not feeling smug as hell, then drop my underwear and step into the shower. The warm water burns as the cold seeps out of me, and when I feel human again, my cock decides it's done with waiting. Through the foggy glass, I can make out Brandon leaning against the counter.

I wrap my hand around my needy dick and relax into how good it feels. "Dude, I'm about to start jerking off. Might wanna get out."

"You're not supposed to tell people when you're about to jerk off."

"My dick is literally in my hand."

He doesn't answer, and I can only imagine he ran out of here as fast as he ran out on me at the party. My eyes fall closed as I start a slow stroke up and down my shaft. Between my hand and the water pelting down on the head of my cock, I'm in bliss.

And even though he's the cause of this erection, I don't mean to picture Brandon during this, but the image of his water-pebbled torso enters my brain, and I have zero desire to push it out again.

I grunt and pick up the pace.

His torso, his full pecs, and sculpted abs. His cocky smirk and the V that disappeared beneath his towel. I picture stepping closer, tucking my fingers under the material and letting it fall to the floor before following it. Knees hitting tile. The smell of sex.

My head drops back on a gasp as I imagine looking up at Brandon and sucking his cock into my—

"*Fuck* ..." My orgasm hits hard and fast, cock pulsing with every spurt of cum. I milk myself through it, wanting to draw it out as long as possible, because that image was fucking hot. Apparently I don't need to touch a dick to know I'm into it. I only need to picture Brandon's. "Holy shit," I whisper, my body giving a belated shudder. I turn my attention to washing my cum down the drain—I'm a considerate housemate—when a throat clears.

I hurry to wipe a circle in the steamed glass and find Brandon exactly where I last saw him.

"Sounded like a good one." His voice is rough, and when I glance down, his towel is sticking straight out at the front.

"You have no idea."

The shower fogs up again too fast for me to make out the look on his face, but I see him head for the door. "I'll see you downstairs."

And as desperately as I want to call him back and offer to take care of his problem for him, I let him go. I meant what I said to Marshall. Brandon is off-limits as long as he has a girlfriend.

No matter how much I really, really want to touch him.

And maybe he should have left for break, because suddenly, these two weeks have become a whole lot harder.

10

BRANDON

THE LAST FEW DAYS HANGING OUT WITH HIM ONE-ON-ONE HAVE been … interesting. I thought us kissing, and then standing there, listening to him jerk off while barely being able to see more than a flesh-colored blur, would make things awkward or tense, but Robbie is Robbie. Nothing gets to him.

I'm glad for it too, because I don't know where to go from here.

It's a weird feeling to have the house to ourselves. He spends a lot of time knitting while I scroll through social media or play video games. I'm so used to the constant noise, even late at night, the movement of people coming and going, the cars passing up and down Greek Row. With all the houses empty or close to it, things are quiet.

Too quiet.

The line between peaceful and boring is a thin one.

I finish drinking my coffee, looking out at the clean,

untouched snow on our front lawn before grabbing my phone and calling home.

Mom answers on the first ring. "Merry Christmas, oh wayward son."

"You've been waiting all week to say that, haven't you?"

"She wouldn't have to say it if you'd come home," Dad calls from somewhere in the background.

"You're both making me regret calling you."

"Brandon Blakely, you show your parents some respect."

"Careful, you're starting to sound like Grandma." I chuckle when she pretends to gasp. "Must be a side effect of getting old."

"Where did I go wrong with you?"

"I thought you kept a list?"

"Now, children …" Dad says in a familiar exasperated tone.

I drop the joking. "You guys okay up there? It's not too late for me to drive up for the day."

"I thought you wanted to spend your last Christmas there."

"I do." Well, with Robbie, at least. But no way am I taking him home for the day, even if it is only an hour's drive. "But I miss you guys."

"You know you're welcome home whenever," Mom says. "Just let me know and I'll throw lunch on."

"Way to make me feel guilty. It's our first Christmas apart," I admit.

"Yeah, we're unsupervised," Mom says. "No telling what we could be getting up to."

"Don't need to know."

She laughs. "I miss you."

"You too. I'll call you later, okay?"

"Okay, sweetie. We love you."

"I love—"

"Even if we're not important enough to spend the holiday with …"

"*Mom.*"

"Don't listen to her," Dad says.

"Thank y—"

"I'm sure you had your reasons for abandoning us."

I sigh. "You two are worse than my frat brothers."

"Love you, bye," they chorus.

I hang up, exasperated but smiling.

My gaze drifts to the Christmas present on the table beside me, and I grab it before heading up to wake Robbie.

If I was at home, this morning would be a mad rush of presents with the family, then cleaning and cooking—while I hid outside—ready for everyone to come over. I'm surprisingly happy with my choice to stay behind.

I push Robbie's door open to find him asleep on his back, mouth open, large chest rising and falling with each deep breath.

After the conversation I overheard the other day about him wanting to see me naked, I can't stop thinking about it. Trying it while our brothers are gone and it's only us here makes sense, but I'm nervous.

And excited. But mostly the nervous thing.

It's why I haven't mentioned to him yet that Jenny and I broke up.

My thoughts about wanting to try more are hard enough to work through, let alone having him suggest it outright, which he would if he knew. And selfishly, I like this time we're getting where we get to be idiots without having a list of worries hanging over my head.

I grab one of Robbie's discarded pillows, lift it high, then whack him as hard as I can with it.

"The fuck?" He grunts sleepily, eyes squinted as he sits up and looks around.

"Merry Christmas, douche nozzle."

He collapses back against the bed. "The fuck you waking me for? We didn't go to sleep until early."

"Because we have a day of festivities ahead. You promised to teach me how to make eggnog."

"Yeah, but not *now*."

"No time like the present."

"Bro my god, get *out*."

I flop down on the bed beside him and prop my head on my hand. "Is that any way to talk to Santa?"

He cracks his eyes again. "What?"

"Here." I place his present on his chest. "It's nothing exciting."

Robbie frowns at the brightly wrapped package. "Fuck, Brandon, I didn't get you anything."

"Actually, that's the best thing you could have gotten me."

"Huh?"

"Now, whenever someone mentions Christmas, I get to point out how I got you something and you didn't get me anything. I get full-on bragging rights over who's the better friend *and* get to use it against you."

"That's not a present."

I stretch one arm up over my head. "And yet, it's made me happy. I'm going to be all, 'Hey, Robbie, remember that time we exchanged Christmas presents? Oh? We didn't? Huh. Guess you better fetch my next drink for me.'"

He sits up. "This present better be good."

I cringe. "It's something small. Not important or anything …"

And yet, I'm nervous as he unwraps the gift. It's a dumb gift—an essential, really—that I hadn't thought about twice while I bought it, and yet now I'm off-balance, sure he's going to hate it.

"Is this …"

"Wool underclothes? Yeah. You're welcome." I force false bravado. "Now your dumb ass can stop whining about the cold."

He still hasn't said anything when the ten packets of mini M&M's I bought fall out of the wrapping with the rattle of little candies. Róbbie's whole face lights up. "Brando … this gift … it's kind of awesome."

And when he looks at me, his blue eyes are unexpectedly soft. I'm not used to seeing anything other than cocky derision in them.

So I try to channel some of his usual energy. "I *am* the greatest gift giver in the history of ever. You can thank me later."

"And now I feel like a shithead that I didn't think to get you something."

Yikes, this has taken a turn for the serious. "Dude, stop. I'm not used to genuine. Call me an asshole."

"Yeah, how dare I appreciate this."

"*Exactly.*"

"Fine." He shrugs and climbs out of bed, wearing only his boxer briefs, and I give myself a moment to take him in. "Thanks for the gift, *asshole.*"

I try to picture walking over there and running my hands over his barrel chest, stroking the hairs on his thick torso, dropping my hand and slipping it into the waistband of his underwear.

Considering my interest in chicks is so strong, I'm legitimately surprised at how enticing that whole image is. There isn't a single feminine thing about Robbie. Nothing I can look at and be like, "yup, that's why," other than the fact he so unashamedly went after what he wanted, and for a short time there, what he wanted was me.

I think I want that back.

We're good friends, frat brothers, and he's made it clear he's interested in exploring his sexuality, so it makes sense that if I'm also curious, he should be the one I go to. So why am I holding back?

Despite his objections to the wake-up call, it's almost eleven, so while he jumps into the shower, I go downstairs and pull everything out for our feast. Robbie better not have been lying when he said he knows how to cook these things, because I'm already anticipating golden potatoes and juicy meat swamped with gravy.

He joins me a few minutes later, hair a damp mess, and wearing only the undershirt I got him and a pair of joggers his legs look ready to burst out of.

"Why don't you have Christmas music on yet?" he asks.

"We're doing Christmas music?"

He laughs as he disappears, and then a minute later, carols are blasting from the TV speakers.

For the next two hours, I'm treated to Robbie's terrible singing while he teaches me how to cook a Christmas lunch. He knows his way around the kitchen, and that laid-back confidence is unexpectedly attractive, especially coupled with his focused attention.

The whole time we work, he doesn't goof off once.

It's … disconcerting.

"You all right?" he asks.

"Yeah, fine."

"You were staring into space. I thought you were stroking out or something."

I scoff. "There's no getting rid of me that easily."

"Total opposite of what I want to do with you."

My gaze flies to his, and we have a beat where we look at each other. I have no idea how to respond, and it's clear he isn't sure what he meant by that.

Robbie shifts, and his light laugh is fake as shit. "You know, because if I get rid of you, I can't annoy you. Obviously the reason."

"Of course." We still haven't broken eye contact.

"So stop looking at me like that."

"Like what?"

"Umm …" He clears his throat and turns away. "Like you're plotting how to give me food poisoning."

"Maybe then I'd finally get to watch what I wanted."

"I can't believe you're still complaining about that. We watched *Die Hard* last night. *Die Hard*. You can't tell me you didn't want to watch the most epic Christmas movie of all time."

"Ehh."

"Ehh?" His mouth drops. "Fucking *ehh*?"

"It's overrated."

Robbie attempts to say something but can't seem to make noise happen.

"Shit, look at that. I made the big man quiet."

"I … I just …"

"And Christmas movie?" I push, because annoying Robbie is fun. "Can it actually be classified as that?"

"You need to stop."

"Or …?" I know I'm pushing my luck, but he's too fun to rile up.

"It's *Die Hard*!" he splutters. "That's it. We're watching it again tonight, and I'm going to point out all the most epic moments and why it's a Christmas movie, and you're going to *sit* there and like it."

"Well, I'm glad you didn't get dramatic about it."

He points at me. "I'm onto you, Brando. Keep it up and no eggnog for you."

"You'll keep your piece-of-shit drink to yourself? Oh no. I've learned the error of my ways."

Instead of responding, he takes my shoulders and steers me toward the small table we've set up the ingredients on. "Time to learn how to make the best-tasting thing you'll put in your mouth today."

"Did you mean to make that sound dirty?"

"Not on purpose, but it's me. Are either of us surprised by this point?"

"Nope." And because I can't stop myself, I ask the question that's been on my mind since the party. "How did you go with that twink guy anyway? Finally fulfill your lifelong dream of cock?"

"Lifelong." He snorts. "And nah. I passed on that."

"Why?"

"No reason. Just did."

I let it go for now, but I want to know more. For someone who's been so full steam ahead on finding a guy to hook up with, I would have thought Robbie would be all over that. We focus back on mixing the eggnog, and Robbie puts way more nutmeg and vanilla in than should be legal. Which is probably a good thing when he adds almost a full bottle of bourbon.

"Are you trying to get me drunk?"

He winks. "You're more fun that way."

"If I didn't know any better, I'd say you were trying to hook up with me again."

"Nah, no worries there." He nudges me. "I know better than to go after someone with a girlfriend."

"Good thing I don't have a girlfriend, then."

His whole head snaps toward me, and I'd tease him about his over-the-top reaction if I wasn't freaking out over what the hell I was implying. "You …"

"We broke up. At the party."

"Why?"

I almost say because she wouldn't let us kiss anymore, but that would be a bullshit lie. "I knew I had to, and before break seemed like the best time."

His stare is fixed on my mouth, and I wait, wanting to see what he'll do next and hoping like hell he makes a move. If he takes it out of my hands, I won't have a chance to think through what's happening. I can lean in, enjoy it.

Instead, Robbie fills two glasses with our eggnog and hands one over. "Merry Bromas, Brando."

"You can't just add 'bro' to words and make them work."

"Sure I can. With enough conviction, you can make anything work." He lifts his glass and takes a long gulp of eggnog, watching me over the rim.

With enough conviction, anything works.

I guess I'm going to test that out.

But first, a drink. Or … two.

And even though the eggnog tastes every bit as disgusting as I remember, I choke it down, needing the liquid courage.

11

ROBBIE

THE EGGNOG GOES DOWN TOO EASILY, AND BEFORE WE'RE even through our lunch, I am tanked off my tits. The room is a bit spinny, and Brandon's face blurs in and out of focus.

We stumble into the front room, where we try and fail to play video games while continuing to drink ourselves stupid. Maybe writing myself off on Christmas Day wasn't a smart choice, but it's a whole lot more fun than sitting around the house on my own.

Besides, if I'm drinking, I can't think about the fact Brandon is single or that I want my mouth on every body of his inch.

Wait.

Inch of his body?

I scrunch my face up and try to wade through my swampy thoughts.

"Dude, your eggnog is lethal."

I squint toward where Brandon is lying across the couch,

arm hanging over the side, while the other is nursing a concerningly full glass that keeps sloshing over the edges. "Good though, right?"

"I'm so drunk I could drink gasoline right now, so your eggnog is one step up from that."

I try to self-five and totally miss my other hand. "I knew I'd convert you."

"I think converting is a stretch."

"You're totallyyy converted." I pump my eyebrows at him. "You can kiss me as thank you if you want."

He studies me for a moment. "You'd love that."

"Nah, been there, done that."

"Ohhh, look who's playing hard to get."

"I am hard to get. Allll the ladies want me."

"No, they wanna tame the beast." Even his words are sounding slurred.

"I am a beast, aren't I?"

"I was talking about your dick."

Oooh, let's do that some more. I reach down to adjust myself, and Brandon's gaze follows the movement. So I give it an extra squeeze, just for funsies, and try not to get worked up at how hard he's staring. "No woman can tame this dragon."

"Needs to be a man, huh?"

"Not sure a guy could tame it either."

Brandon runs his tongue over his lips, and my whole body heats. He's so attractive, even before dipping my toe into the queer paddling pool, I've noticed shit like how his hair always sits perfectly and the way his body is photoshoot ready. I chalked it up to envy over not looking like him and being able to pull chicks like him, but … fuck. The thought of touching Chad's dick is whatever. The thought of touching Brandon's?

My cock is mildly interested, chubbing up enough to press against the crotch of my sweats.

Brandon laughs so hard he slips halfway off the couch. "Did the dragon hear us talking about it, did it?"

"My baby is always ready for attention."

When Brandon claws his way back upright again, his legs fall over my outstretched ones. The couch isn't large enough for us both to lie down on, but fucked if either of us cares.

His eyes are hooded when he replies. "What kind of attention does it think it's getting from me?"

"Just talking about him is enough to awaken the dragon."

"Stop. Calling your cock the dragon is as bad as calling yourself Rob-dog."

"If you'd seen it, you'd understand."

He kicks me, and I swear the room tilts. "You're so transparent."

"Your vision messed up too?"

"No, I'm not that drunk." He sits up, and I can't tell if he's swaying or it's the room. "I know you want me to touch your dick."

"Do I?"

"You're practically begging for it." He flashes me a full-fanged smile.

I push myself up to face him. "Funny, because it almost sounds like *you're* begging for it."

"I would never."

I eye him and the way he's leaning forward. Is he leaning forward? Or is it me?

Fucking fuck, why did I drink so much? "What's wrong, Brando? You wanna kiss me again?"

"About as much as I want my balls forcibly removed."

"I can do that too, if you ask nicely."

"You're obsessed with seeing my dick, I swear."

"Technically, any old schlong will do," I say.

"Of course, because why have standards when you can have everyone?"

I crack up laughing at the dumb one-liner I used to pull back in freshman year. "Okay, maybe I've gnome—*grown* up since then."

"You've grown up, but you haven't matured."

My grin stretches across my face. "You have no idea *how* much I've grown up."

"But I'm sure you're willing to show me, aren't you?"

"What can I say? I'm a generous guy."

He tugs his bottom lip between his teeth, and I zero in on the movement. It's hot as fuck. When he lets it go again, it's darker pink and wet, and I can't tear my gaze away.

"You, umm ..." He sounds sort of breathless. "You're staring."

"You want me to be staring."

"Says who?"

"Says the way you keep licking your lips."

He does it again. Slower this time and so fucking deliberate. I groan as my dick decides it's well and truly ready to take over.

"What are you going to do?" he taunts.

"Lick your lips again and you'll find out."

At first, nothing.

Then the tip of his pink tongue darts out.

Fucking Brandon.

I all but tackle him onto the couch. He grunts as his back hits the cushion, but then my mouth is there, and I swallow the sound down. He doesn't play coy, doesn't try to fight me; he kisses me back as deep and desperate as I kiss him, and even with my brain moving as sluggishly as it is, the need inside me settles.

His mouth is hot, his kisses hard. It's both new and exciting and overwhelmingly familiar.

Brandon's hands knot behind my head, holding me close, tongue surging forward as deep as he can manage. Our teeth knock, my hand bunches in his shirt, while the other grabs his back.

I'm not trying to be precious about this. I'm following how it feels and what I want, and when I lower my body and press against him, all the nerves inside me light up and fucking sing.

I want to feel his skin under my hands, his cock pressed to mine, while he desperately clutches me closer. I love when I can feel how much my partner wants me, and between his hard cock and commanding mouth, Brandon leaves zero doubts in my goddamn mind that he wants this as much as I do.

"This doesn't mean anything … right?" he manages between mauling my mouth.

"It means we're taking advantage of college."

"Experimenting …"

"Having fun …" I add, wanting him to shut up and let me enjoy kissing him.

"It's all curi—"

My lips attack his neck.

"—*osity*. Oh. Fuck. Yeah, right there." Brandon tilts his head, offering his throat up to me, and I suck and nip and kiss my way down to the dip before his shoulder. His skin is warm, stubble rough. Strong hands clutch my shoulders and fill me with sensations I've never experienced before.

I want to kiss further. Run my lips over his shoulder to

his pec, his abs, his cock. I'm so turned on by the thought, I'm going cross-eyed, and look at that. I think I can mark my experiment as a success, because now I'm here, now I'm touching a man and wanting more, I know with total certainty that if he whipped out his cock, I'd choke myself on it.

Though …

I pause in my attack.

This must be what it was like last time. Freshman year when I hooked up with that guy, I was drunk then as well. I don't remember hesitating or overthinking; I only remember being swept up in the moment. It's left a lot of blank spaces in my memory. Blank spaces I'm desperate to fill … and hooking up with Brandon, while I'm half-shitfaced, isn't the way to do it.

Motherfucker.

I pull back and look down at his lust-drunk expression.

"What's wrong?"

Goddamn it, even his voice is pure sex. "I think …"

Brandon catches my lip with his teeth, and an honest-to-god growl leaves my mouth. "Don't start doing that now," he rasps.

"I *think* I need to—*fuck*—we need to stop."

"W-what?" His gaze slowly sharpens. "Did you change your mind, or …"

"Oh, nah, I'm sure. I'm about ready to tear your clothes off and take advantage of you."

"Is it taking advantage when I want this as much as you do?" He rolls his hips and drags his long, hard length along my thigh.

My brain short-circuits, and he almost has me giving in. I hurry to scramble off him. "No. Nope. Stop confusing me."

"Confusing *you*? One second you're eating my face, now you want to stop? What's going on?"

The panic in his voice is amusing. "Relax. It's not you."

"Then what …" He tucks his legs up underneath himself. His lips are swollen, hazel eyes tinged with confusion, and the longer I look at him, the wider my smile grows. Nerves are a mosh pit in my gut, because not only is Brandon sexy and kisses like a champ, but he also cares. The present he got? Hot damn. Bros being solid bros is frat as fuck—it's not like he bought me a six-pack of beer.

"I've been with one guy, and this whole mess is because I don't remember it. I was drunk off my face then, and I'm pretty sloppy now."

"We've been drinking, but it's not like we don't know what's happening here."

"Hot as hell, am I right?"

"Then what are you doing?"

I lean in and kiss him again, immediately realizing my mistake when I struggle to pull back. "If we hook up, I want to be sure I'll remember it."

"Dude, you really think I'd let you forget?"

"I'm counting on burning it into my memory." I stand up and stumble to the other couch. "Tomorrow."

He lets out a long-suffering groan. "How do you know I'll even be interested tomorrow?"

"You better be, brother."

Brandon's stare trails over me, and I'm worried for a second that he's about to say fuck it all and join me. But he doesn't. Thank fuck. Because if he touches me, I'm not strong enough to stop him.

"You can't call me brother when we were kissing like a minute ago."

"Why not, brother?"

He aims a cushion at my head. "It's weird, dude."

"But you *are* my brother."

"I'm your *frat* brother."

I tuck my hands behind my head and relax into the back-rest. "Either way, tomorrow I'm going to see your dick."

12

***

BRANDON

I STAY IN BED LONGER THAN I PLANNED, MY STOMACH AWASH
with alcohol and nerves. Kissing Robbie again was a mistake
… because I don't actually regret it. I want more. I want his
large body pressing me into the couch as he controls our kisses
and whatever else we do next.

It's not only the hangover keeping me in bed though; it's
the confusion over what comes next. Robbie said he wants
more, while we're sober, but then we stayed up until 2:00 a.m.
playing video games and raiding the Christmas leftovers. We
got drunker and drunker, flirted ridiculously, trading heated
glances, until we both hauled ass up to bed.

And now … well, one of us needs to make a move. I don't
for a second believe Robbie has changed his mind because
once he gets something into his head, he's full steam ahead.
Like a freight train. All I can do is hold on for the ride.

The question is, does he make the move or do I? He's been
the one to push this thing between us every time, and while I

love him taking control when we're kissing, I don't want to be passive in this. Making him come to me every time runs the risk of him thinking I'm only humoring him when, honestly, I think I'm in this as much as he is.

Kissing another guy is hot, and now I know what he meant about being curious about dick. Unlike him though, I don't need to see one to know they do it for me. Or … at least Robbie's does. The shower jerk-off the other day, and then feeling him hard and needy on top of me last night, turned me on as much as any woman ever has. Maybe more because I knew it was him.

The thought of trying to do this with another guy isn't appealing though. If Robbie put the brakes on and decided fooling around with a frat brother is dumb, I don't think I'd go looking for someone else to try this with. Robbie would. Which is … annoying.

I like that we could do this together. That we could figure out how much we're comfortable with and go from there. Share some laughs, some orgasms, maybe some butt stuff, see what happens.

I roll off the side of my bed, hitting the floor with a thump that echoes in my head. Okay, so maybe no butt stuff for today. Or laughing, probably. A long whine leaves me as I crawl to my feet. Might as well get this over with. I don't even know if the big man is awake yet, and if I'm basing it on the rest of break, he'll probably sleep in until after lunch.

I can't wait that long to face him.

My dick agrees with me.

Like I predicted, he's not awake, so I hurry through my morning shake, then take a quick shower and sort out manscaping. You can never be too prepared.

The fuck knob keeps me waiting until after midday, and

when I hear his thundering footsteps on the stairs, the nerves that had drizzled away come back in force.

"Morning," he says happily, passing me as he heads toward the kitchen.

"Morning is long gone," I point out. He disappears, and I try to resist following him, but next thing I know, I'm on my feet, heading in his direction. "You're in a good mood."

"I had a great sleep."

"I woke up hungover as a motherfucker, and you drank way more than I did."

"Yeah, but I'm used to abusing my liver. That asshole gave up on me years ago."

I snigger. "Bet it was on our Big/Little night when you ended up bent over the banister, puking your guts up onto the ground floor."

"How *did* I survive being a pledge?"

Robbie and Chad might be a lot to control now, but back then, they were complete mayhem. Being free in the world for the first time went to all of our heads, and while I was never as wild as the two of them, I'm surprised *any* of us survived freshman days. Thinking back to then, it's hard to believe, but we've all calmed down a lot. Even Robbie.

I watch as he devours a banana in three bites and let my gaze drop to his ass. It's huge, like the rest of him, and *so* round. A bubble butt on roids. Could I touch it? Pretty sure yes. Would he let me … do other things to it?

I remind myself that baby steps are the way to go here.

I'm struggling just to bring up the topic, let alone bend him over the counter and fuck him.

"So are we going to do it or what?" The question flies from my mouth before I can chicken out.

Robbie tenses for a second before slowly turning back to me. "Do what?"

"You know, hook up. Experiment. Touch some dicks."

The corners of his lips creep upward. "You wanna touch my dick?"

"Isn't that what we were going to find out?"

He takes a moment to answer as he checks me out, and instead of calling him on it, I cross my arms and lean against the table, waiting for him to be done. "What are you proposing?"

"Careful, that almost sounds like you want to talk parameters."

"Fuck off." He snorts. "I'm not Charles."

"Then why don't we do what you normally do and not think too hard about this. We can go upstairs and see what happens."

"Fool around this once."

"Sure." I shrug. "We can't be the only ones in the house who have done it. We'll have some fun, figure some things out about ourselves, and then move on."

"No relationship bullshit."

"I love you, Robbie, but the day I want a relationship with you is the day no one else on the earth exists."

"Agreed."

"Cool, so … we're doing this."

His sudden grin looks dangerous. "Lead the way."

I know Robbie was right to put a stop to things last night, but the whole way up the stairs, I wish I was just a little drunk to get through this. Not so that I could use it as an excuse, or so I could forget, but because it'd give me confidence, and I could really use some of that right now. I have no idea what I'm doing. I've never been with a guy. Never watched porn with two dicks touching, though I probably should have spent my morning doing that instead of lazing around the house.

Halfway up the stairs, Robbie reaches up and grabs my ass.

"The fuck, man?"

"You got a problem with me touching your ass?" he asks.

"I just wasn't expecting it."

He chuckles. "I dunno if you've realized, but for us to do this, I'm gonna have to touch your no-no parts."

"Okay, smart-ass."

"I really want you out of these pants."

"Can you at least wait until we get to my room?"

His groan comes out gravelly. "No guarantees."

And when I reach the landing and glance back over my shoulder, his cock is already making its presence known. Mine perks up at the sight, and thankfully, I reach my bedroom before I can get fully hard.

We both hover in the doorway for a minute.

"Think we need to get naked," he says.

"Is this going to be awkward?"

"Probably." He yanks his shirt over his head. "I think that's inevitable when it's us."

"You're right. Maybe we should have tried this with someone else." But even as I say the words, I don't like them. Maybe we bicker and get on each other's nerves. Maybe we rarely see eye to eye. But I trust him, and I know it goes both ways.

"Nah," he says. "You were the best option." Then he shoves his sweats down and stands there buck naked.

Clothes. Right. Off. I'm too busy staring at his body to remember, well, anything.

Robbie eyes me. "I can't suck your dick while you're still wearing pants."

"You want to …" I can't get out of my clothes fast enough.

Then we're both standing there in nothing, eyeing each other's boners.

"You'd think I'd never seen another dick before," he says.

"I've never seen one that big. And hard."

He gives himself a lazy stroke, and I swallow.

Neither of us makes a move.

"Okay, this is ridiculous. We're not a pair of virgins." I flop back onto my bed. "Get over here."

The nerves radiating off him are so unlike Robbie I'm not sure what to think.

"Unless you want to back out?"

"Nope." He crosses the room and drops down next to me. "I want this, but I'm not used to being out of my element."

Dude, you and me both. I push past my nerves and bring a hand up to his neck. "Let's start with kissing, and then …"

"See what happens?"

"Exactly."

His big hand finds my hip, and then he leans in. The kiss isn't the fast scramble of lust I'm so used to from him. It's tentative, unsure. We work to set a rhythm while I try to ignore the gigantic dick between us. He's not touching me, not yet, but the heat from his body radiates toward me, making me want to close the distance.

I need my brain to clock off. To stop thinking and let myself fall into this thing.

Fuck it. I cup his face and press forward. Our bodies come into contact, cocks trapped between us, and as his hand slides from my hip to my back, a shiver runs through me.

Okay. This is more like it.

My cock that had been flagging with the awkwardness surges to life, responding to Robbie's loud growl.

"Yup," he mutters. "Kissing is good."

When his lips find mine again, the cautiousness is gone, replaced with the familiar need flowing through both of us. There's nothing like the feel of a naked body against mine, and apparently I give zero fucks if that body is twice as wide and way hairier. Instead, letting my hands roam down to grip his football-sized biceps sends lust bubbling up to my head.

Robbie tugs me closer, then rolls onto his back, pulling me on top of him. My legs tangle with his, and the new position brings our cocks together in the most amazing way.

"Fuck me …" I'm struggling to think. "This is …"

"Oh, yeah …" He looks dazed. "One of my better ideas."

I roll my hips, sliding our erections together, and our hoarse moans mix in the quiet room.

Then he reaches between us and wraps his hand around us both.

"Oh shit." My head drops as he squeezes us and then gives a long, dry stroke.

"I need lube," he says.

I scramble to grab it from my drawer and toss it to him before getting back in position. This time when he grips us, it's enough to make my eyes roll back. Who knew that another dick could feel so good against my own?

"Any idea what you're doing?" I ask.

"Just what feels good."

"Excellent. Carry on."

And he does. The smooth glide of his hand over us both is so far removed from anything I've ever done before but so goddamn hot. I don't even have time to compare our cocks, which is something I definitely thought I'd do because the second the thought jumps into my head, Robbie rolls his palm over the head of my cock, and my mind goes blank.

I shudder and thrust into his fist. It feels so good I do it again, and again.

"I can't figure out whether I want to kiss you or watch you," he says.

Shit, that's a tough call. I greedily take in his solid chest, gaze following the light hair from there, down his thick body, into his pubes.

I whimper and plant my hands on either side of his broad shoulders so I fuck his fist with purpose.

"Watch," I say between heavy breaths. "We've kissed before. And we can kiss after. But right now, I need to see all of you to believe this is even happening."

And I know Robbie said he wanted to suck my cock, but there's no stopping me now. For two dudes who have no idea about gay sex, we're fucking nailing the assignment because I'm already about to nut like this is my first handy.

Robbie grunts and spreads his thick thighs wider, giving me more room to move. From this angle looking down, I can see the heads of our cocks pressed together, and with every thrust, I almost fool myself into thinking I'm fucking him.

Which I can say without a doubt that I am down for.

Him fucking me would be a challenge because that thing is even bigger up close.

"Holy shit, Brando, I'm close."

"Good." I pant. "Not just me, then."

I focus on his chest again, loving how sexy and solid it looks. I want to tease his nipples, run my hands all over him, but since those are occupied, I use the only thing I have left.

I latch onto his nipple with my teeth.

Robbie lets out a cry, and at first, I think I've hurt him, but then he stiffens. I release him in time to see ropes of thick cum shoot out onto his gut. Seeing him let go, the way he milks himself through it, the flush to his face, and the knowledge I'm responsible for it all goes to my head.

My balls are already tight when he scoops up his cum and wraps his hand back around my cock.

"Come on me."

Oh shit.

His strokes are hard and fast, the pressure insane. He knows exactly the way to handle a cock, and there's no nervousness left as he hooks one hand behind my neck and draws me into a kiss. The feel of his tongue filling my mouth and his hand working my length has my thighs tensing, shaking, as I chase that need to let go.

So ... damn ... close.

My cock gives a throb, and finally, the building pressure releases. I gasp with relief as I come, completely overwhelmed at what's happened, and when I collapse against Robbie's chest, we take a moment to catch our breaths.

"That was …"

"Mhmm."

Heavy arms wrap around me.

"So …" he says. "I guess we have answers."

"That cock is a fun time?"

"Damn straight."

We grin at each other for a moment.

He clears his throat. "Thanks."

"Yeah, man, of course," I say like my mind hasn't been blown as well. "I'm glad I could help out."

13

ROBBIE

THE ONLY CLASS I EVER DID HALFWAY DECENT AT WAS English. And can you be surprised, really, when I come up with evocative poetry like this?

Thanks for the frot, your cock's kinda hot. I'm after some more, so will you be my whore?

I know if Brando propositioned me like that, I'd be impressed.

"What did you get up to these holidays?" Holly asks. She's the office manager where I intern in the labor relations division and has worked her way up from exactly where I'm at now. Her question also reminds me that I'm about to be asked the same thing a lot once my brothers start returning back, so I better work on a damn good answer.

"Hooked up with one of my frat brothers." Hmm … probably shouldn't lead with that.

Holly stares at me for a second. "Okay. You ever done that before?"

"Nope, first time."

And like she can't help it, she giggles. "And you had to tell someone, huh?"

"It's been killing me." And it has. I'm back doing that overthinking thing that I hate. We hooked up over a week ago, and since then, all we've done is share a New Year's kiss because why the fuck not? "I don't have anyone to talk to about it."

"Is this the same brother who just came out?"

"Nope, this is the one who I pretend gets on my nerves."

"Oh …" Her smile turns sly. "The notorious Brandon."

"Calm down, he's nothing special."

"Right. You only hooked up with him."

"Exactly."

She laughs at me. "You know, I've always thought the dumb jock stereotype was mean and overdone, but come on, babe. You complain about him always, and now you guys have crossed a line that most friends don't. Can you at least agree that he's a *little* special? At least as a friend?"

I hate when people throw logic at me, but she's right. When I think of Brandon, it's not the same way as when I think of the rest of the knuckleheads I live with. There's something … softer, more protective there. "Okay, fine. I like him. Maybe more than a bro is supposed to like their bro."

She squeals and fist-pumps and does a bunch of weird-ass shit.

I wait for her to be done. "You good now?"

"That was very cathartic, thank you." Holly leans against my desk. "So what's next?"

"Dunno. We agreed to a one-time thing. It happened, it's done, and the rest of the house will start showing back up any day now, so that's that."

"You want it to happen again though?"

"I do."

"And him?"

That's the question, isn't it? I haven't asked outright, but if sticking my tongue down his throat to start off the year didn't lead to sex, I dunno how else to broadcast that I'm very interested in a repeat. "I don't think so."

"Bummer." We're both quiet for a minute. "You could ask him though."

"Nah, if he wanted more, he would have said something. I'm not a hard guy to read."

"Well, everyone thinks they're easy to read, but it doesn't mean they are."

True. I drum my fingers lightly over my keyboard, listening to the rhythmic clack. Maybe I should say something. Just come right out and suggest we make doubly sure this cock thing works for us. Being with him answered all of the questions I had, and I've gotten myself off to the memory of his sexy body working over mine more times than I can count.

Dudes do it for me.

But Brandon … he's one sexy dude. It'd be a shame to replace all that with someone else. For now. We're both single —why shouldn't we take advantage of regular sex with someone we know won't be trying to latch on and force us into a relationship? It seems like the perfect solution to me.

The hours of work drag on, and by the time I leave, I'm ready to hit Brandon with my offer. We're going to talk it out, then hopefully fuck it out. Then grab something to eat and maybe do it all again.

At least for tonight, before our brothers get back, but hopefully for longer than that. It'll depend on whether he wants this thing kept quiet or not, because in our house, it's almost impossible to hide when you're hooking up with someone. I say almost because Chad managed, though I don't think they were banging at Sigma house before we found out about them, because we definitely would have heard something.

So either Brandon doesn't do this thing, or we work out how far to take it. I give zero shits about my brothers knowing I'm with guys—I've never had an ounce of shame when it comes to sex, which is probably good since I'll fuck nearly anyone—but I've also come to terms with the fact I'm bi. This is who I am. Chad and I can be bi bum brothers together— screw anyone who has an opinion on that.

Brando will need time to figure out where he's at though.

The least I can do is let him know more dick is an option.

But when I get home, longing for another night of video games and hopefully orgasms, we're not alone.

Because of course some of the guys have come back early.

I find Brandon in the kitchen with Champers, Zeke, and Miles. I'm surprised Miles is back already, given how home- sick he gets, even two years into college.

I hold out my arms when I walk in. "Let me guess, you missed me."

Zeke snaps his fingers. "That's what it was. My head hurt from a lack of obnoxious loudmouths who drink too much and party too hard and have Charles constantly blowing up my phone."

"Speaking of obnoxious loudmouths, where's Doomsen?" Brandon asks.

"They were stopping by to see Bailey's fancy family before coming back," I say.

"Still can't believe that," Miles says. "Dooms all hooked up with a moneybags boyfriend."

"It's none of our business who anybody dates," Zeke points out.

I wonder if they'd be saying the same thing about Brandon and me hooking up. "Speaking of dating." I turn to Champers. "Ever find out if your girl was cheating?"

He shrugs. "We broke up, so it doesn't matter now."

"Sorry, man," I say, the other guys echoing the sentiment.

"Looks like we've got our own little Bro-motions happening," Brandon teases.

"Speaking of," Zeke says. "I need you two there more over the next few months. We've only got until graduation to make sure that whoever takes over from us has the right attitude. There's still a lot of traditions between now and then, so I need all of us involved. Full force. Total brotherhood bullshit, got it?"

"What do you mean bullshit?" I ask, kinda hurt. I know some people think fraternities take things too far, but there's nothing better than having a team of people at your back. Through thick and thin. Since we were thrown together in the pledge hall—not so much a hall and more two adjoining rooms with four sets of bunks crammed into each—we've been thick as thieves. I don't want that to ever change. Not when we graduate and move away. Not when we get jobs and families and do all that grown-up stuff that we're supposed to do.

Zeke gives me a patient look. "You know what I mean."

Do I though? We're all close, there's no questioning that. We're all about the frat life, but sometimes I think my brothers see graduation as the end date to all this. That our fraternity is something fun to do through college, but when we leave here, it'll end.

Am I the only idiot who doesn't think that way?

Brandon stands from the table. "Come on, Robbie. We

were supposed to keep the driveway and walkway clear while everyone was gone. Let's go do it before anyone else is back."

"Make the pledges do it," I whine.

"They're not back yet, and you know how I feel about hazards." He grabs my arm, and I let him pull me, sulking, from the room.

We both throw on coats and boots before grabbing shovels from the back shed.

"It's always so weird to see you when you're back from work," Brandon says as we shovel snow from the paths.

"Why's that?"

"You're so corporate-looking."

"I'm anything but corporate," I throw back.

"Hence why I added the 'looking' part." Silence kicks in for a moment before he says, "You okay?"

"I'm shoveling snow. And it's cold. What do you think?"

He waves a hand. "I don't mean that. You got all sad inside."

"Ehh. Nothing."

"I'll believe that never."

I pause what I'm doing and look over at him. His cheeks are flushed from the cold, and his wool hat is covering his hair, but when his hazel eyes meet mine, I get this little thrum through me. "Fine. So it's hitting me that we have not even six months left of all this, and then what? Everyone takes off to different sides of the country and never sees each other again?"

"Yeah, it's hard to imagine, isn't it?"

"It feels like everyone is ready to get on with their lives and end all this, but I love it. We have it made here. This is the shit college dreams are made of, and I don't want my friendships to end."

"Then don't let them." He goes back to work. "Dude,

nothing has to happen that you don't want to happen. There isn't a script here. You want to keep your friends, then put the effort in and make it work. Maybe the end of college isn't the end. Maybe it's just kick-starting whatever fuckery we get to go through with each other next."

My mouth falls open.

"What?" he asks and awkwardly shifts his weight to the other foot

"That's probably the smartest thing you've ever said." I hold up my hand, and he high-fives me, clearly with no clue why. "To the next chapter of fuckery."

A smile splits his face. "Hells yeah, brother."

"Huh ..."

"What?"

I glance around, and there's no one dumb enough to be out here with us. Do I bring up my offer now? Why the hell not? "You called me brother. I guess throwing out there that I'd be down to hook up again is out of the question."

"What?"

"No pressure." I shrug like I'm not desperate for it. "It was fun. It'd be cool to do again. Like you said, it could be the next stage of fuckery we get to do together. College is almost over, so I'm all set to take advantage of every moment between now and then." I'm talking way too much for something that's supposed to sound like a casual suggestion.

"You want to do it again?"

"I jizzed so hard, you really think I'm going to say no? Besides, I never got a chance to suck your cock, so I got ripped off."

He laughs so loud I'm worried someone from inside will come check on us. "Fuck you. There was nothing half-assed about what we did. But I can't believe you waited until now to bring this up. I've been trying to get you back into bed every day since, and you goddamn wait until everyone gets back?"

He has? "You *have*?"

"You think I normally walk around shirtless in the middle of winter?"

"We had the heat on."

"My *nipples* were ready to snap off."

Holy shit. "Why didn't you say anything?"

"Because when do you hook up with the same person more than once? In all the years I've known you, I can probably count it on one hand."

"Well, true, but you're not just a hookup to me. You're one of my closest brothers."

"Again, please don't call me your brother while we're talking about getting into each other's pants."

I'd apologize, but I'm way too happy with the direction this conversation is heading. "So, we're doing it again?"

Brandon glances back at the house. "Yes, but discreetly. You know the meaning of that word?"

"Of course." I pretend to think about it. "It means to shit, right?"

He screws up his face. "I *think* you mean secrete, and wrong on both counts."

"Either way, let's keep this quiet."

Brandon rolls his eyes, knowing I'm messing with him. "Sure. Just for you."

We both get back to work. "For what it's worth, I can't wait to see your cock again …"

"I'm with you there—"

"Brother."

His snowball slams into the back of my head.

14

BRANDON

As expected, Charles comes storming down the street to "talk" to Zeke about Robbie's and my Christmas decorating. Robbie and I watch from the front window as he goes red in the face, growing more and more agitated. Zeke is leaning against the house, arms crossed, small smile on his face, and not rising to meet Charles on his level. Whenever I see the two of them together, I'm reminded of a cat toying with a mouse.

Eventually, Zeke shrugs and says in his low, deep voice, "Where's your festive spirit?"

Charles gapes. "If I went to the dean—"

"But you won't. Because it was only a few decorations, and we've both done way worse."

He scowls. "Fine, but get your boys under control."

"Sure thing, buddy." Zeke pats his shoulder before turning for the house. "Now go home before you hurt yourself."

Robbie and I grin at each other and scatter before Zeke can

come in and give us some half-assed speech about forcing Charles on him.

First Bro-motions night back from break is always a big one. The main concerns are jumping back into classes and keeping up with grueling schoolwork. Some brothers have had issues with their families, and others, like Miles, are wondering what they're doing so far from home. He's got a huge family back in Tennessee, so I sort of understand, but as an only child whose parents gave him everything, college was my first hit of freedom.

I love them, but I also love breaking out on my own.

I guess it's not hard to forget about homesickness when you're only an hour from home.

"… dunno if I should transfer closer," he says. That catches my attention. And Robbie's, apparently.

"Leave?" he asks.

Miles shifts. "I dunno, man. I thought I would have settled in by now, but it still don't feel right."

"Family's important," I cut in before Robbie can get started on brothership and make Miles feel guilty. "And you have to make the best choice for you and your mental health. It's always number one, dude. But if you do stay, we're all here for you."

The other guys agree. And that's the amazing thing about Bro-motions night. We're here to support and listen, even if we don't have the answers. There's no judgment. No sly comments. No one made to feel weak. It's what we need when we're all so involved in sports that still come with a heavy side of toxic masculinity. I know Miles moved here for hockey, and he has a decent shot at the NHL after he gets his degree, but that shot isn't a guarantee, and it would be fucked for him to go through all this stress and missing everyone to not reach his dreams.

But that's the gamble we all have to make.

It's the gamble everyone makes with college. We're sinking four years into a degree that might do sweet fuck all for our futures, yet we're pressured to go through the motions and rack up debt on something that's a total crapshoot.

My gaze strays to where Robbie is sitting. He takes up half the couch to himself. Everything from his body to his confidence to the way he owns a space is *big*, and damn if that isn't catching my attention in an inappropriate way. He's turning me on, and all he's doing is knitting whatever misshapen thing he's working on.

I wrench my attention back to the others and try to be a good brother and listen to their problems instead of my dick.

Even if my dick is making a compelling argument.

The meeting can't wrap up fast enough. Seriously. It can't. Especially since it ends up running way later than they normally do.

When we finally end things and people start making their way home or to their rooms, I all but drag Robbie out of the room and down the hall.

"Tonight," I whisper as soon as we're out of earshot.

"For …"

I punch his shoulder because the look on his face tells me he knows exactly what I'm talking about. "Wait until everyone is in bed, then sneak into my room."

"Why does it have to be your room?"

I narrow my eyes. "You don't want to do it again?"

"Damn right I do. But you're the little one. You should do the sneaking."

"Little? I'm six foot, you dick."

He snorts. "Well, that's a stretch."

"Fuck off, you know I am."

"With shoes on, maybe."

"Sorry we can't all be behemoths."

He chuckles and leans in, lips alarmingly close to my ear. "Lucky I like bite-sized things."

I shoulder check him and walk off before I remember we didn't actually work out who was going to who. Fucking Robbie. Is it humanly possible for us to have a conversation where we don't get at each other's throats? Not six foot? Maybe some of us enjoy not being giants, thanks. And sure, I'm not built like a brick shithouse, but I've never had complaints about my size. Height, muscle, dick … I'm totally in proportion. My proportions just happen to be normal-people standards.

I'm still annoyed when the house falls quiet, and I give in about a second later. I'm too desperate for this to play games. When I get to his room and duck inside though, I find Robbie stripped down and lying on his bed with his hands behind his head, wearing nothing but a shit-eating grin.

"Good thing no one else walked in," I say, zeroing in on his cock as I lock the door behind me.

"Definitely. I'd hate to give my brothers self-esteem issues."

"Uh-huh." I cross the room, pulling off my clothes as I go. The same awkwardness from the last time is trying to take hold, so I do my best to ignore it as I climb up to lie beside him.

"Hold up." He pulls back and takes a moment to check me out. "Your abs are insane."

"I think the same about your arms."

He lifts one and flexes, and even though I know he's being

a cocky dick, the sight is incredible. Fat chance I'm going to tell him that though.

"Have you been working out since the season ended?" I squeeze his bicep. "Not as impressive as I remember."

"Fuck you." He laughs and nudges his cock into my thigh. "What about that? Still impressive?"

"Okay, *that* I can't even joke about." I roll my eyes. "No need to look so smug."

"I'm an impressive beast. I get it."

"Beast is right." Because fuck him I'm into it. "Can we get started yet?"

"Someone's impatient."

"Dude, you've been edging me for over a week."

"Everyone wants the Rob-dog."

I make a show of going to climb out of bed. "No. Nope. Can't do it with someone who calls themselves Rob-dog."

He pulls me back down and rolls on top of me, pinning me to the mattress with his bulk. "You jealous? Want me to call you Bran-diddy-dog?"

"Sure. If you want me to completely lose my boner."

"I can call you brother if you like."

"Okay, Bran-diddy-dog is a step up from that, at least. Not a big step. Maybe more like an uneven crack in the footpath."

He hums and leans down to brush his lips over mine. Like every time we're together, it sends a warm ripple through me. "So since we're keeping this discreet, I guess we need to be quiet, right?"

"Mhmm. Otherwise, everyone will know."

"Yeah, and the walls are thin. But I'm not exactly known for being quiet, and judging by our practice run, you're a vocal motherfucker too."

"I can hold it in."

Robbie runs his hand over my cock, and I suck in a gasp. "You were saying?"

"Fuck off, you don't make me lose that much control."

"If you want to risk it …" He very slowly strokes me from root to tip, and even that small amount of friction from him has me feeling all shivery. Okay, so maybe control isn't a thing I'll have for much longer.

"Fine. *Fine*," I say. "What are we going to do about it?"

A devilish spark hits his eyes. "How do you feel about being gagged?"

"Gagged?"

"Do you need me to explain it, or are you unsure?"

"Explain *this*." I whack his head. Goddamn moron.

"It'll keep you quiet." He leans in and licks along my ear.

I melt. Even the lightest touches are too much that when he gets his mouth on me, I can barely think.

"We don't need to decide now since I'll be gagged by your cock anyway, but think about it. If we're going to be *cum*panions—"

"I'm sorry, what?"

"Like companions, but with cum. I thought it sounded better than bum buddies."

"Neither of those is great."

He thinks for a moment. "What about fap brothers?"

"*Dude*, no." I wrinkle my nose.

"Like frat brothers who fap together."

"I know what you meant, and it's still a hard no."

"*Cum*panions it is, then."

I cringe, but I can't deny it is the better of the three. "Back to what you were saying."

"Oh yeah, if we're going to do this, you know, regularly, we have plenty of time to figure it out." His thick fingers drag over my bottom lip. "And I'm not gonna lie, thinking of you gagged is hot as hell. Especially if it's because your lips are wrapped around my cock."

The familiar nerves are back at that, because I have no idea what I'm doing when it comes to blow jobs anyway, let alone when the cock I'm working with is a monster. But I want to try. Even if the thought sends enough butterflies through my gut to make me feel sick, I *want* to do it. To feel my mouth stretched around him and taste his cum on my tongue. "Better get to it, then," I tell him.

Robbie's stare sharpens. "Let the bro jobs commence."

15

ROBBIE

I TALK A BIG TALK, BUT THE ACTUAL *DOING* IS HARDER THAN I thought it would be. My usual confidence is abandoning me, so I dip my head and kiss him again. There's something about the way he feels under me, so pliant, head tipped back and mouth stretched wide so I can fuck his face with my tongue, that calms my nerves.

Even though I know he won't judge me, and this is a safe space for us both to explore, I *want* to make this good for him. Maybe it won't be the best blow job of his life, but like in class, I'm going to put in the effort and hopefully scrape together something passable.

Because not giving your partner one hundred and ten percent during sex is the anti-frat.

I break from his mouth and trail kisses down his jaw. Brandon draws in a shaky breath, and I grab his face to push it aside and continue along his neck. He's shaved since we were last together. I miss the scrape of his stubble, but his smooth skin shows off his defined jaw and is somehow just as manly as when it was rough under my lips.

"How is this so hot?" he whines.

I chuckle into his neck. "Because you're with me. Duh."

"Uh-huh." His hands run along my sides, then around to grip my ass. "I'm sure it wouldn't be the same with any guy."

His words come with a heavy dose of sarcasm.

I turn his face so he can see me. "You trying to break my heart here?"

"Oooh, is someone feeling threatened?"

"Someone is already under a lot of pressure to perform. I'd like some appreciation for my efforts."

He laughs and nips my jaw. "Put some effort in, and I'll appreciate it."

"Dick …"

"Asshole." He smiles, flashing those white teeth at me, and I can't help releasing his face to press my thumb against his eyetooth.

"I think I have a vampire kink."

Then he sucks my thumb into his mouth, and *holy fuck*, my mouth drops. He looks sinful with my thumb between his lips, and I can't wait until that's my cock. Brandon's grip on my ass tightens as he rocks his dick up against mine.

I free my thumb, then grab his hands and pin them to the bed.

"Nope. We're not falling into that trap again." Because as hot as it was last time, I refuse to be distracted from my goal. I push up onto my knees and drink him in. He's beautiful. All that smoothly sculpted muscle. His long, toned thighs. And his perfect red cock that's demanding attention.

Balls up, Robbie, we're going in.

I release his hands and slide down his body until his dick is right in front of my face, and I gotta say, it looks a whole lot bigger from down here. And where I expected nerves over doing this right, all I'm hit with is a desperation to get started. To make it good for him. To see Brandon squirming as I drive him out of his mind.

I lean in and run my tongue from his balls to the tip of his cock. The taste, the way he sucks in a breath, goddamn, it makes my dick throb. My nerves disappear as I wrap my lips around his head and suck it into my mouth. The salty taste floods my mouth as I sink lower, loving the stretch, the feel, and just the *thought* that I have a mouth full of cock is so fucking hot, I want to keep it there and jerk off.

The only thing that stops me is wanting Brandon to touch me this time.

I hum with satisfaction and glance up.

The humor is completely gone from his face as he watches. He's propped up on his elbows, eyes heavy with the same hooded look from last time. His hands are gripping my sheets, and having the evidence, the un-fucking-deniable truth of how turned on he is right now, is blowing my mind.

I try to keep eye contact as I move, but damn it's a big ask. There are so many thoughts racing through my mind—to go deeper, move my tongue, play with his balls—that it's helping keep the edge off, but the expressions playing out on his face are like my own personal porno.

I release his cock with a soft *pop*. "You know what I wanna do?"

"Put my cock back in your mouth?"

Definitely that too. "I wanna suck you off while I finger your ass."

His cock jerks. "Ah, shit. That could be …" He swallows,

and his legs twitch wider. "Yes, but shouldn't we … I dunno, work up to it or …"

"Do you want to work up to it?"

His forehead is scrunched in confusion, almost like he's struggling to think. "Ah … you know what, fuck it. Just do it."

"For real?"

He drops back and spreads his legs. "Be gentle."

I kiss the inside of his thigh. "Yeah, I'm gonna want this to happen again, so my only focus is making this feel good. I got you, bro."

I'm quick to grab my lube and get back into position. It's surprisingly easy to switch off my brain when I suck his cock back into my mouth and cover my fingers in lube. I give his balls a quick tug, then rub along his taint and dip my fingers into his ass.

"Fuck this is weird," he says.

If it wasn't for the dick in my mouth, I would have laughed. What the fuck is weird about letting your frat brother shove his fingers up your ass?

Well, maybe I'll start with one. I've never tried this before, but thinking of even one finger up my ass makes that fucker clench tighter than a steel trap. I'll try it, of course, because I'm not letting Brandon outdo me, but I can guarantee if I'm not a gentleman about this, he's gonna make me pay when he returns the favor.

And also, there's a part of me that really wants to make it good.

We're going through this together, so we're both gonna remember this maybe more than any other hookup, but I don't wanna be memorable by default. I want us both to look back at this time one day with complete and total fondness.

My fingers find his hole, and I take some time to give that

thing a little love. I'm gentle, just like he asked, and all my focus on his ass is making my blow job sloppy. And yet, when I glance up to find him watching me again, he doesn't look like he has any complaints. His bottom lip is trapped between his teeth, and his eyes are unfocused.

I try to give him a questioning look as I press against his hole, and he must get it—hey, maybe sharing bodily fluids is giving us ESP or some shit—because he nods.

"Do it."

Yippee ki yay, motherfucker.

I press in, and even though he tenses, he doesn't ask me to stop. I've only just breached him, but I pause, giving his cock lots of attention before working in some more.

His body is so tight and warm, and by the time I'm in to the first knuckle, it's like his ass is trying to suck me in farther.

I've totally got this.

My lips tighten, tongue working madly as I suck him off with purpose. His hard-on hasn't flagged, so the pain mustn't be too bad, and when I finally have my finger buried inside him, I glance up again to check in.

He makes a strangled noise and gives a little thrust. Unfortunately, the "little" thrust bumps the head of his cock against the back of my throat and immediately triggers my gag reflex. The choking sound is loud in the quiet room.

"And you said I'm the one who'll be loud," he teases.

"That was sabotage. You tried to choke me."

"It was hot though." His hazel eyes are darkened with lust.

Feeling evil, I move my finger slowly out and back in again. Brandon shudders, thighs inching farther apart and abs clenching tighter. His ass clamps down on my finger, and goddamn, I wish it was my cock so bad. "You know what's hot?" I do it again, and again, Brandon reacts. "Seeing you squirm on my finger."

"Dude, I'm gonna tease the fuck out of you when it's your turn."

"You can—"

My words cut off when I pass over a spot deep inside him, and Brandon cries out, almost jerking off the bed. We both freeze. Then I lose my shit laughing.

"What was that?"

He drops onto his back. "I think I saw heaven."

"Dramatic, much?"

"Just you wait."

And yeah, after that, I'm curious as hell.

"I need you to get on with it now," he says.

Gladly, because not only do I want to make him come, but my cock is getting impatient. I dive onto his dick and aim for the blow job of my life. The whole time I'm sucking him, I work my finger in and out, wanting to add more but not willing to push my luck. And when he thrusts into my mouth and back onto my finger, making delicious needy noises, it boosts my confidence. I try to work him deeper, fuck him harder. I gag more times than I can count and make a total mess of his cock, but when he grips my hair painfully hard, I know I'm on the right track.

"There …" He gasps. "Right there. Just keep … keep …"

His fingers tighten, and then cum floods my mouth. I'm unprepared and almost choke but do my best to swallow every drop, and when he finally stops throbbing in my mouth, I release him.

"Damn, dude. That was …"

"Uh-huh." I push to my knees and climb up his body until I'm hovering over his chest. This part I know. This part is where I'm experienced as fuck, and I'm going to give it to him like I would anyone else. "Open up for me."

His mouth immediately drops, tongue slipping out, and I try to restrain my groan as I slide my cock along it.

"It's so hot when you don't question me. Makes me think you're as into this as I am …"

Brandon pulls back. "I might not be as assertive as you, but don't think for a second I'm not totally into this. Because I am. Completely. I wouldn't be here otherwise."

Even though I know that, I didn't know how much I needed to hear point-blank that this isn't all to help me out. Because there's a difference there. A curious frat brother helping out his bro is one thing; two frat brothers, in this together, figuring out who they are at the same time, is another.

"Then like I said, open up."

This time he leans forward and wraps his lips around me.

And if seeing Brandon's lips stretched around my cock isn't a beautiful sight, I don't know what is. This guy who I've known for years, who I have verbal sparring matches with daily, who's gotten me buckets to throw my guts up in, and had my back when I was too drunk to walk, is working my cock like a pro.

He barely takes much more than the head at this angle, but the inexperience isn't even on my radar as I thrust into the warm suction of his mouth. He feels too damn good. Looks too damn good.

Desire floods my bloodstream, and my balls are already so tight, so ready.

"I want your teeth." My words come out on a moan.

His eyebrows bunch.

"Just a little. Let me feel them."

The first scrape of them over my sensitive shaft makes me

lose control. I grip my bed with one hand and my cock with the other and jerk myself in time with the small thrusts. Brandon's deep grunts when I push too far, his hands clenching my thighs, the heat in his eyes … it overwhelms me.

Pleasure shoots along my spine, and my cock pulses right before I unload. It's mind-numbing bliss, the force of the orgasm taking me offline for a moment, and when I blink Brandon back into focus, the fucker is trying to smirk around my softening cock.

I stop stroking myself and pull out.

Something about the set of his mouth makes me ask, "Did you swallow?"

He opens his mouth to show me my load pooling on his tongue. Then he crooks his finger at me to come closer.

Sexy bastard.

I meet him in a kiss, where we pass my cum back and forth until it's all gone. I can safely say I've never even thought about trying my own cum until now, but that part of it barely registers. All I know is that sharing this with him, doing something so fucking intimate, is incredible.

"Well," he says when I let him up for air. "I think we can safely tick blow jobs off our list."

"Our … list?"

"Of what we like. Isn't that what this experimenting shit is for?"

Huh. I guess he's right. I mean, I'm here because it feels good, and since I know I'm into whatever now, I'm not ruling out who I'll end up with one day. So the more practice I get with him, the less of an inexperienced idiot I'll be once I find someone I want to settle down with.

Brandon … I'm not sure what's going on in his head. I want to ask, but I don't want to push, and since we're already messing around, I dunno if us trying to talk out our sexualities will be one step too far.

Either way, we're here for the same thing. Me for experience, him for some imaginary checklist. And both of us for mind-blowing orgasms.

16

BRANDON

I SWEAR EVERY CLASS THIS WEEK HAS LATE-NIGHT STUDY sessions, and this semester my frat duties are on crack.

After a night of incredible blow jobs, I'm ready to get Robbie back into bed immediately, but our schedules never line up in a way it can happen without us having to stay up late or skip early morning classes.

And something about going into January of graduation year has made our brothers clingier than ever. Rick is always asking to hang out and constantly has treasury matters to talk through. Chad has scheduled mastering mayhem meetings nearly every week, and Larken has amped up our schedules with more philanthropy tasks than I can count.

Plus, my coursework is heavier than ever. Thank fuck our team didn't make it further because there's no way I'd be able to handle all this as well as practice and games.

"Okay," Chad says. "Which one was the best?"

Robbie sniffs loudly, drawing my attention to him before I turn back to the file on my computer.

I scroll through the proposals our pledges submitted and highlight two. "This one is my favorite, but it's way too cold for a street-long Slip 'N Slide, so we'll table that for a few months. Which leaves this." The prank submission is a simple one. Fill all the Kappas' cars with plastic balls and cover their windows in shaving cream so they can't see inside before they open the doors.

Chad and Zeke read over it, but instead of doing the same, Robbie's stare flicks up to meet mine. Heat flares deep in my gut. I could have tried to find another guy for the times Robbie is busy and I'm not, but it holds zero appeal.

Outside of this thing we're doing, guys in general don't interest me. I've tried checking out dudes in class. Pretty ones, built ones, ones who give off the same energy as Robbie, but the thought of going down on any of them almost makes me cringe.

I'm just *not* attracted to men, so why can't I get enough of *him*?

He sniffs loudly from across the table and rubs at his reddened nose, and fuck, even that looks hot. What is wrong with me?

"Any risks?" Zeke asks. He's punching info into his tablet, keeping tabs on everything in a way only he can manage. Where Chad is the most go-with-the-flow VP I've ever seen, Zeke always knows what's up.

He might be laid-back, but that's because he's usually two steps ahead of the rest of us.

Other than that dumb Kappa prank and Chad's relationship with Bailey, I've never seen anything catch him by surprise.

What would he think of me and Robbie?

Not that he'll find out.

It's clear this is all a bit of fun, and I don't know where Robbie's head is at. I'm pretty sure he's ready to own his sexuality and doesn't give a fuck what others think, but if that's the case, how soon will he want to start exploring with other guys?

As much as I'm enjoying this, I think that will be the point I'm out.

I focus on Zeke's question. "It's all relatively standard. Since it's winter, the shaving cream will likely get close to freezing, so it'll be easy for them to clean off. That means there won't be any issues with obstruction while driving unless they're dumb enough to try it without cleaning their windshield. Worst that will happen is they get a bit messy and then have to put all that time into getting the balls out."

The second I say *balls*, I glance toward Robbie, who grins at me, and there goes my gut again. I have no clue if sexy balls are a thing, but if they are, he's got them.

I shift to ease the pressure on my dick as I remember how he looked towering over me. It needs to happen again. It needs to happen soon.

And while we're at it, we're going to need to talk about there being no one else while we fool around because the thought of Robbie with some other guy makes me uncomfortable. I don't like it. Sure, I'm a relationship guy, even though I postponed committing to anyone during college, but I always pictured settling down not long after.

Robbie hasn't had a relationship the whole time I've known him—he's never even wanted one. I'm worried that asking him to keep this thing between us for now might be pushing it, but then I look at him again and know I'm going to do it anyway.

Fuck, I want him.

It's almost unhealthy how much.

He rubs a big hand over his rough stubble. "How do we get the keys to the cars?"

"The suggested idea is room raiding in the middle of the night."

"No need," Chad says. "The night we plan it, I'll stay over there and relieve the Kappas of their keys while they're busy."

"And I'll call some bullshit meeting with Chuck and offer to pick him up for it."

"Chuck?" Robbie sniggers before sniffing again.

"Charles hates it." Zeke looks way too pleased by that.

"In that case, I'd say the plan's a go. We'll let the pledge who came up with it call the shots and coach him through it."

"Deal."

Even though he says that, I can't imagine Chad following some lowly pledge's orders.

Zeke taps his watch, and it lights up. "Better go. I have a study session for the next hour."

I have no idea how he does it all. High grades, championship swimmer, president of our house. All without breaking a sweat.

"And I have a hottie to take on a date," Chad says.

"You're taking me out?" Robbie says. "Aw, you shouldn't have."

Chad whacks his head on the way out.

Leaving me and Robbie.

"Well, this is convenient."

"Isn't i—" Robbie launches into a coughing fit.

"Shit, dude, you okay?"

He clears his throat. "Been feeling a bit flat today."

I study his face and for the first time notice he looks drawn. "You getting sick?"

"I'm sure it's nothing." He waves the question away. "You were saying?"

"Nuh-uh." I hold up my hands. "You can keep those germs to yourself."

His face falls. "Don't be like that."

"Concerned for my health?"

"Cockblocking. You're here … I'm here … most of our brothers are out …"

Goddamn that's tempting. So tempting. It's probably only a cold, and hooking up with him is definitely worth the risk.

Then he coughs again, louder and phlegmier. Suddenly, I'm no longer horny.

"Call me crazy, but I'm going to pass."

Robbie grunts, and his whole body deflates. His head drops against his hand. "I think I'm sick."

"Yeah, dude, though you can take the 'I think' out of that sentence." I stand and round the table to him, then press my palm to his forehead. He leans into it, and I'm not surprised. He's burning up. "Go to bed. I'll get you some drugs."

He shakes his head. "I'll be okay."

"Interesting …"

"What?"

"Nothing … you just seem to be under the impression I was asking." I grab him under his arm and coax him to his feet. Thank fuck he gets the message because there's no way I could have lifted him myself. "There we go."

"You gonna be my little nursemaid, Brando?"

That gives me an idea. When Robbie first bought the sex doll that he left in my bed to scare off the chick I was hooking up with, he'd dressed her in a nurse's outfit. A barely there nurse's outfit. I took it off when I deflated the doll and buried it somewhere in my drawers. It might be time to dig the flimsy thing out.

And unlucky for Robbie, because he's sick, he'll have to deal with looking and no touching. It's evil, but it's guaranteed to make sure that when he's better, I'm the one he comes for and not some other guy.

We might have agreed to regular experimenting, but we didn't agree to only hooking up with each other, and I regret not bringing it up when I had the chance. Is doing it while he's sick kosher? Who knows, but in my head, locking down my frat brother for regular orgasms is frat as fuck, and apparently Robbie is the only one I want to do that with.

He better buckle up because I have ideas.

Lots and lots of ideas.

And I wanna try them all out with him.

17

ROBBIE

I've felt like someone's been taking a jackhammer to my head all damn day, and the second I flop back onto my bed, I stop fighting it. I'm motherfucking sick. This is obviously the universe's way of fucking with me because Brandon looks goddamn incredible today. I can't work out if he's done something different, or I'm wearing O goggles, but my sexy little fap brother had my dick standing at attention.

The only part of me with any energy left.

He's right though. Hooking up probably wouldn't be sexy or smart. I can barely breathe through my nose, so blow jobs are out, I can't kiss him, and as much as I want to suggest he reverse cowboy this bitch and take a ride, I think he's gonna need some practice before he's ready for this rodeo.

I sink into my mattress and pray he hurries up with the drugs.

When he *finally* slips inside my room and locks the door, he's wearing his coat.

"You going somewhere?"

"Nope." He sets the bowl he's carrying aside, then opens his coat and lets it fall to the floor.

All I can do is gape at him.

He's wearing next to nothing. And what he is wearing …

Holy goddamn fraternity ancestors, no man has ever looked so hot.

It's a nurse's outfit that consists of a tiny white skirt, attached by a small strip of white material up to the bra. Then he slides a white headband with a red cross down over his floppy blond hair.

I remember to close my mouth. "Bro my god …"

He blows me a kiss. The damn thing looks obscene on his broad, muscled body, and my cock has forgotten we're sick because he's begging me to get on that. And I want to. I *really* want to.

But my head hurts, and now I'm lying down, the thought of getting up again is too much.

"Nurse Blakely at your service." His deep voice is pure sex.

"I'm already sick. Why are you torturing me?"

He knows he is too. His hazel eyes are alight with mischief, and while I want to be pissed that he'd tease me like this, seeing him having fun is too irresistible to get annoyed over. Brandon rattles a pill bottle as he crosses to my bed. He shakes two out onto his palm.

"I don't know what you're talking about, dude. I'm simply being a top-notch *cum*panion and looking after my patient. Now, are you going to be a good Rob-dog, or am I going to have to grab the restraints?"

A desperate sound leaves me. "Good. I'll be good."

"Then open up."

My mouth drops, and Brandon pops the pills and his fingers inside. He strokes over my tongue, pressing back until I gag.

"Good reflexes," he praises before holding up the water. "Now drink. We have to get your fluids back up—before I make you lose them all again."

"T-today?" I follow the question up with a sneeze so hard my head flies forward. When I look up again, Brandon's cringing.

"Gotta say, you're making it *really* hard for me to stay in character."

"I'm leaning into the sick patient part."

"Spraying snot over the room isn't what I meant about body fluids." He shudders, and it seems to take real effort to get his face to relax again.

I want to defend myself, but I feel too pathetic. "Look after me."

"That's what I'm here for." His stare rakes over me. "Now, let's get you comfortable."

I'm about to ask what he means when he reaches down and pushes my sweater up and over my head. A shudder races through me. My skin comes alive.

Brandon reaches for my undershirt and pushes that up too, his fingers gliding over my skin, and I lift my arms to make it easy for him. With him leaning over, the top of the costume gapes down, revealing his perfect pecs. I want to touch them, to trace his nipples with my tongue.

Even without asking, I know he won't let me. So I resist. Fight the need to pull him on top of me and drive him crazy. I let him do whatever he wants to, trying to ignore my cock that's getting needier by the minute.

Once my top half is bare, he moves on to my pants. He

slides them slowly down each leg, scraping his nails over the insides of my thighs, then running both hands up my calves.

I'm only in my boxer briefs, and I should be freezing, but his attention on me has my blood running hot.

"You're being a very good patient," he says, voice husky. He's hard, tenting the front of his skirt. We ignore it the same way he's ignoring my dick.

Brandon lifts my leg and presses a kiss to my ankle, my calf, the inside of my knee before his lips run along my thigh. "And good patients should be rewarded."

My hips lift off the bed. "Yes. Please."

He drops my leg and stands, crossing to my closet. "Let's get you dressed first though."

"What?"

"Once you're dressed, I'll make you dinner and tea, and then we're going to have a little movie night."

I groan. "Why do you hate me?"

"This is for your own good."

"Bullshit."

"I'm looking after you."

I grip my cock. "You should be looking after this."

His taunting mask slips as he huffs a laugh. "Don't make me restrain you."

I release my cock and sigh. "This is going to be a long, painful night for me, isn't it?"

"Probably. But the important part is that *I* have fun."

And maybe he's only joking, but it's true. Seeing him enjoy himself gives me more pleasure than it should. "Fine," I grumble. "Do your worst."

"You're going to regret that."

"Like you can make my cock any harder than it already is."

He smirks, and I realize my mistake a split second before he bends over. The skirt rides up, and the man is going commando.

"I fucking hate you," I say, unable to tear my eyes from his ass.

"And yet, you're stuck with me." He walks back over, carrying a stack of my clothes. "Exclusively."

"Huh?"

"While we're hooking up. *Cum*panions, or dick dudes, or whatever you want to call us. It's just us, okay? While we figure out where our heads are at."

I'm so in shock at his request, I can't answer it. Do I want to keep hooking up with Brando? Abso-fucking-lutely. Exclusively? That's harder to answer. There's zero desire whatsoever to find anyone else, which is weird for me, and I love the idea that Brandon won't be seeing anyone else, but … I've never done the one-person thing. Not even casually like this. I'm not sure I have it in me, even though I picture myself settling down one day. And if I fuck up? It's not just a fap brother I'll lose.

Brandon is … important. That can't change.

I run a hand over my face.

"It's okay if you're unsure," he says.

"Nah, it's not that."

"Then why do you look like you're about to shit yourself? Gotta tell you, man, that's not in Nurse Blakely's job description."

The bastard gets a laugh out of me, even as my gut is in knots. "It's … a lot."

"Sorry." He doesn't sound it. "Those are my terms though. If you think you've experimented enough with me, then go find some other dudes to suck your dick. But I won't be hooking up with you while I'm worried about you comparing my sloppy-ass blow jobs with some professional deep-throater."

"I wouldn't—"

"Don't care, Robbie."

Fucking Brandon. Mitigating risks even where there's none to worry about. Maybe some gay guy could deep-throat me like a porn star, but that isn't nearly as appealing as him kneeling, gagging, eyes watering as he gives it his all. "You know I've never been with only one person."

"I do. Which is why I'm laying it out now."

"Calling me a slut, Brando?"

"If the empty jumbo pack of extra-large condoms fits …"

I kick him, and he chuckles.

"You don't have to answer me right now. You're sick, and we're fucking around, and it's all good. But I want an answer soonish. Think you can do that?"

"Yes." It's the least I can do for him, even if it means a shitload of thinking ahead for me.

"Now relax," he says before grabbing the bowl he carried in with him.

"What's that?"

"Can't let you go to sleep without a bath, can we?"

I let out a body-shuddering cough. "Yeah, at this point, I'm not moving."

"Lucky you don't have to." He sets the bowl down beside my bed, revealing the soapy water inside.

"What are you …"

"Shh …" He reaches in and pulls out a washcloth that he squeezes the water out of. "Just relax."

I feel like I should object, but as Brandon starts dragging

the cloth over my skin, washing every inch, I can't because my tongue feels too big for my mouth. So I watch him. He takes his time, making sure he doesn't miss a spot.

He's concentrating hard, eyes locked on my body, and every nerve ending in me is vibrating under his attention. My neck, my face, both arms and legs. He washes my chest and stomach, paying extra attention to the places my boxer briefs meet skin.

"Oh no," he says.

"Huh?" I'm losing touch with reality.

"Here I am trying to clean you, and all you're doing is making a mess."

"What do you mean?"

He grabs my cock and sweeps his thumb over the spot of precum staining my briefs. I swallow hard, hit with both relief and so much want.

Brandon *tsks*. "You were being so good for me."

"I was." I shift my thighs open. "I am."

"Making a mess isn't being a good patient."

"I can't help it. You haven't cleaned there yet. And heads up, it's about to get a whole lot messier if you don't help me fix my problem."

His grin is evil as he lifts my waistband and works my boxer briefs down my thighs. "What kind of nurse would I be if I didn't attend to your needs?"

I'm so close to begging him to get on with it when he reaches down to dip the washcloth in the water again. He doesn't drain it as much this time, and when he wraps it around my cock, it's like a warm, wet hug. His hand squeezes tight, and I drop my head back on a loud pant.

"Yes. Fuck. More."

His hand stills. "Is that any way to talk to your nursemaid?"

I almost kick him out, but I'm too turned on. Bastard. "Please, Nurse Blakely. Help me."

"Better." He sets a fast pace, stroking over my needy cock with the exact roughness I need. I don't know if he can sense how close I am, or it's what he would have done for himself, but it's goddamn perfect.

I can barely breathe, but nothing is going to stop me from blowing my load. Except when I fuck up into his fist, Brandon stops again and presses on my hip.

"You're supposed to be relaxing. Let me do my job."

I force myself still, and it's one of the hardest things I've ever had to do.

To his credit, he's nailing this position. It makes me want to get sick more often so he'll take care of me like this. Over and over. He jerks me hard, fast, and the force of keeping myself still is ramming my pleasure home. Tingles race down my spine, my balls draw up, and I shudder, right on the edge.

Then Brandon's hand is gone, and his mouth seals around my cock.

The change from cooling water to his warm, tight mouth sets me off. My cock jerks, unloading into his mouth, and he swallows me down like he's been sucking dick all his life.

I sag against the bed.

"Okay," I manage through heavy breathing. "I'm relaxed now."

He laughs and dries me off, then helps me into warm clothes. His cock is still hard, and I reach for it.

Brandon bats my hand away. "I'm looking after you, remember?"

"Let me return the favor."

"Nope. You're sick." He pulls the wool shirt he got me down and smooths it over my gut. "I'm going to go and take care of myself, make you dinner, then we'll watch some … educational videos."

I scrunch up my face. "Educational?"

He picks up his coat to put back on. "Can you trust me?"

"I dunno. An animal documentary, sure. Climate change details, not so much."

"Noted."

I mourn the loss of his nurse's outfit as he pulls on his coat. "No fair."

"Yeah, I'm not wearing this thing all night. It's way too tight."

Then he grabs the bowl and ducks out into the hall. I'm left with silence, feeling warm and cozy, wrapped in happiness.

The only thing unsettling me is his request that we don't see anyone else.

Not because I don't want that.

But because until he said it, it hadn't occurred to me that was already what I had in mind. We're experimenting. It's fun. I hadn't thought through any specific plan, but I guess I'd already assumed we were going through this together.

So it should be an easy thing to say yes to.

Right?

A few weeks or so of fooling around? Easy orgasms? *Fun?* Because sex should always be fun.

Whenever someone has suggested booty calls and repeat hookups in the past, I ran hard and fast the other way.

We're in *college*. There are thousands of people out there I haven't even met yet, and once the year is up, we'll all be disappearing to other sides of the country anyway. Why get tied down and have to deal with all that mess?

A large part of me wants to remind him that keeping things casual is the way to go.

So why am I holding back?

18

BRANDON

WELL, THAT ENDED UP GOING FURTHER THAN I'D PLANNED. Sure, I wanted to tease the guy, but there's something about Robbie that makes it hard to stop once I get my hands on him. And seeing how desperately he wanted relief had been all the encouragement I needed.

I jerk off, which takes approximately seven seconds to do since I'm so worked up, and then I take a quick shower, get changed, and head down to make soup and tea. It's what Mom always does when I'm sick, and it never fails to make me feel better.

When I get back upstairs, Robbie is under his covers, looking so fucking snuggly I kinda want to climb in and wrap myself around him.

But first, sick.

Second ... that's not something two bros tend to do, *cum*panions or not.

So I wait for him to sit up, then pass him his soup.

"This smells incredible."

"Eat up."

He doesn't need to be told twice.

I push him over, then drop onto the bed beside him, on top of the covers of course—because frat bros.

"What are we watching?"

This is the fun part. I grab his laptop and open some porn.

He cracks up laughing. "This isn't a movie."

"No, but it is educational. You ever done anal before?"

"Nope, you?"

I shake my head and navigate to a clip with two guys. "I figure this will give us some idea for when you're all better, and since we have no experience in the field, let's look up whatever other things there are out there that two dudes can do together."

He drains his soup, and I switch out the bowl for his tea. "Take notes. I'm going to want to try it all."

I'd laugh, but I know he's serious. So that's what we do. We spend most of the night watching and note-taking until Robbie curls up beside me and falls asleep. His breathing is heavy and loud, nose red, face tense even in sleep. I watch him for a moment before reminding myself not to be a creep, but even then I can't look away. Robbie is … well, fuck, he's an absolute pain in the ass. Outside of the bedroom, I want to wring his neck sometimes, but … damn if there isn't some-thing about him that's softening me to his wild ways.

That won't do.

I creep out of his bed, careful not to wake him, and cross to his desk to retrieve a marker.

Then I channel my middle school self and draw a giant dick on his face.

He doesn't wake, even as I smile down at him, something twisting in my chest.

I remind myself I've set my terms.

Robbie might not be into the exclusive thing, but I have boundaries, and now is as good of a time as any to set them. It'll suck if he turns around and says he's had his fun, but if he does, I'll have to respect that.

Then I head for the door, and when I reach it, I glance back at the giant monster snoring under his covers, and I'm hit with that same urge to join him. Just to be near him. Am I going insane? This is *Robbie Harrows*.

Thorn, splinter, pest. Creator of migraines that last for days.

What have I gotten myself into?

And why don't I want to stop?

ROBBIE'S WIPED OUT FOR THE WHOLE WEEKEND, AND NOT IN A cute way. I'm honestly worried he's going to cough up a lung at some point, and unlike the other night, I keep my distance.

And damn he's being a big baby about being sick.

Needy and whiny, he wants me at his beck and call, but dude, I *also* have homework and shit to get through. Think I can tell him no though?

Of course not, which is why I'm perched on a chair five feet from his bed, watching a movie on his laptop, while I balance mine on my thighs and try to hide my screen full of sex toys from him. He might not have given me an answer yet, but I'm going to place an order so I'm ready for when and if he does.

"How can you even see from over there?" he grumbles.

"Easily. I'm not missing things by coughing every two minutes."

He *humphs* and tucks a pillow under his arm. I probably shouldn't find that adorable, right? *Right?*

My ringtone blares suddenly over the sound of the movie, making us both jump.

"Fuck," I mutter, grabbing it and checking the display. "My mom. I'll—" I go to get up and take this outside when Robbie pauses the movie.

"Stay there." He sinks back onto his pillows, and his eyes fall closed, so he doesn't see the cringe I send his way. Can't wait for him to witness this conversation.

I answer before it cuts out. "Hey, Mom."

"Remembered who I am, did you?"

Ah, the old guilt trip. "I was planning to call you later."

"Uh-huh. I bet."

"Seriously." Sure, I normally call home on a Saturday, but I've been babysitting a giant man child, and time got away from me. "How's the week been?"

"Great," she says, forgetting to play mad. "We went to the winter markets yesterday, and it was lovely. I got a bit too tipsy on rosé, but your dad got me home safe."

"You're my parents. I don't need or want to know about you having fun."

"Please. You think I'm oblivious to what you boys get up to at those fraternity parties? No point acting all uptight now, Brandon."

"Well, this has been a great conversation …"

She tsks. "I'm just calling to make sure you're coming home for your birthday next month."

"Ah …" My eyes dart to Robbie. He shouldn't be the

reason I hesitate to answer. A month is a long time, and he hasn't even agreed to a short-term thing yet. "I'm not sure."

She fake-gasps. "You neglected to come home for Christmas, and now you're going to make me miss my only son's birthday? Twenty-two years ago, you were nestled so sweet and cozy in my belly, waiting to make your way out through my—"

"Stop. You win. Okay." I can't be subjected to my birth story again.

"Cutting the crap, why don't you want to come home?" she asks.

"There's … no reason."

"Brandon."

"Seriously. I wanted to stay at the house since it was my last Christmas here. No big deal." I'm overly aware of the way Robbie tilts his head to watch me.

"And your birthday?"

"It's … nothing."

"That wasn't even halfway convincing."

"It's not that I don't *want* to come home for my birthday. I…"

She gasps, but this time, it's real. "Holy shit, you've got a girlfriend."

"What? No? No girlfriend."

"Steve, come here!" she shouts, and I make out the sound of Dad approaching as the phone is switched to speaker.

"No, Mom." I sigh. "There's no girlfriend."

"Well, there's *someone*. I can tell. Is it new? Is that why you don't want to tell me?"

"No, it's—" I know they're not going to let up. "Fine. One of my brothers was staying for the holidays, and I didn't think he should be left here solo. That's it."

My words are met with silence, on and off the phone. I risk a look over at where Robbie's lying and catch his eyes. Jesus fuck, imagine if my parents knew about him and what we've been doing. How would they take it?

Like she can read my mind, Mom asks, "Is it romantic between you?"

And apparently Robbie can hear the whole conversation because his booming laugh fills the room.

"Who's that?" Mom asks.

Could this get any worse? "The frat brother I was telling you about. He's sick, so we're watching a movie."

Mom releases a long, drawn-out *aww*. "My Brandon is such a good friend."

"Or more than friend," Dad says.

Someone help me with these two.

"Put us on speaker," Mom says.

"No, I'm not going to—"

"Put us on speaker, Brando," Robbie echoes.

"No, I'm—"

"Please, honey. We just want to make sure he's okay."

"She wants to make sure I'm okay." Robbie's grinning like an idiot. "Do it do it do it."

"Do it," Mom and Dad start chanting too.

I sit there gaping, like how the hell did I end up in a three-way conversation with maybe the most immature people I know?

Whatever. "You asked for this," I remind *all* of them before I switch the phone over.

"Mrs. Blakely," Robbie says. "Heard you had a fun time yesterday?"

"*Thank* you. See, Brandon? Your friend knows adults have a life as well."

"The winter market?" I say skeptically. "Hold me back."

Robbie throws his pillow at me that I throw back before I remember there are probably germs all over that thing. We're both laughing, and I almost miss Mom say, "If I'd known you were there by yourself for Christmas, I would have invited you here. You're always welcome."

And thank fuck she didn't know, because *no* thank you.

"What about for his birthday?"

My head snaps up at Robbie's question, and I madly try to indicate to him to stop talking. Apparently, my throat slashes aren't very intimidating because he just blows me a kiss.

"We'd love to have you," Dad says.

"*I* don't even know if I'll be back," I say. "Let alone Robbie."

"Oh, Brandon, of course you will be. After three days of labor—"

"Stop."

"And my water breaking in the middle of a restaurant—"

"Please no."

"And all that pain."

"*Fine*," I relent. "I'll be there."

"With your friend," Dad says.

"Wouldn't miss it for the world," Robbie tells them.

This is a nightmare. "Can I please clarify that everyone here knows how horrible this whole experience will be for me?"

"So dramatic," Mom says like she isn't exactly where I got it from.

"It's supposed to be my birthday. Why do you all hate me so much?"

"What's the problem?" Robbie asks. "Are you embarrassed of me?"

"Well, no—"

"Then it must be us."

"*Mom*." I force myself to take a breath. "For the record, I hate you all. And the three of you meeting can only be a horrible experience that all four of us will regret."

"Your concerns have been noted." Dad's clearly trying not to tease me. "Talk later, son. Looking forward to meeting you, Robbie."

"You too, Mr. Blakely."

"And, Brandon?" Mom says. "We want you to know, we love you very much. No matter what. And I'm sure we'll love your *friend* too."

"Please don't say friend like that."

"We're so proud of you, Brandon."

I huff. "You're still on speaker."

"I hope you make our son happy, Robbie. And remember, man or woman, it's equally as important to wrap—"

"*Argh*." I quickly hang up, while Robbie almost breaks a rib laughing so hard he ends up in a coughing fit.

"There is no way you're coming with me," I tell him.

Robbie tucks his hands behind his head. "I guess we'll wait and see."

19

ROBBIE

OTHER THAN FEELING TIRED AND SLOW, WITH A LINGERING cough, I've recovered enough to head back to work the next day. The office for policy and management is off campus, in a covered laneway with lampposts and twinkle lights.

"You look like shit," Holly says. "Big weekend?"

"Nah, I've been sick."

Her face falls. "Are you okay to be here?"

"Yep, all recovered." Thanks to a very sexy nurse. I don't even know what all that was about, but I'd be an epic liar if I said I didn't enjoy it or hope that it happens again.

"Question for you," I say as Holly goes through the files she's holding, dropping the ones meant for me to file on my desk.

"Shoot."

"Things with Brando happened again."

She looks up in surprise. "Well, good for you."

"Yeah, but he said they can only keep happening if we're not hooking up with anyone else."

"Like …" She frowns. "A relationship, or …?"

"I don't think so. He said while we're figuring this thing out, we should stick to each other, and he won't keep doing it if I see other people."

"And you want there to be other people?"

"*No.*" It's not until the word is out of my mouth and she's blinking at me in surprise that I realize how over-the-top that response was. "Ah, I don't know. Maybe not."

"Are you hearing yourself?"

I huff out a laugh. "What a mess, right?"

"Actually, I think you're making it a bigger mess than it needs to be. You guys are friends, why shouldn't you figure things out together? If you're having fun, go with it."

"See? This is why we're besties." We have the same philosophies. Lean into the fun, don't run from it.

"Except I'm not your friend, I'm your boss."

I wave her comment aside. She loves me. "Besides, I guess we need to make this thing last a month."

"Ah, why?"

"We're going to visit his family for his birthday."

Holly watches me for a moment. "Okay, are you only hooking up, or are you actually boyfriends?"

"We're bros. Who hook up. And are friends."

"So you're brofriends?"

Holy shit, that makes perfect sense. "That's what we are."

"Huh?"

"Brofriends. We're not dating, but we're not just brothers anymore either."

"Context *really* is key here."

Context schmontext. I hurry to grab my phone.

"I know you're not going to text and work."

I pout at her. "Brolationship crisis, babe."

"Again. Boss." She side-eyes me. "You have two minutes."

Holly dumps the files and heads into the staff room. I love that girl.

Me: *I figured it out*

Brandon: *Figured what out?*

Me: *What we are*

Brandon: *Which is?*

Me: *BROFRIENDS!*

Brandon: ...

Me: *No, hear me out. We're brothers. Who have sex. But we're not dating. So we're brofriends*

Brandon: *JFC*

Me: *Perfect, am I right?*

Brandon: *You're certainly something*

Me: *I'll take that compliment*

Brandon: *That doesn't surprise me*

Me: *Naww you love me*

Brandon: *You're an idiot. You here for this meeting?*

Me: *Is Betty White the greatest actress in history?*

Brandon: *Well, I'm gonna go with a no on that one, so you won't be here?*

Me: *What is wrong with you?*

Brandon: *The greatest actress? The GREATEST? Really?*

Me: *The woman's an icon*

Brandon: *I could name at least five others who slap more than her*

Me: *How the fuck are we friends?*

Brandon: *Given you're wrong about literally everything, I have no clue, dude*

Me: *kdfklgfsdglj*

Brandon: *Did you just keysmash me?*

Me: *I'll do more than keysmash*

Brandon: *Don't threaten me with a good time*

Me: *Oohh now there's something we can agree on*

"Time's up!" Holly calls, coming back through with a coffee.

Damn it. My phone vibrates with another text, but I reluctantly put it away without checking because I know if I see what he's written, I won't be able to stop from writing back.

So I spend the whole final hour there, counting down the minutes as I file all the useless paper documents away. Like, come on, who hasn't switched to digital these days?

When I'm finally let out, I have one message there waiting.

Brandon: *So are we still doing this? You never actually answered me*

And now I'm glad I didn't open that message, but it also means that he sent that an hour ago and probably thinks I'm blowing off giving him an answer. I have been. Kinda. But it's not that I don't want to answer him; it's the *how* that's the problem. I won't walk away from this thing, so I'm gonna say yes, but how do we work out a time frame on it? Cross off his imaginary list and then move on? Butt sex, then bail? Get a five-star rating on our BJ skills?

We're gonna have to *talk* and shit.

I always tell my bros that open communication is key, and look at me not taking my own advice. It's different when it's your brother and not a chick though. Girls come and go, brotherhood is forever.

Look who's pulling up his big-boy panties and asking his bro to go exclusive with him.

Is it hot in here?

The house is full when I get there. Constant energy and

noise wraps around me like a sweaty football jersey, and just like when I take the field for a game, I'm hit with a surge of love for my life.

Does this get any better? I'm gonna go with a no.

And instead of viewing this thing with Brandon as a scary unknown, I need to jump in like I do with everything else. Trading mind-blowing orgasms should only ever be viewed as a good thing—I'll put it in the Sigma rule book if I have to— so no more holding back.

I catch him on the way to the war room—literally. The second he goes to walk by, I hook my arm around his waist and pull him into the empty laundry.

"What are you—"

I cut him off with my mouth. As we kiss, I back him into the wall, crowding him up against it and bending my knees so he doesn't hurt his neck. *Fuck, I've missed his mouth.*

I keep waiting for this feeling to dull, for the way he kisses to stop making my head spin, to be able to look at him without wanting to do filthy things to his body. But it's not all physical either. I *like* Brandon. As a friend, as a person, as a sexy little nurse.

His mouth breaks from mine, and his puffy lips make me groan.

"What …" He swallows. "I mean, hey."

"Hey." I grip his jaw and pull his mouth open before kissing him again. And he must get as lost in it as I do because his arms wrap around my neck, and he pulls me tight against him. Our cocks line up with delicious friction, but for once, I'm not in a hurry to move things along. I wanna kiss, and touch, and worship this sexy guy with everything I have to give him.

"Shit!" He jerks away from me but doesn't get far. "The meeting."

"They won't start without us." I pull his earlobe between my teeth.

"No, you idiot." Brandon pushes my chest and I back up but don't let him go. "They're going to take one look at us and know we were kissing."

"And?"

He freezes.

Pulls back to study my face.

"Seriously?"

I shrug. "Does it matter? They're not going to judge us for liking some D."

"No, but they might judge us for liking each other's. You really want to deal with all the dumbass jokes and constant ribbing?"

"True. But then we wouldn't have to sneak around anymore. We can hook up whenever we like. Be as loud as we want."

Brandon rubs his thumb over my bottom lip. "I dunno, dude. I'm kinda looking forward to gagging you."

"Someone's kinky."

"*Someone's* looking for a way to finally shut you up."

I kiss him again. A quick one. Just because. Then I put on a cheesy porn voice. "Baby, I'm gonna make all your fantasies come true."

He laughs and shoulder checks me as he passes. "Let's get this meeting out of the way. I kinda hate that you gave me a hard-on before we got started."

He's about to leave when I remember what I was supposed to talk to him about. My fingers circle his wrist.

"I wanna do it."

"What?"

"Just us."

Brandon stares at me for a moment, like he's sorting through our options and weighing up whether it's what he wants. I have a whole second anxiety spike thinking he's about to change his mind, when his face splits into a smile. "Yeah?"

I point to my dick. "The dragon likes you. Who am I to argue?"

"Thank fuck one of you has good taste."

Before I let him go, I reach up to fix where his hair got all rumpled during our make-out session. His eyes meet mine, and we share a look that feels heavy and light all at once.

"Ah, thanks …" he says.

"Got your back, bro." I let him go.

And don't mention the epic stubble scrape blooming around his mouth.

Oops.

20

BRANDON

We're in the war room waiting.

We met up earlier to go over the plan before everyone headed to bed for a few hours' sleep.

Zeke is already back from his meeting with Charles, Charles's keys successfully swiped, and now we just need Chad's go-ahead. He's supposed to be waiting for Bailey and the rest of the Kappas to fall asleep before creeping through the house and lifting us the rest of the car keys we need.

We have trash bags full of plastic balls and cans of shaving cream on standby.

I take the thermos of coffee Robbie offers me. "Thanks."

"Of course." He's had a smile stretching across his face all afternoon, and I'd love to think it's because of what we decided earlier, but I know better. There's prank fever in the air, and Robbie's getting high from it. "You good? You ready?" He's practically bouncing.

I set a hand on his thigh to still it. "Would you calm down? You're going to make me anxious."

"Nah, this one is straightforward."

"I'm sure that's what the Kappas thought too."

For the first time, the smile drops, and he gets that same worried expression he's looked at me with a few times since it happened.

I hold up my hand. "Don't."

"*You* reminded me of it."

"Because it's not a big deal."

He grumbles something under his breath as he takes the thermos from me and has a large sip.

I nudge him. "Hey, you're about to stuff balls into holes and piss some Kappa dudes off. Focus back on that."

He hums, but he's not feeling it, and I want to kick myself for bringing his mood down. As much as he might drive me crazy with his pranks and tendency to overdo the parties, there's something so pure about his overeager excitement. I want to protect that.

"Think about the look on Charles's face when he realizes his Mercedes has been creamed."

He finally sniggers. "Think he'll burst a vein in anger?"

"We can only hope."

Robbie lifts his hand for a high five at the same time as I do, and we both laugh and follow through. The wuss is wearing gloves and a wool hat, pulled down to his eyebrows, and the three sweaters he's wearing make him look bulkier than usual.

I want to tease him about the cans of shaving cream he has filling the pockets of his cargo pants. He's wearing his fanny pack, and I have no idea why, but his whole outfit looks ridiculous ... and somehow so *Robbie*.

I think I like it.

There must be some heavy drugs in his cum, because I never would have thought the sight of a fucking *fanny pack* could make me feel soft, and yet, here we are.

With me not taking the opportunity to laugh at his clothes.

I look down at what I'm wearing and wonder for the first time if it's too safe. Too boring. Fucked if I know, but I don't like that thought. Robbie is Mr. Fun. Fun and boredom don't mix.

Which doesn't matter when all we are is *brofriends*.

The reminder that hooking up is temporary shouldn't be as heavy as it is.

"What's the bet he's fallen asleep?"

I turn to the voice and look at Shifley, who's playing on his phone. His Big, Colby, whacks the back of his head.

"This is Doomsen you're talking about. No matter how magic his boyfriend's dick is, he knows the score. Frat first, everything else second. He's got our back, just you wait."

And an hour later, at 2:00 a.m., Chad proves him right.

Zeke gets a text with a photo of a pile of keys down the side of Kappa house.

"All right, brothers," Zeke says. "It's go time. Everyone remember their roles?"

There's general agreement before we start to move.

Since this is a training mission, the Bigs will observe but not actually be involved in the prank, and Zeke will act as lookout. He's never been as big on the pranks as we have, mostly happy to let us do our own thing, even if it means having to take the full weight of Charles's disapproval of our mayhem.

I'll be there making sure nothing goes wrong, and Robbie

will be making sure the future deviants of Greek Row play their parts to precision.

Shifley is the pledge who came up with the prank, so once we reach Kappa house, he disappears down the side of the house to grab the keys while his Big and Zeke watching from the next yard. The rest of us split off.

We've had the pledges spend the week scoping out which car belongs to which Kappa, even though we could have easily told them, and the plan tonight is to hit Charles, Lucas, Jordan, and Sam, partly because they're the biggest pains in the asses, and partly because they have sunroofs. If it was up to Robbie, Bailey would have been on that list too—favoritism is *not* frat —but since he's the reason Chad was able to get us the keys in the first place, I guess that gives him a pass.

The only regret I have, as I watch the pledges scramble to their assigned cars, is that I can't be more involved. I'm hands-off. Which is fine. Being risk manager is important. I *know* that.

But even as I watch Robbie dart after the pledges and their Bigs, I wish I could be right there with them.

Shifley gets back with the keys and runs them out to each group. Charles and Sam, being president and VP, park in the driveway, but the other two cars are out on the street, in plain view of anyone who happens to look out their window or drive past.

And apparently letting off cans of shaving cream and shaking plastic balls from plastic trash bags is not as quiet as I would have thought it was.

Each group gets their car unlocked and the sunroof open. Robbie distributes the shaving cream from his pockets and rubber gloves and wet wipes from his fanny pack. Because of course he's thought of everything.

As they work, I keep an eye out for hazards—not that there should be anything with a plan so straightforward. I guess one of them could end up with shaving cream in their eye or something, I dunno, but otherwise … this shit is boring.

I turn from the group doing Charles's and Sam's cars and head for the street, when a handful of shaving cream flies at my face.

"The fuck—*oomph*!"

I'm wearing it before I can finish the sentence. Robbie's suppressed laughter gives him away, and as soon as I swipe the cream from my eyes, it's on. I lunge at him, and he sprays more shaving cream at me until I manage to wrangle the can from his grip. We wrestle back and forth, a laugh that I'm only just able to hold back building in my chest as I return the favor and douse him with it.

"*Dick.*"

Robbie tries to tackle me, but I flip us around, leg behind his, and send the big man down. Only I don't wriggle out of his grip fast enough. He grabs my waist, and my feet disappear out from under me. We land in the snow, covered in sticky shaving cream, panting against our suppressed laughter, limbs a tangled mess.

I glance up to see Shifley slashing his hand across his throat, but fuck it. This prank will be the first of many for them —this moment, this fun, this is the shit college was made for, and if we fuck up their prank, they'll get another.

I'll never have another moment like this with Robbie.

Either we're not as loud as we thought, or it's late enough that no one's awake, but the guys finish up, and Zeke directs us all to head back to the house.

"Sorry, prez," Robbie says, and Zeke waves him off.

"Dude, you think I give a shit about messing up a prank?"

"Don't let Chad hear you say that," I warn.

Zeke doesn't look worried. "Some brothers take this too seriously. Maybe if it had been interrupted, we could have reminded them this is for fun. Nothing more."

Robbie shoves me again, starting another wrestling match the whole way back to the house. I'm out of breath by the time we walk in, and the sudden change from the cold outside to the warm inside makes my already struggling lungs burn.

I shrug Robbie off me and head for the stairs, coughing the whole way there. That'll teach me to leave my goddamn inhaler behind.

"Shit. *Shit*. Brando."

I glance up directly into Robbie's panicked expression. I'm coughing too hard to talk, and while it's uncomfortable, I *know* it's nothing serious. There's just no way for me to let Robbie know that though.

When I keep walking, he's hot on my heels, crowding my space. "Are you okay? What do you need?"

You, to get out of my way.

"Fine, I—" The coughing takes over again, so I push him aside, take the remaining stairs two at a time, and shoulder my way into my bedroom.

My inhaler is where I left it on my desk, and as soon as I get my first hit, my airways instantly feel better.

Fuck asthma.

I use my inhaler until I feel good again, and while breathing is easier now, there's the usual lingering burn in my chest and weariness from coughing so hard. It doesn't take long to pass, but it's always a pain in the ass.

"You okay?"

I look up at Robbie, who's standing so close we're touching and looking way too concerned. His eyes are wide, and he's pale. I want to tease him for being such a drama queen, but actually ... it's sort of nice. "Dude, that was nothing."

His expression doesn't change.

I force myself to laugh, just so he can see it's not a big deal. "It was only a small one. Nothing to worry about, I promise."

"I didn't like it."

This time, my laugh is real. "It wasn't a fun time for me either, cowboy."

Robbie grunts and then does something that catches me totally by surprise. His arm wraps around my shoulders, and he pulls me against him, crushing me in a hug.

I'm not sure what to make of this. Or ... anything really. But I return it, confused and overwhelmed by how good it feels.

"It scares me every time."

My throat feels thick. I squeeze him tighter. "Dude, it's asthma. That kind of thing happens a lot."

"Great. I didn't know whether I needed to call an ambulance or what. If I hadn't been such a dumbass, you never would have—"

I slap my hand over his mouth. "Yeah, no. You were being you, and I had a fucking blast." I slowly move my hand from his mouth to stroke his cheek. "Actually, that was the most fun I've had outside of the bedroom in a long time."

"I'm glad, but ..."

"What's going on? You've seen me have an asthma attack before."

"Yeah, but ..." He lets me go and whistles through an exhale. "Ah, fuck. Sorry. I ... Yeah. It was like the Kappas' prank all over again. I didn't know what to do."

"Well, at least all the doors survived this time."

He laughs. Just a small one, but it's something.

"Sometimes when I have a little attack like that, trying to talk makes it worse. So … what about a code-type thing? Like, if I … I dunno—pat my head, that means I'm fine. Nothing to worry about."

He thinks for a moment, then nods. "Yeah. Yeah, that works."

"Good."

"Cool." He hesitates a second, then steps forward and pecks me on the lips. "Let's go down to the debrief."

And even though I've convinced him, he doesn't leave my side the whole time we're in the war room, and when we finally haul ass back upstairs, he sneaks into my room as soon as the hall is clear.

"What are you doing?" I ask as he climbs into bed with me.

"Being a good brofriend."

"Sorry, dude, it is *way* too late for sex stuff."

"Ah, yeah. Sex stuff. Damn." He punches the pillow, then settles in. "Good night, then."

"Umm … yeah." I lie back down, acutely aware of him in the dark. "Good night."

21

ROBBIE

I'M WOKEN TO THE SOUND OF SHOUTING.

"Zeke! Zeke! Zekezeke!"

Brandon groans as something hits the side of the house. "What is that?"

"Sounds like Chad."

The front door slams. "Zeke!"

"Come on." I slap his ass and climb over him to go and see what the shouting is about. When I get downstairs, I find Chad in the front room, peering through the curtains in nothing more than his underwear. Another volley of—I'm going to say water balloons based on Chad's wet hair and drenched briefs—hits the side of the house.

"It's minus two out, brother. Put on some clothes."

"My boyfriend sold me out!" he shouts. "The *audacity*. The sheer *nerve*."

"Start again, from the top."

"When they found out what we did, Bailey told them all I

was there, and they woke me by pouring a bucket of cold water over my head." He turns to me. "Can you believe it? My *own boyfriend*?"

There's a chuckle as Brandon joins us. "Dude, didn't you zip-tie him to a chair the other week?"

Chad opens his mouth and closes it a few times. "That was different," he sputters.

"Why?" It goes against everything in me, but I think I'm team Bailey on this one.

"Because ... because ..." I swear his lips are turning blue, and he shivers. "So not frat."

Brandon and I start to laugh.

"I'd use you being half-naked as an opportunity to ask to touch your dick again, but I have a feeling none of us would find it right now."

He flips me off and storms past. "F-fuck ... you all."

He passes Zeke on the stairs, who watches him for a moment before turning to us. "What was that about?"

"Kappas retaliated."

He nods. "Well, I'm sure they owed Chad for something, so he can take this one for the team."

Zeke heads for the kitchen, and I turn to find Brandon watching me.

"What?"

He glances around, grabs my hand, then pulls me toward the stairs. As soon as we're back in his room, he kicks the door closed then presses me against it and kisses me. It's hard and needy, leaving me with no room to wonder what he wants from me, and when his tongue swipes over mine, we're suddenly on the same page. I pull Brandon tighter against me, and he slips his thigh between my legs, giving me friction against my hard-on.

"I had a thought," he says before tugging on my lip with his teeth.

"Oh yeah?"

"Let's skip class today."

"What …"

"I want to try more sex stuff."

I grin and grab his ass. "Oh no, did you catch my cold, man? Rob-dog will stay home and take care of you."

"Will you wear that costume?"

"Hard no. It wouldn't fit. That's all yours. The memory will live rent-free in my brain forever."

He sniggers and tugs me toward the bed, kissing me the whole way. I palm his ass through his sweats, greedily kneading the full cheeks, and Brandon moans into my mouth. When he pulls back, his face is flushed, his lips are swollen, and I want to grip his perfect blond hair until it's standing on end.

"You sure about this?" I ask. "Classes have been crazy lately, and you never have a free minute."

"I don't. So I'm making one. Now, do you want to fuck me, or am I fucking you?"

The question short-circuits my brain. "Both. Definitely both."

Brandon's eyes darken, and then he turns us and shoves me onto the bed before ridding me of my shirt. "I think for our first time trying this, we should keep things simple."

"Fine. Be a killjoy."

Something crosses his face too fast for me to pinpoint. "If you're not having fun, we can stop."

I yank his sweats down, and his long cock slaps back against his abs. "No way is that happening." My mouth instantly waters at the sight of him. The head is red and swollen, shiny with precum, and so hard the thing could do serious damage. I lean forward and suck him into my mouth as Brandon strips off his shirt.

"Damn, your mouth is magic."

"Wait until it's my ass." I look up at him, still standing over me, and he runs his fingers through my short hair.

"Your ass?"

"Well, I think we're probably going to need some practice runs before you can take me."

Brandon hesitates, and I know he's trying to work out whether he should be offended or not, when he shrugs. "Fair point. That thing is a monster." He drops to his knees next to the bed and helps me out of my pajama bottoms. "But I'm gonna bottom for you one day, dude." He licks me from balls to tip. "Don't think you get all the fun."

"Somehow, I think you'll have plenty of fun with your cock in my ass."

He snorts. "This is about trying new things, so you better believe I want a turn."

I pull him into another long, deep kiss that makes my cock throb. "Remember what to do?"

"I've been researching."

"Good." I shift farther onto the bed and drop back against it. "Then get a move on. I'm horny."

"You're about to get hornier."

I eye his sexy, naked body. "Not possible."

Brandon smirks and walks over to his side table. "After watching that porn the other night, I placed an order online."

"For …" My eyes widen when Brandon lifts a silicone butt plug and a long strip of material. "What are those for?"

"This"—he lifts the plug—"is for me to wear while I fuck you. The gag is for you, dude."

"Do you think it's healthy to feel jealous of a butt plug?"

He lets out a burst of a laugh. "Think of it as your friend. It's getting me ready for you."

"Yeah, but it still gets to play up there first."

"Are you sulking?"

"Yeah, a little."

"You're ridiculous." He tosses me the lube. "Why don't you start me off at the same time?"

"What do you …"

The bed dips as Brandon crawls onto it. He leans down over me and tugs my ear between his teeth. It sends heat into my bloodstream. "You like that, don't you?"

"So, so much."

"Noted." His voice is tinged with amusement. "But what I thought could be hot is … sixty-nine while we finger each other, then you fill my ass with the plug while I fuck yours."

Bro my fucking god. I wrap my arms around him and haul him against me. "Yes to all of that."

"What are we waiting for, then?" Brandon kisses his way down my body, alternating between soft and sensual and biting so hard and fast, my eyes water. Instead of being a turnoff, my cock throbs at the attention. When he gets to my dick, he wraps his hand around it and gives me a long, firm stroke.

My thighs shudder.

"This thing is goddamn insane." His tongue flicks out to run along the slit, and I watch him, desperately needing to feel his mouth. "Someone likes me."

"I told you he did. You're like a Pokémon, and my dick chooses you."

Brandon sniggers. "You've never been more nerdy. Which is saying something. Because you own a fanny pack."

I'm about to bite back when his mouth closes over me, and

suddenly, I'm A-OK with being called whatever he needs me to be called. "See how much you can take."

He sinks down onto me and gets about halfway before he gags and pulls off with a cough. "I'm determined to get that whole thing in there."

I grab him and tackle him to the bed. "Well, until then, let's go back to the original plan. Because I gotta say, it's one of your better ideas." Then I kiss him through his laugh, hard and demanding, until the amusement dies between us, and the atmosphere shifts. His breathing has gotten heavier, and every touch feels heightened. I kiss my way down his body this time, letting myself explore each muscle, each dip between his abs. I take note of the things that get a reaction and file that information away in my Brandon smut notes. Once I reach his flushed, hard cock, I turn around to straddle his face.

"This good?"

"Oh, yeah." His voice is strained.

"Hey, no coming until you're fucking me."

"Yeah, I'm not making any promises there."

In that case, I need to be very careful about how I go about this. I grab the plug and click open the lube, coating it and my hand with a shit ton of the stuff before passing it back to Brandon. Not only do I not want to hurt him, but I also know he's enough of a bastard that if I do, he'll hurt me right back.

And maybe that shouldn't turn me on, but it sort of does.

I'm learning a whole new world of things about myself lately.

Once I hear Brandon close the lube, I can't hold back any longer. I feed him my cock while I turn my attention to his.

And fuck, this is hot. The suction around my dick while I work on his probably wasn't the smartest way to start this out when it's been nearly a week since we were last together. All I know is I can't get enough of touching him, sucking him, listening to his grunts and labored breathing.

A heavy dose of precum hits my tongue and reminds me to ease off, even though I'm desperate to drive him crazy. Instead, I do what I came here to. I slide my fingers between his cheeks until I reach his hole, and like he was waiting for my go-ahead, Brandon does the same to me.

It's … weird.

Definitely not what I'm used to, but he keeps sucking on the crown of my cock, while he rubs his fingers over my ass, and it's like my body is at war with itself. Is this how it feels for him?

Simultaneously amazing and terrifying.

Because I'm sure this shit is gonna hurt, but Brandon is gentle with me, softly working me open until he's able to slide a finger inside.

Surprisingly, it's not painful. I'm undecided how to feel about it, but I'm determined to be dicked down at least once, so I'm gonna suck it up and get on with it.

And when he works his finger slowly in and out, my eyes almost roll back. I press my finger inside him too, then get lost in the feeling, overwhelmed by sensory fucking overload.

We give each other's dicks enough attention to keep them interested while we work on getting each other ready. Brandon gets a second finger this time, and it takes all my limited concentration to make sure I go slow and take care of him, but once they're in there and I fuck him with them, he begins to push back against me.

He releases my cock on a groan. "Are you ready? I think you're ready."

If I'm not, I'm past caring at this point. I need him inside me. "Yeah, just give me a second."

I grab the butt plug and remove my fingers.

Brandon tenses under me for a second before he lets out a long breath and spreads his thighs.

"You good?"

"Do it."

Hells yes. I work it in slowly, giving him time to adjust, and my eyes are glued to where he's stretching around it. He's right that I was jealous before, because I wanted it to be my cock first, but I'd underestimated how hot it would be to work the toy in and out of his body. To see his hole stretch and his cock jerk. To witness the little tremors racing through him.

By the time it's fully in, I'm breathing as deeply as he is.

"Goddamn, Brando ..."

"Yeah."

I scramble off him and drop onto my back. "My turn."

He chuckles as he grabs a condom, and I watch him open it and roll it down his long cock.

"Look how desperate you are for me."

"I'm not even going to bother trying to deny it. Fuck me."

He kneels between my legs, stroking himself slowly, focus locked on my ass. When his eyes flick up to meet mine, there's a flash of vulnerability through his heated gaze. "I want to make this good."

I tug him down against me and draw him into a long kiss. I'd thought that once we started fooling around, the kissing would lose some of its effect. That I'd get used to it. Immune. But instead, every kiss is like a hit of drugs to my system, and I can't get enough.

Brandon reaches down between us and lines his cock up to my entrance. The blunt head pushes forward, and I get this weird *oh shit it's happening* moment. I'm letting a guy fuck me. And not just any guy. *Brandon*. And not just letting, but *needing*.

He shakes as he pushes in, and the more it burns and stretches, the more of the feeling I want. It's not exactly painful, but there's a tinge of something that slowly gets more pleasant as he fills me completely. His hips hit my ass, and he pulls back from the kiss to let out a long breath.

"Jesus, fuck, dude. You have no idea how it feels."

"Right back at you." I gasp as he shifts.

"The plug is right on that spot. Between that and how tight you are, this isn't going to last long."

I scramble to grab the gag and pass it to him. "Put this on me and do your best."

"I think I might need it more than you."

With how loudly he's breathing, he might be right. But then he flashes me a small smile, and his teeth give me an idea. I tilt my head to the side. "Use me."

"What?"

"If you can't be quiet, bite down on me."

"It won't hurt?"

"I want it to."

He groans, and his eyes almost flutter closed. "Okay. If you want me to stop and can't talk, pat your head."

"Like your asthma thing?"

"Exactly."

I shouldn't find it so adorable that he wants to look out for me like that. "Not that I couldn't overpower you anyway, but sure. Good idea."

With my help, Brandon manages to get the gag on one-handed. It's some kind of knotted material that sits tight in my mouth and across my face, and even when I try to make noise, nothing more than a muffled grunt comes out.

A wicked look crosses Brandon's face as he gives his hips a roll. I suck in a breath through my nose as my ass comes alive, and I'm already cursing the gag because I want to tell him to do it again.

The pain is completely gone, and now all I want is for him to fuck me hard and fast.

I slap his ass, and Brandon laughs before it slowly turns into this husky moan. "Okay."

His eyes are locked on my face as he moves, slow and unsure at first. It's a frustrating tease, nowhere near enough. I want him to unapologetically take out our years of bickering on me.

I reach down and grab his ass, fingers biting into the round cheeks, and match each thrust with one of my own.

"Yes …" He picks up pace, getting more confident, and it doesn't take long until he's pounding into me. His grunts echo in the room, but the insane pleasure shooting through me makes it impossible to care.

All I can focus on are his sexy muscles, rippling with each thrust, his parted lips, the wave in his hair flopping down over his hooded eyes, and the sudden, amazing, mind-blowing need.

My cock is aching, but I don't want this to end.

Brandon looks out of his mind as he alternates between hard and fast thrusts and slow and deep ones that make me squirm desperately, and bite down so hard on the gag my jaw is going to be dead by the time we're done.

"Fuck, Robbie … Fuck …" Brandon grabs the backs of my thighs and pushes my legs up to watch. "You're so hot. This is insane … This is …"

I try to grunt my agreement.

"I shouldn't love you gagged as much as I do."

My grip on his ass tightens. Coaxes him faster. I love that

he loves the gag. I love that he's losing his mind fucking me. I love that it's my body he's going wild over because there's no denying the effect he has on me.

My attraction to him is out of this world crazy, and when he grunts loud enough that it gets even my attention, I card my fingers through his hair and tug his face to my neck.

His teeth sink in, and *oh holy fuck*. I scramble for my cock, getting lost in the mix of pain and pleasure surging through me.

I sound like a desperate fucking whore behind this gag, and even *that's* turning me on. I jerk myself hard and fast, matching Brandon's thrusts, and I have a moment to wonder if this is how it feels for him—to be filled so perfectly while my cock is worked over. My orgasm builds and builds, my balls tightening, and then Brandon releases my neck and lets out a hoarse cry right next to my ear as his whole body shudders.

Feeling him come sets me off. I lose track of everything but the goddamn relief in my pulsing cock, and when Brandon slumps against me, we both take a minute to catch our breaths.

He pulls back, still looking out of it, and gently removes the gag. His stare traces my cheeks, and then he leans down and softly kisses both of them.

"You've got marks."

"They'll fade."

He strokes my neck, right over the bite. "This won't. At least, not quickly."

I close my arms around him and flip us so I'm on top. His dick slips out, and now my ass feels kinda raw. But totally worth it. "Good," I tell him. "I don't want it to fade. I want more." I kiss him. "So many more."

Again and again.

I'm starting to freak out that I'll never be done with this.

22

BRANDON

Robbie and I don't skip classes again, but even though our schedules are intense, we catch up as much as we can. And the nights when he's busy, I work on myself. I'm taking the plug way easier and even managed to get two fingers in there next to it last night, so I'm getting confident I can take him.

Who knew having a brofriend could be so fun?

But while I love everything I'm doing with Robbie, and I wouldn't change us fucking around for the world, I'm nervous about this visit home. My mom and dad know me a bit too well since I'm all they ever had, and I'm worried that as soon as they see me with Robbie, they'll call me out for the thing I'm trying not to think about.

The *thing* that causes butterflies when he's around.

The *thing* that makes me get lost in sex above and beyond the pleasure of it.

The *thing* that has me reluctant to name an end date for whatever we're doing.

Technically, once he fucks me, we'll have covered all the experimental bases. Sure, there are always things to learn sexually—especially if you try out the kink side of things—but when it comes to knowing what positions do it for us and what we're comfortable doing with another man, we've got it covered.

Almost.

So once he tops me ... what's the point of us continuing this thing?

Other than I really, really want to.

"Gear up, motherfuckers!" Chad says, handing out the water guns.

"Or in our case," Robbie mutters, "brother fuckers would be more accurate."

"Dude, stop." I laugh as I jostle him, and he fires a spurt of water at me in retaliation. "Dooms is gonna kill you if you're not taking this seriously."

"Relax." He pats his pocket. And okay, for maybe the first time ever, Robbie's cargo pants and fanny pack make sense. He's got them stuffed full of as many small water guns as he could fit in there.

They're going to have fun.

And I say "they" because I don't get to play.

Risk managers need to look out for their houses. My role will be to stand back and observe, fill our drum of colored water when it gets low, and make sure any out players get their asses inside and changed once they've been hit. It's only five, but it's already dark out, and it's going to be a cold one.

All fourteen houses on the row are playing.

"All right, you animals," Zeke says. "Most of you have played Guard Duty before, but for the pledge bitches, this is how it's gonna go down."

I try not to sulk at the fact even the *pledges* get to join in. Most of the time, they're the ones stuck with the grunt work. In something like our scavenger hunt, it makes sense for the risk managers to play and be on the ground with the others. We're all first aid trained, and if anything happened, having us spread out all over campus means that one of us is going to be close if needed.

In the street, keeping each of us at our houses is the smarter choice.

I get it.

Of course I do.

Keeping the frat houses and our members safe means continuing to operate. We need to keep this bubble of brother and sisterhood operating so future Sigma Beta Psis get to experience everything we have—unless they're the risk managers too, and then they're shit outta luck.

Though, I don't miss out on as much as Zeke. Unlike him though, I care. I want to be involved. I really didn't think this executive position through. And yeah, it has its perks like a single room, which I'm definitely taking advantage of, but the previous risk manager didn't warn me how isolating the whole thing can be.

"This is our totem." Zeke holds up a small marble statue with our letters stamped across the bottom, backlit from the light on our porch. He'd tried to have a butt plug approved, but when he told the other presidents he wouldn't confirm whether it was used or not, they vetoed that idea fast. Pity. It would have given us the advantage if the other teams didn't want to touch it. "Every house has a totem. It's your job to capture theirs and bring them back to our porch while protecting our own. First house to three wins—and you can steal totems back. If you're shot, you're out. The more people you shoot, the more points our team gets if everyone is out before the three totems are gathered."

Today, there's no time limit for how long the game can go for. When I played during sophomore year, we ended up going well into the night, until most houses gave up from the cold. We won, of course, because not even a little frostbite can make a house full of athletes quit.

Stubborn and competitive to the core.

It should be the Sigma Beta Psi motto.

"Other than those rules, there are no rules," Chad says. "Any questions?"

There never is. All we want is to get started already. Zeke says into his radio that we're good to go, and then everyone gets into position.

Robbie nudges me. "You okay?"

"Fine." I force a fake as shit smile. "Love playing waterboy."

He hesitates in joining the others. "Did you want to play? We can switch if you want to."

"Switch, huh? We're gonna." I pump my eyebrows at him.

"As much as I love where your mind is at, you know that's not what I mean."

I wave him off. "It's fine. I know what I'm doing here."

He's clearly conflicted, not sure whether to take me at my word or not, but as much as I might want to join them, I don't want to do it at Robbie's expense. These are the days he lives for, that he spends a good chunk of his free time planning, and there's no way I'll be the one to take it away from him.

Besides, it wouldn't be as fun if he wasn't involved.

I give him a push. "You better win this for us, big guy."

"I'll make you proud, Brando."

"Good. Because if you get this over with quickly, we'll have the rest of the night to do whatever we want."

He sucks in a sudden breath. "I'm gonna hold you to that."

What I don't tell him is it doesn't matter if this thing goes all night. I'll still be waiting for him.

I don't know how to stop.

23

ROBBIE

I CAN'T REMEMBER EVER WANTING TO GET A GAME OVER WITH before it's started before. These street-wide games are one of the things I look forward to most, and this time playing them is going to be the last—so why do I wish it was done already?

Well, I know why.

Brandon.

No matter how much we hook up, no matter how much we say we're in this for fun, it's never enough. His butt plug has become my wingman. Touching him is my obsession. Whenever I'm supposed to be concentrating on something that isn't him, my thoughts are overtaken, and I lose hours thinking about him, wishing we had more time together.

It's cold out, but at least with the wool clothes on that Brandon got me for Christmas, I don't feel like I'm about to lose a foot, and as soon as the siren sounds to get started, running will warm me up as well.

We only have to wait a few minutes until the Kappas let off

a low, keening alarm, and it's game on. Everyone scatters. We have one minute to disappear before the street becomes a Hunger Games arena, and I make like fucking Rambo as I bolt and throw myself into the bushes alongside our house.

Sometimes these games work better through teamwork; other times it's every man for himself. The fewer people you're around for Guard Duty, the less chance you have of being seen, and not only do I want to win, but I want to win fast.

The bushes run along the Sigma-Lambda boundary, then loop around the back of the property and reach the Deltas' yard on the other side. Everyone playing is in all white, partly as a terrible attempt to blend in with the snow, but mostly so when we're hit with a water gun, the color shows up and the right house can be awarded.

Shooting people has never been so fun.

Especially since I've never been hit before, and I plan to keep my perfect record intact.

Normally I go straight for the Kappas' house, but if I was them, I'd be expecting it and would have an ambush set up and waiting. So tonight, I have my sights set on the Deltas. They're not usually one of the first targets because of where their house is set. The houses either end of the street are usually hit first because of the corner blocks, but tonight, I'm throwing strategy out of the window and hoping that works for me.

The siren sounds again to let us know the one minute is up, and almost as soon as it cuts off, the unmistakable sound of mayhem breaks out. There's shouting and cheering, idiots hollering as they go head-to-head with the enemy. Someone has clearly tried to go straight on the attack judging by the war cry, and I'm hoping it will distract whoever is guarding the back door at the Delta house.

I'm getting well experienced with back-door entry.

I snigger as I reach the side of the house and press myself against the wall, shuffling along so I'm not seen. Before I come into view of the back porch, I grit my teeth and drop down onto the snow in an attempt to stay hidden. I try to ignore the way my body instantly seizes up and wants to freeze as I shuffle along. The Delta guy is on the back porch, staring out into the night. The porch light is on but only reaches so far, so where I am should be mostly out of sight unless he senses movement in the shadows or he randomly shoots in the hopes of getting someone—like he does right now.

I watch the jet of water blast from the gun, catching light from the porch, and thank my frat forefathers that he chose to shoot in the opposite direction. I got lucky.

Before he can turn around, I jump up from my position, lift my gun, and take aim. My shot gets him right between the shoulder blades, leaving a large blue stain.

"Oh, shitty shit fuck." His back arches against the freezing spray. "Fucking Robbie. That's *cold.*"

"I iced it up special for you," I taunt.

He flips me off.

"Where's your totem?"

"As if I'm going to tell you that. Good luck finding it."

He disappears back into the house to get changed, and I follow him. Now he's out, he's not allowed to interfere, but I know if I was in his position, I'd give my brothers the heads-up anyway.

I sneak into the house, gun raised, pretending I'm a police officer in a crime drama.

Theatrics for the win.

Every house only has two people guarding it, so I know there's another Delta out front. I'm quiet as I check my phone for what I'm looking for—a rubber ducky—and sneak through the house.

If I was a rubber ducky, where would I be?

The bathroom is too obvious, but I poke my head inside on the way past anyway as I try to rack my brains for where else it could be. There's nothing in the living room, and I can make out the Delta on the front porch while I'm in there, so I hurry through the room and into the kitchen.

Only, when I cross the threshold, I step on a loose board, and a creak goes through the house.

I freeze.

Hold my breath.

Ears strained for a sound.

I've just counted to three in my head when I hear the front door quietly click open.

Goddamn fuck damn.

I barrel across the room on my tiptoes, trying to stay as stealthy as possible, and head for the back door. If I leave though, this whole venture was pointless because walking away empty-handed feels a lot like failure.

So I take a risk, push open the door, and then slam it closed.

Footsteps sound in another part of the house, so I race back up the hall and throw myself into one of the ground-floor bedrooms and pray like fuck that I'm not caught. My heart is pounding out a serious rhythm, blood rushing in my ears, and even though I'm low-key sick and need to pee over the idea of being caught, I wish Brandon could be here with me.

It's not fair he has to miss out.

On a whim, I pull out my phone, press my finger to my lips, and snap a quick selfie to send to Brandon. Hopefully it'll make him smile, at least.

Then I put my game face back on and strain my ears for any hint of movement.

After probably a minute or so, I pull out my phone again and text Chad.

Me: *You still in, brother?*

Chad: *Who do you think you're talking to? Do I look like a dumbass pledge?*

Me: *My mistake*

Chad: *What do you need?*

Me: *Think you can cause a stir out the front of Delta house? I took out their back guard and got inside, but I think their front guard is in the house looking for me*

Chad: *Wow. Amateurs. It's like they want us to walk in the front door*

Me: *Just get him out of here*

Chad: *I got you*

A minute later, I hear a series of tiny explosions and heavy footsteps thumping back through the house. I wait for the sound of the front door opening and closing, then sneak out of my hiding spot.

My adrenaline is running high, and I'm working to keep it in check as I glance into each bedroom as I pass. I loop back around to hit the kitchen from the non-noisy side, and when I'm checking out the space, I spot a flash of yellow inside the oven.

I carefully pull open the door and *bingo*.

I got the little ducker.

I'm out the back door, not caring when it slams behind me, before the front guard even knows what happened. Then I dive back into the bushes, run along the perimeter, and check our front lawn is empty before I make for the porch.

I toss the duck to Zeke.

"Damn, that might be a new record, Robbie."

"Gotta get through this fast." When my back is to Zeke, I send a wink Brandon's way. He's watching on, bemused, wool hat covering his hair and ears, scarf almost pulled up over his mouth, but even though he's half hidden, the heavy *ba-dump* in my chest has no chill. I want to kiss him. Grab him. Be the one to keep him warm out here.

Even if I'm half freezing my ass off.

And if I'm already starting to feel like this around him, how the fuck do I show up for his family birthday thing and act like he means nothing? When I'm beginning to suspect he means so much more than that.

My phone vibrates in my fanny pack, and I quickly pull it out.

Chad: *I'm almost in at the Kappas, but there's a group of them waiting along the side of the house where I can sneak in. I need something that will draw them all out*

Damn, a whole group of them? That would require something big. Something that's bound to break my perfect streak of never having been hit.

I could sacrifice myself easily, but we've only got one totem, so even if I did draw them out before they got me, that's still only maybe two. Two isn't enough of a lead when all it takes is for one of them to be stolen back.

I need armor. Or a tank.

I laugh, and then my stare falls on my car parked in the street. Well, actually …

"Zeke?"

"What's up?"

"Doomsen needs me to fuck shit up so he can get into Kappa house. But I need Brandon."

He shakes his head. "He's needed here."

"Okay." I stuff my hands in my pockets as casually as I can. "I guess I'll drive my car while trying to shoot out of the window. Totally safe, after all. In the snow? At night? What could go wrong? Definitely not something a risk manager needs to worry about."

His attention flicks from me to Brandon and back to the dark street. "Do it."

Fuck yes.

I text Chad back to be ready, grab my keys, and gesture for Brandon to follow me.

"Keys?" He holds out his hands.

I toss him the gun instead.

"What are you …"

"Tell me you have good aim."

The smile that breaks across his face lights me up inside. "I've got this, Rob-dog."

I crack up laughing, unlock the car, and we both jump in. "Quick, what's the most dramatic song you can think of?"

"Ah … 'Eye of the Tiger'?"

Yes. I find it in my phone, then switch on the car, link it to my sound system, and blast that fucker on loud. I'll do anything for attention. And if this doesn't score me massive mayhem points against Chad, I might as well pass him the crown.

"Let's do this."

The key to getting attention? Being as obnoxious as goddamn possible. I rev the engine before pulling into the street, headlights on high. Brandon cracks his window, and points his gun out of the gap, ready to take out whoever he needs to. The problem is, on the street, no one gives a fuck.

So I do what any frat brother trying to cause a distraction

would do. I mount the gutter and take us through the front yards.

"Robbie …"

"I'm going slow, man."

Brandon gives a nervous grimace. "Please don't kill anyone." He shoots suddenly. "And that's one."

"Game on, bitches."

I steer us carefully through the snow, doing burnouts, blasting the horn, flashing the headlights over and over. People from other houses converge on us to try and take Brandon out, but that bastard has perfect aim, and they drop like flies. We reach Kappa house, and Brandon shoots the front guard before he has a clue what's happening. When none of the others show their ugly faces, I reach over and take his gun, then hand him one of my smaller ones.

"I'll cover you."

"You want me to go in?"

Before I can think it through, I lean over and press a quick kiss to his lips. "Watch out for the guy around back."

He strips off his coat and scarf, then jumps out of the car as I put it in park and let down my window.

"Come out, Kappa bitches!" I shout. "The Rob-dog reckoning is here!" I hold down the horn long and shrill, sure I have everyone's attention on the row. Whatever it takes to keep the focus off Brandon.

Charles watches him pass, unable to do anything to interfere except shout at me about rules.

Fuck him. There are no rules.

I shoot him for funsies and cut off every one of his protests with a blast of the horn.

Zeke will be hearing about this tomorrow.

Brandon's gone for a few minutes before he comes thundering out at a dead bolt, clutching the goblet and throwing himself at the car. He's reached the hood when Sam appears on their front porch and aims at him.

I throw open my door, line him up, and he swings his attention to me. We shoot at the same time, and I gasp as the freezing cold water hits my sweater.

Motherfucker.

The only good thing is I get him at the same time, so there's nothing he or Charles can do as I slam the front door and jump into the back of the car.

Brandon glances back from the passenger seat. "What are you doing?"

"I'm out." I show him the green stain on my front. "You'll need to drive."

He slides over the console, throws the car in drive, and we head back onto the road.

"Holy shit," he says, out of breath. "That was crazy."

He doesn't stop smiling the whole way back, not even when he hands the goblet over to Zeke.

Zeke shakes his head at us. "Twenty bucks says Guard Duty will suddenly have a new rule by tomorrow."

"I'd be disappointed in Charles if it didn't."

His gaze drops to my sweater. "Holy shit, you're out?"

"Yup."

"Streak's over, then?"

"I guess so." And I'm nowhere near as annoyed at that fact as I thought I would be. Because seeing the happiness radiating from Brandon made the whole thing totally worth it.

BRANDON

WE EASILY WIN GUARD DUTY THANKS TO ROBBIE'S EXTREME ambush, and even when the other houses try to call foul, they have no grounds to stand on. Zeke's right that Charles ends up pissed, and before the party even kicks off, the no-cars rule is in place for next year.

But that doesn't change the fact we won tonight.

The party is pumping at the Lambda house, everyone getting drunk off their tits, and having the party at a house other than our own means I would normally be able to let loose a little.

But I'm stone-cold sober and horny as fuck.

Who knew I'd have a hard-on for immature fun?

I text Robbie to meet me back at the house and sneak out. I have no idea if he got my message or not, but it's not like it matters. I'm going to get things ready and hope he joins me at some point.

There's no one at home, and even from next door, the

music is still loud. Perfect conditions for two brofriends to fuck each other's brains out.

I walk into my room, ready to strip off and get that plug in my ass, but the second I step foot inside, hands grab me and shove me into the wall.

Robbie kicks the door closed, lifts me off my damn feet, and kisses me stupid.

I grip his hair tight, kiss him back hard, and try not to shiver when he grabs my jaw and forces my mouth wider. He kisses me like he owns me, like he's desperate for me, and fuck if that doesn't go to my cock. The unapologetic way he takes what he needs shouldn't be such a turn-on, but here I am, cock hard and ready to shoot bullets.

He lands a powerful whack on my ass before squeezing the cheek tight. "How are you so sexy?"

I smirk as I lean in and drag my teeth along his throat, and Robbie immediately tilts his head back, exactly like I knew he would. He might be bold in what he needs from me, but he's not scared to make himself vulnerable either.

"My bite mark is gone," I say, kissing him right over the spot where it was.

"Better give me another one, then."

I laugh. "Did anyone notice it?"

"A few people."

"What did you say?"

"Best sex of my life."

I pull back and study his expression. "Are you shitting me?"

"Nope."

My mouth drops, and I don't know what to say to that, because holy shit he's right. "Dude, you're not even going to try and play it cool?"

He grins and kisses me softly. "Why bother? You dicked me down good. Are you going to do it again?"

"Actually, I thought it could be my turn this time."

Excitement lights up his face. "You think you're ready?"

"We're going to find out."

Robbie shudders, and I love when his powerful body does that. When he's so overwhelmed he needs to let the energy out somehow. "Bed?"

"Actually …" I squirm until he sets me down. Then I turn around and arch my back at him. "Maybe we could do it like this?"

"Wall sex?"

"There's no one here." I shake my ass at him, and he immediately reaches out to grab it. "We can be as loud as we want."

"You're on."

He grabs the lube and condom while I strip out of my clothes. No matter how much I've practiced for this moment, I have a good feeling it'll probably hurt anyway, but I don't think there's anything I've ever wanted as badly as I want to be torn apart by his cock. Maybe I'm starting to understand why so many people want to tame that beast.

I watch him peel off his clothes until he's down to his briefs, and my cock throbs at the view. He's so *big*. All over. Chest, arms, middle, ass, legs … My mouth fucking waters at the sight of his dick pressing forward.

I squeeze my eyes shut to try and get myself under control.

"You okay?" he asks, pressing a kiss to the back of my neck. That small touch has my muscles relaxing.

"Yeah. I want this so fucking much."

"Okay." His hands stroke up and down my sides, thumbs tweaking my nipples, and he buries his nose into my hair and runs kisses along my neck. "That's good." One of his hands disappears, and I hear him suck on his fingers before sliding them down my crease. "Relax for me, Brando. I've got you."

I shift my legs apart, and he kneels.

It's a strange feeling, knowing he's watching as he works a finger inside me, but then I think of how hot it looks to see my dick filling his ass, and instead of getting self-conscious, I tilt my hips back toward him, spread my legs wider, and fold my arms against the wall.

His groan tells me I'm on the right track.

Robbie's finger disappears, and when he slides it back in, it's covered in lube and moves more easily. He fucks me with it for a few minutes before he works his second one in there.

"I'm going to stretch you right out for me," he says, voice low and scratchy. "I won't hurt you."

"I dunno if I can wait that long."

"You can and you will." He takes his time, spreading my ass with one hand and fucking me open with the other. The stretching burns, but he's slow and careful, and the appreciative sounds coming from him are keeping my cock rock hard.

He spends more time than I expected down there, and I have no idea how many fingers he's got inside me, but I'm taking them easily now.

"I've gotta be ready by now," I say, hands balled into fists and forehead pressed into my arm.

He rumbles an appreciative sound. "You're fucking gaping. Jesus fuck, Brando."

Then he leans forward and drags his tongue around my rim.

I pound the wall at the jolt it sends straight to my dick and strangle back the unconscious grunt. "Please. Do it."

He stands, dropping his boxer briefs, and tugs my head

back into a filthy kiss as he covers himself with a condom. "I'll go slow."

"Just do *something* already."

Robbie steps away to lube up, and then his body closes in behind mine. He plants one hand on the wall above my head while he guides his cock to my hole with the other. I'm filled with nervous expectation and desperate need as I push back, and the head fills me.

He's so goddamn big, no amount of stretching could prepare me for my first time with that thing, but I refuse to give up, and Robbie keeps his word to go slow.

He reaches around to gently stroke me with his lubed hand as his cock inches inside me, bit by bit, both filling that need coursing through me and stretching me to what I think is my limit before stretching me some more.

"You okay?" he asks.

"Uh-huh. Nearly done?"

"Halfway."

I almost back out.

"You can do it," he says. "You're doing so good. There's no way I could do what you're doing."

I shiver. "Next time we argue who's tougher, you remember this."

He kisses my neck. "No competition. It's you. I'm blown away by you right now."

"How does it look?"

Robbie shifts back a little and pushes farther inside. I breathe through it, and when he gasps, it makes me more determined than ever to see this through. I fuck myself back on him slow at first, then getting more and more confident.

"I can't wait to see how stretched you are once we're done."

"Dude, don't make me laugh."

"Nothing funny about this." The gravelly, lust-drenched tone kills my amusement, and with one quick thrust, he's in. "You good?"

"Kiss me for a bit."

His hand leaves the wall and grips my hair tight, tugging my head back. His kiss is rough, consuming, everything I need it to be. It makes me dizzy and distracts me from the pain that ebbs away, replaced with the uncontrollable urge for him to move.

I roll my hips, and Robbie growls. He releases my hair and my cock and presses both hands to the wall this time before he starts to fuck me.

He's careful, controlled, but the more I get used to him, the easier it is. There was a small worrying voice that this would be an epic disaster and I'd hate it, but somehow we're doing this … and it feels incredible. I'm so full, his cock is setting all my nerves alight, hitting that spot deep inside me that makes my toes curl. We find a rhythm, steady and so deep, but the needier I become, the more I push back into him.

Complete instinct and want is taking over, removing all my worries and replacing them with something that feels so amazing it was worth all the prep work.

Without the gag, Robbie is vocal and so loud that even with the music, if there was anyone in the house, they'd hear us. I'm bracing myself against the wall, but every time he drives into me, it sends a thump through the house, a grunt rattling from my chest, so much goddamn desire flooding into my balls.

He finally releases the wall to grab my hips and pounds into me so hard and fast his balls slap against mine. It's a completely new sensation that's jumping right to the top of my *yes* list, and I moan long and loud enough to give Robbie a run for his money.

Then he suddenly pulls out, spins me, and hoists me into the air. My back hits the wall, and he presses back inside. He's sweaty and completely checked out.

"Touch yourself."

The second I wrap my hand around my cock, we both groan. Robbie pins me to the wall, taking everything he wants and giving me everything I need. He fucks me hard as he chases his orgasm, and I'm so blindingly close, I can barely keep my eyes open. But I don't want to miss this. I want to witness the exact moment he lets go.

I'm close though. Worried I won't make it. Struggling to keep control so I can see him go first.

Pleasure ripples along my spine, making my ass clench, and then Robbie gasps and lets go.

"Brandon. Oh, fuck, Brandon."

His lips slant over mine, not quite kissing but claiming all the same. I shake as my orgasm takes hold, and the first jerk of my cock is bliss. My eyes fall closed, and I sink into the feeling, wanting to draw it out forever.

Suddenly, Robbie laughs.

"What's so funny?"

"Nothing." He kisses me. "Everything."

"You are one weird dude."

He lets me down, cock slipping out. "Okay. *That* was officially the best sex I've ever had."

I want to ask, to test him out, see if he's done now we've covered that off or if he wants more as much as I do. I'm nervous. Not sure how to even bring it up. Fuck it. "Think we can go for top three?"

"I reckon top five."

"Top ten?" My nerves are bubbling up to something like excitement.

"I bet you could take out all top fifty places if you wanted them."

I tug him down and sink my teeth into his neck. "Let's test that theory out."

25

ROBBIE

HAVING A BROFRIEND IS POSSIBLY MY FAVORITE THING. AFTER Bro-motions night, we fuck. Before classes, we have a quick morning jerk together. During the day, we argue and bicker and are exactly the same as we've ever been, but now I can admit to myself that I really like those back-and-forths with him.

They don't annoy me.

If anything, they turn me on.

And now it's February, and we're heading to Kilborough to visit Brandon's family. Maybe we should have come up with some kind of lie for if our brothers noticed us both missing all weekend, but with people always in and out of the house, it's unlikely. Instead, we snuck out, and I figure we'll deal with it if we need to.

For now, all my focus is being given to Brandon's parents.

This isn't going to be awkward as balls at all.

I swear Brandon is sweating bricks.

"You okay?" I ask, taking a long slurp of my Icee.

"Of course."

"You could at least try for convincing."

"That *was* convincing."

"If you say so …"

He throws a glare my way. It makes me laugh.

"Do you need to house-train me before we get there?"

"House-train?"

"You know, warn me about my bad habits and teach me all the shit you need to for them to like me."

That makes him smile. "You have nothing to worry about."

"You sure?"

"Yeah. They're never going to like you, so there's no point in trying."

I'd whack him if he wasn't driving. "You're a fucking dick."

"Dude, don't stress. You already know they're excited to meet you."

They are. We talked on the phone to them last night, and both Amber and Steve were excitedly running through their plans for the weekend.

"Do you think they were serious when they asked if they should set up separate beds?"

He cringes. "I still can't believe she said that."

"I can. She totally knows we're hooking up."

"Yeah, well, while we're there, we're not. We'll sleep in separate rooms and act like the friends we are. There's no need for them to get invested in a relationship that doesn't exist."

I get what he's saying, even if I don't like it.

Which is a first for me.

I've never been tempted to do the relationship thing once during college, and here I am, right at the end of it, thinking I might want one with *him*. Brandon's special. I think that's the thing that's always drawn me to him. All that posturing and showing off for him freshman year, the drinking, the dumb pranks, the being over-the-top at parties just because I knew his attention would be focused on me … our verbal sparring matches that can last all day, and then the video games and breakfast together, and quiet moments while we walk across campus.

When it comes to college, he's there in almost all of my memories.

Chad and I might be thick as thieves—or at least we were before we both started focusing on other dudes—but even though we're close, it's never been like it is with Brandon.

Instead of trying to voice all that, I lean forward and turn up the music.

"Oh no …" Brandon moans when I start to sing.

And sure, I don't have a great voice, but it's fun, so sue me.

We get to Kilborough in good time and pull up at a large property outside of town. Even from here I can see the huge abandoned prison that drives the town's economy. We drive down the long driveway until we reach a large single-story house.

"This is big for two people," I say.

"All the back half of the house is rooms for our farmhands. Some of them prefer to stay on-site when they're rostered because of the early mornings."

"What's the farm do?"

"Fresh produce, mostly. Mom sells at a market in town, but most of it is sent up to Boston."

"That's cool."

He nods. "It's not something I'm interested in, but it was cool to grow up here with all of this land. I knew kids from the properties near here, and we all used to sneak out at night."

"That's not very safe of you, Mr. Risk Manager."

"I haven't always been a stickler for rules, fuck you very much."

"Nah, but you've always been more sensible than the rest of us."

He doesn't like that, judging by the way his face falls.

"Hey, that doesn't mean you don't know how to have fun. You're just smarter about it."

"Yeah, okay," he says like he doesn't believe me.

"Hey." I grab his thigh before he can climb out of the car. "I think you're really fucking cool, Brando."

He gives my hand a quick squeeze. "Thanks."

We separate and climb out of the car to meet his parents, who are waiting on the porch. There are warm hugs all around, even for me, which is awesome.

I pull back from hugging his mom, who barely reaches my shoulders, and turn to Brandon. "I see where you got your height from."

"Fuck off. Dad, tell Robbie I'm six foot."

His dad tilts his head to the side. "Are you? I thought you were five nine."

I roar with laughter at how indignant he looks.

"Mom."

"*Mom*," I mock.

He flips me off.

She wraps her arm around his waist and steers him inside, putting on a baby voice. "Come on, dear, let's get away from those mean men."

"At least someone loves me," he throws back.

I'm still snorting back my amusement when I grab our bags and follow them.

"How long have you and Brandon known each other?"

Steve asks, following me into the house. He's where Brandon got his blond hair from, even though Steve's is streaked with gray, and he's got a thick farm-strong body. Brandon's dad is a total DILF, and I can't wait to mercilessly tease him about it.

"We rushed together freshman year. I haven't been able to get rid of him since."

Steve eyes me. "Yeah, he's mentioned you a few times. Nothing like making lifelong college buddies."

"Exactly. I swear some of my brothers don't get that, but we're bros for life. That was the whole point of joining a fraternity."

"It was nice of you to come back here for his birthday."

"It was nice of him to stay with me for Christmas."

Steve smiles suddenly. "I bet. That big old house, all to yourselves."

"What? No. I just mean—"

He slaps me on the back. "I'm messing with you. I have to duck out and check up on some things, but drop the bags at the stairs and follow the hall. They'll be out the back."

I thank him, still not sure what to think of that exchange. I know they're both suspicious that there's something between us—their hints haven't been subtle—and it kinda seems like he likes me anyway.

My chest fills with some sort of bullshit pride, and I swear I fucking inflate at the thought. I dump the bags and follow Steve's directions, but when I hear Brandon and Amber talking, I pause.

"I'm only saying, honey, no judgment."

"Stop. I get it. You're fine if I'm gay—"

"Or bi."

"Or that." Brandon sighs. "Look, it's … complicated, okay? Please don't make things weird."

"Weird? Why would I make things weird? I'm offended you'd assume such a thing."

I can't see what look he's giving her, but she chuckles.

"Fine. I'll drop it even though I don't understand what's so complicated. You either like the guy, or you don't."

"I don't want to label anything, because … You know what, I don't want to talk about it."

"Oh no, not with your mother. You do know what your father and I did to put you on this earth, right?"

I cringe at the same time as he groans, because parents should never, ever act anything other than virginal in their kid's presence.

"If I tell you, can you promise to drop this entire conversation? For the whole weekend? No talking about any of it?"

"Of course."

"Robbie's the only guy I've ever even thought about like that. I've never been attracted to a dude before him, and even now, I look at other guys and there's nothing. Once this thing ends, I'll be with chicks again, so is there even any point in having this conversation?"

My jaw doesn't hit the ground, but damn it comes close. He doesn't think guys are attractive? So what the fuck are we doing, then? Why me?

This sinking feeling hits my gut as he confirms everything I've known but have been ignoring.

We're a fun time. A college fling. And when we end, Brandon goes back to being the straight boy.

It was always going to happen, so it shouldn't hit so hard.

"I know I said I'd drop it, but I have one more question," his mom says. "Why are you so sure it's going to end?"

And Amber just became my favorite person.

There's the scrape of a chair, and I chance a quick peek to

see Brandon has dropped into it. "Robbie doesn't do relationships, and even if he did, he lives in Arizona. College is almost over. And no college relationships last anyway, so obviously this thing is going to end whether it's soon or not. And it will be fine when it does, because I don't want to lose him as a friend."

"Interesting."

He grunts. "What is?"

"Just that was a whole lot of excuses, and not one of them was because you want it to."

"It doesn't matter what I want. Robbie is not the dating kind."

Ouch. I duck away from where they are in the kitchen and make my way to the living room. His words are fair; I can't dispute them. I'm *not* the dating kind. I've never done a single thing to make people assume I'm capable of settling down. I've never wanted to.

I've been trying to convince people I'm not boyfriend material for years, even if most of them don't listen.

And now I've finally found someone to hook up with, someone who knows the score and isn't trying to push for more, and … I don't like it.

For the first time ever, I'm ready.

Too bad he's already written us off before we even had a chance to try.

26

BRANDON

ROBBIE IS ON HIS BEST BEHAVIOR. HE GETS ALONG WITH MY parents and keeps a friendly distance from me. Exactly the way I asked him to. Exactly like he does when we're at school.

And I hate it.

I'm beyond frustrated with myself and this growing need inside me for his attention. He ends up spending a lot of the afternoon outside with Dad and then on the couch across from me as we play Monopoly with my parents.

Which would be some wholesome fun if Mom and Robbie weren't taking this shit way too seriously. Dad rolls his eyes at me across the board, and I laugh, catching Robbie's attention.

"Don't start." He points at me. "This is clearly life or death."

"And clearly you're all terrible at business," Mom says as she adds another hotel to her arsenal, "because you're about to be whipped by a little old lady."

"Ohh, let's talk about whipping some more," Robbie says.

I throw the dice at his head. "Dude, don't hit on my parents."

"Why not? They're both hot."

I bury my face in my hands.

Dad tsks. "Where do you find these friends, Brandon?"

"I was scraping the bottom of the barrel with this one," I answer. Only, when I look up, a strange expression crosses Robbie's face before he covers it with his typical grin.

"You're all jealous because I'm about to land on Board-walk." He rolls a five and throws his hands up. "Holy shit I can't believe that worked."

Mom and Dad rib him as he showboats and fills the property with houses. This whole day has knocked me off-center. Even watching him with my family feels like I'm waiting to wake up from a strange dream where somehow my two lives are colliding.

I want to hate it.

But I don't.

This shivery sort of happiness is filling my limbs, and I can try and fool myself all I like that it's because I'm home and have missed my parents. I know it's total bullshit.

Robbie is the cause.

And that shit is not okay.

All the reasons I gave Mom are valid, but there was one very big one I left out. I'm scared.

I'm catching feelings for the big idiot, and I know that should be my warning sign to call things off, but I'm scared I'm already in too far.

I love being around him. Whether we're sleeping together or hanging out, he makes things better.

I'm a sucker for his company.

I haven't looked at anyone else in months.

I don't even give a shit that he's a guy and it's not something I ever pictured for myself.

When we say good night and Robbie ducks into the spare room with nothing more than a pat on the shoulder, I tell myself not to read into it. He's being respectful. He's *listening* to what I asked of him.

The next day at the Killer Brew, where we meet up with extended family for my birthday lunch, I try not to focus on Robbie hanging back and keeping his distance. Or the way he doesn't sit with me at lunch. Or how he never tries to join in the conversations I'm having even when I wave him over.

I'm supposed to be enjoying my birthday, and sure, I appreciate my parents getting everyone together for me, but fuck, I'm so distracted that it's frustrating even me.

This isn't like Robbie. Even when we're around our brothers, he's nonstop teasing, and we're in each other's space. We act exactly the way we always have, which isn't like this. Something's changed.

I'm trying not to freak out.

Was meeting the family too much for him?

Is this hitting too close to a real relationship and going to be the thing that ends us?

I throw back my drink and try to let go of the worries. Whatever happens will happen. We're not long-term, and I need to stop forgetting that.

But as much as I tell myself to keep away, when we're home that afternoon, I corner Robbie alone while the others disappear to who knows where.

I don't let him get a word out before I press him against the wall and kiss him.

"Shit, I needed that," I say.

He wraps his arms around me. "What's this about? I thought we were doing the friends-only thing while we're here."

"Around my parents, yeah. When we're alone, we're still brofriends, right?"

"In that case …" He leans down and kisses me long and slow, neither of us in a hurry to separate.

I don't sense any hesitation on his side, and it helps to settle that gnawing worry inside me.

"So kissing is still okay?"

"Dude, always." I nip his bottom lip. "While we're here, kissing in private is cool. Broning is not."

He jerks back. "Broning?"

"Bros who bone. Duh."

"You made up a word for me." Robbie cups my face. "I think I just fell in love."

He's teasing me, but damn if my heart doesn't do some acrobatics shit. And because I don't want him to know what those words do to me, I shove him and laugh.

Before I can walk off, he hooks an arm around my waist. "Sneak into my room tonight?"

"Dude, I *just* said—"

"No broning. I got you."

"Then …"

His blue eyes soften as he runs his hand through my hair. "Maybe it's only me, but things have been feeling awkward. Everything's okay with us, right?"

It's almost on my tongue to tell him that I don't think it is. That I think I'm going to ruin everything. I can't say it. "Yeah, of course. You good?"

"I'm good."

"Then we're good."

And when the house is finally quiet that night, I sneak down the hall to Robbie's room and let myself in. My parents wouldn't have cared if we shared a room the whole time here, but then they would have assumed we're more than we are, not that they haven't been doing that anyway. I swear if I told them we were dating, they'd throw a fucking party.

The second he sees me, Robbie pulls back the blanket, and I climb in beside him. Thankfully, he's clothed too, so the temptation isn't as bad as it would be if he was only in his underwear.

It's dark, so I can't see his face, but his hand finds my abs under the covers, and he lightly traces his fingers over them.

"I ... have a present for you," he says.

"You do?"

"Yeah, it's nothing. Just something dumb and small." He leans over the other side of the bed and grabs my gift. "It's not wrapped."

I can't see it properly, but the material under my fingers is smooth and soft.

"It's a scarf," he tells me.

I can make out the knit pattern. "Did you make this?"

"Ah, yeah. Didn't have the money to buy something, so ..."

"I love it."

"You haven't even seen it. Maybe it's in that shit-green color you love so much."

"Damn, I hope so." But I don't need to see it. He made it for me, and the thing could look like fucking vomit for all I care. I'll be wearing it anyway. I fold it and place it on the floor beside the bed before curling into his side again.

"It would have been cool growing up here," he says.

"It was. Mostly. I mean, when you're a teenager, small towns aren't the most exciting place, but I know I was lucky."

"You think this is a small town?" he asks. "There were ten kids in my grade at school, and you could walk from one end of the town to the other in a few hours."

"Ouch."

"Yeah, it was fun though. We used to get up to some shit. Especially me and Marshall."

"You guys are close?" I ask.

"Yep. I love him like no one else. He's the quiet one in the family, but he's not quiet-quiet. He's more subtle snark, and the others don't get him, so he always feels a bit left out."

"That sucks."

"Yeah, but at least when I was there, we'd take off all day and go swimming in the creek or sit in the parking lot of the gas station drinking Icees and heckling the people grabbing gas."

"You? Being a pain in the ass?" I snort back a laugh. "That doesn't sound right."

"Fuck you."

"You do. Frequently."

His fingers flex as he groans. "Don't start. No broning, remember?"

"But it's fun to tease you."

His hand flattens to my stomach, then runs slowly up to my chest and back down again. "I like when you have fun."

"Me too. Not enough of it these days though."

"But you liked Guard Duty, right?"

There's something about the way he asks, like he needs my approval, that warms me. I wriggle closer and grab his arm, pulling it around me so I can rest my head on his shoulder. "I did. You know, when you're not being a walking hazard, it's kind of impossible not to have fun around you."

He presses his lips to my forehead. My eyes fall closed, and I lean into his touch, glad it's dark and he can't see what he's doing to me. The way he's twisting me up isn't right. It's not what we planned.

I clear my throat and pull back. "You miss your brother?"

"Yep."

"At least there's only a few months left until you'll be back with him."

"Maybe …"

I latch onto that one word. "I thought you planned to go back?"

"I did, but now that I have this internship, if they offer me a proper job with them, I'm going to stay."

"Stay? In West Haven?"

"If I get lucky."

The image of him in his button-up and tie makes me smile. "You're gonna be a corporate guy."

"It still needs to happen yet."

"It will." Because it has to. If Robbie stays, even if we're not hooking up anymore, we'll have more chances to keep in touch. Chad and Bailey are heading to New York City, which is only a few hours away, and if Robbie and I end up in the same city, we might get to keep a bit of what we have.

"What about you?" he asks.

"Staying close to a bigger city and finding a design job with a company will be my first step, but when I'm older, I've always wanted to move back here. Or close by. I thought it was a pain in the ass when I was a kid, but I can see myself raising my family here."

He's quiet for a moment. "That's some suburban dream right there."

"Don't make fun."

"I'm not. It sounds awesome. How many kids will you have?"

"Two," I say.

"Yes, me too." Somehow, even in the dark, when I go to high-five him, his hand is already there waiting. "A big farm like this or someplace small?"

"Maybe in the middle. Lots of land for ATVs and shit, but a small house."

"You could do your own vegetable garden," he says.

"And run a design business from home."

"Maybe get some chickens running around."

I press my face into his shoulder. That whole thing sounds fucking perfect and idealistic to me. A relaxed life. No nine-to-five. A family I can spend time with.

"Don't forget the guest room," he says.

Guest room? "What do you mean?"

"Well, if I'm close by, I can come visit, right? And I don't think your wife would want me sharing a bed with the two of you."

My wife … Just when I'm getting swept up in the perfect future, Robbie had to go and mention that. A wife has been what I've always imagined, but now, it makes my heart sink.

I press tighter against him because for one wild fucking moment, I saw myself doing all that with *him*. "Not something we have to worry about for a long time."

"True." He yawns and presses another kiss to my head. "I'm beat."

"Then go to sleep, idiot."

"You gonna stay here?"

"Do you want me to?" I fire back.

There's only a slight hesitation, and then he softly says, "Yeah … I do."

I wrap my arm around him and cuddle into his side. He's big and warm and so fucking comfortable. "Good night, then."

27

ROBBIE

WHEN I TOLD BRANDON I LOVE HIM, I THINK ... I THINK I might have meant it.

Not over *broning*, though that was beautifully fucking epic, but because of everything about him. He's sexy and confident, keeps me on my toes, and has amazing visions for the future. Even that deep-seated responsibility he pretends doesn't exist, I kind of love anyway. He's the perfect balance of fun and cautious, and damn I didn't know what a sexy thing that could be.

But then I'd given him a hint, mentioned I might not be moving back to Arizona after all, and ... nothing.

Not even an opening for us to talk about more, and even when I brought up the wife and the guest room, he'd agreed.

I'd thought the kissing and him sneaking in to share a bed with me might have meant something, and yet ... I'd ended up with blue balls from being near him, and a blue heart from our conversation.

These last two weeks have been harder to act like everything is fine, but I think I'm managing.

I'm trying to remind myself to keep this in perspective, that getting regular amazing sex is nothing to whine about, but that gets harder to convince myself of every time we're together. He's with me most nights, even if we don't have sex, and I'm getting used to having him around and knowing that we're more than frat brothers. Knowing that behind closed doors I get to make him mine.

For tonight's party, we're doing look-alike, and I have the perfect costume. I've borrowed jeans off Rooster, who's almost as big as me, which means these fuckers cling to every inch of me. I snuck a scarf from Brandon's room and even found a blond wig that will do. Then, just in case it wasn't totally obvious, I printed out a hazard log form and hung it around my neck.

It's been a solid two months since Sigma house threw an absolute rager, which is unheard of in frat years, so tonight I plan to remind everyone why we're the shit around here.

Only, when I get downstairs to start pre-drinks with my brothers, I walk into the front room, where people are playing flip cups, and as soon as I catch sight of Brandon, I double over with laughter.

"You little smart-ass," I choke out, eyeing his cargo pants and fanny pack.

"Like you can talk. What do you always say to me? Can you even fit a credit card in those pants?"

"Considering I struggled to fit my balls, I'm going to go with no."

He leans in and drops his voice. "If it helps, those pants are so goddamn hot, they make me want to strip you out of them." He gives the scarf a tug.

"And that fanny pack makes me want to see your fanny."

"*Dude*." He shoves me. "What is wrong with you?"

"Why are you asking me? Aren't you the one with a list?"

He mutters something under his breath, and I grab him in a headlock. "You love me."

"No way, man."

I tighten my arm. "You love me. Say it."

"Like a hole in the head."

"Hey, if you're talking about my mouth hole, that's a whole lot of love."

Brandon tries to tackle me, but I hold firm. "Let me go, asswipe."

"I will when you say it."

"Fuck off."

"*I love you, Robbie.*"

"You're a dick."

"*I love you so, so much. You're superious to everyone.*"

"Superious isn't even a word."

"It is now. It's like the ultimate supreme."

He tries to shove me off him again. "Just like adding 'bro' to words doesn't make it a word, using made-up shit in a sentence doesn't make it a sentence."

"Coming from the creator of *broning*."

"That's the last time I humor you."

"Aw, come on." I squeeze his arm tighter before I let him go. "Admit it. Just once. It'll feel so good to get off your chest."

His face is bright red when he straightens. "You know what's good to get off my chest?" He flips me off.

I probably deserve that.

Doesn't make me any less salty about it.

I'd only wanted some kind of affection as a friend, hadn't

expected the ultimate L word, but damn, he couldn't even give me that.

I leave him and head for where Chad is pouring out a round of shots and quickly swipe two before he can stop me.

"Anyone ever mentioned you're an impatient mofo?" he asks.

"All the time. Now top me up."

He fills the shot glasses again. I'm twice the size of these twigs, so statistically, I need way more alcohol to get drunk than they will. Because blaming it on my size is way easier to do than confronting the fact my college years have been one giant house party and now I practically sweat vodka.

All my brothers have gotten into the theme tonight. Chad's wearing a white button-up and red bow tie, and I have no clue who Pee-wee Herman is, but he and Bailey find it hilarious. Bailey is dressed as Prince Charming, and Zeke is wearing a Speedo and swim cap, a fake gold medal hanging around his neck. He's also shirtless, showing off all his tattoos.

I walk over to him, and before he can even say hey, I flick his nipple. "You're gonna freeze your tits off, man."

"The benefit to being so cold you're numb?" He grabs my nipple through the shirt and twists. "No feeling."

When he releases me, pain burns the site. "Ouch," I complain, but I kinda like it.

Well, not just *kinda* based on the way my dick twitches.

And fucking perfect. Brandon's got me conditioned.

The later it gets, the more the party fills up. Brandon had nothing to worry about with Jenny and her sisters, because look at that, first party we throw and they're all in the door.

And no matter where in the house I am, she's always around.

She's pretty, I can give her that. *Really* pretty. And I know

Brandon isn't interested in her because I take him at his word, but she's a reminder of everything I'm not.

Maybe Jenny wasn't it for him, but another chick will be.

Another chick who's petite and sweet-looking and basically everything I'm not.

Well, hello, insecurities, we finally meet.

This uncertainty bullshit isn't me. If someone's not interested, I move on to the next person who is. Easy as that. The guys like to joke that I don't have standards, but I view it as being open to all women—and men now too. I don't give a shit if someone is tall or short or fat or thin. They only need to be cool as tits and a fun time in bed. Those standards are good enough for me.

So why can't I move on from Brandon? If I do feel the things for him that I suspect I do, ripping off the Band-Aid is one hundred percent the way to go with this. And yet, I know I won't.

Because goddamn do I want to keep him.

The beer goes down too easily, and the insecure thoughts bombard me at a level I've never had happen before.

I try to shake them off. Try to drink them away.

And every time my thoughts circle back to just riding this thing out until it ends, I spot Jenny and the cycle begins again.

She's the gold standard. Well, not her specifically, but that type of person.

Social, good-looking, the type you take home to meet the parents.

I throw back a shot.

He took you home to meet his parents.

Yeah, but not as his boyfriend.

His mom knows you're something to each other.

But he told her it wasn't serious.

Just talk to him.

No way in frat hell will I ever talk to him about this shit.

Aaand now I'm arguing with myself.

I know how awkward it is when your hookup wants more. I'm not being that person to him.

But he took you home to meet his parents …

I throw back another shot. And another.

The night disappears around me, and next thing I know, I'm standing on the upstairs banister, ready to jump onto the chandelier.

28

BRANDON

MY BRAIN IS SUPPOSED TO BE MY WINGMAN. MY NUMBER ONE bro. So at what point did it think focusing on Robbie would be a good idea? I swear one morning I woke up and suddenly my brain was all *him, he's the one*.

Because of course he is.

I look down at where he's sleeping soundly, knowing last night could have been a million times worse. If Zeke hadn't grabbed him before he jumped …

My annoyance at him spikes again, just as he lets out a pathetic whimper. His whole face screws up, and I hurry to grab the bucket I brought up in case he needs to puke.

"Brando …"

"I'm here, big guy."

"What happened?"

Sure that he's not going to bring everything back up, I set the bucket down again. "You got drunk."

"I normally get drunk though. This isn't drunk. This is … torture."

"Well, I'm not surprised considering you tried to swing from the chandelier. While *singing* 'Chandelier' by Sia."

Robbie cringes. "Why am I so dumb?"

His pathetic tone helps my annoyance disappear. "It's part of your charm."

"I'm sorry. Like, *damn*. My liver has already given up on me, so I must have been bad for me to be feeling it."

I frown. "I know you get a bit loose sometimes, but last night was wild, even for you."

And I've never seen such a big guy pout, but that's exactly what he does. "Do you hate me?"

"Dude, if the last three years haven't done it, one night isn't going to change things."

"But you're always going on about what a pain in the ass I am and how you don't get to have fun because of it, and then I go and do that."

He's right. It's irritating, and he was thoughtless. But one thing I know about Robbie is he cares big about his friends, and since we've started hooking up, he's proved again and again that he cares about me, so last night was … well, drinking and having fun is him, but getting so written off he's almost blackout drunk is not.

"Why did you do it?" I ask.

Instead of answering, he folds his arms over his face.

"Robbie?"

Nothing.

"If you don't start talking, I'm going to have to assume it's because you hate me and wanted to make my life difficult."

When he peeks out at me, he's glaring. "You know that isn't it."

"Then …"

"I don't wanna say," he mumbles, hiding again.

"Well, I dunno, I need something. Because I want to think you had a reason, but you're making it very hard for me not to be shitty at you right now."

He huffs and rolls onto his front, looking almost green from the movement. I wrap my arm around him and move closer, because even if the big idiot annoyed me last night, I think his hangover is punishment enough.

"I got scared," he eventually says.

"Of?"

"Jenny."

I almost laugh. "I didn't even see her at the party."

"I did. All damn night."

"Well, was it something she said, or …" I try to think of something she *could* have said that would have any effect on Robbie. Things usually just roll off his back.

"No."

"You need to stop being cryptic, because I have no idea what you're saying." I pinch his chin. "Since when are you all … shy? Embarrassed? What's going on here?" My mood plummets as I'm hit with a horrible thought. "Did you hook up with her?"

"Fuck no."

I breathe a sigh of relief. "Okay, then can you spit it out?"

"She made me insecure."

"Insecure?"

"About … us." He buries his face in my side. "When we were in Kilborough, I heard you talking to your mom."

"O … kay …" Something in his tone makes me hold him tighter. I'm refusing to get excited, because when he says *us*, he could mean he's having second thoughts, but … somehow, I'm sure that's not it. I don't interrupt because I get the feeling he's thinking hard.

"You mentioned all the reasons why we'd never work, and one of those reasons was that I'm not the relationship type."

I try to read his face, wondering where he's going with this and struggling to remember what else I said. "Because you're not."

"But I am. I can do relationships, and I can be committed. I'd be the best fucking boyfriend in history, because if I was into someone enough that I wanted that with them, they'd be my whole world."

My breath catches because is he … is he … "Why are you telling me this?"

He doesn't answer at first, and then, finally, he lifts his head and looks me in the eyes. "The reason I'm not into relationships is because no one has even made me want one before … until you."

"Robbie …"

"Shut up a minute—"

"You're really selling that greatest boyfriend in history line."

"Brando … I've just gotta get this out." He covers my mouth with one of his big hands. "I was insecure because Jenny is your type, and I'm *so* not a Jenny. You're going to get married to some chick one day, and if I'm honest, I don't want you to. When we were talking about that future of buying a property and having babies, it sounded perfect to me. So maybe it's too early to say, or I'm wearing cum-goggles or something, but … *I* want to be the one who gets that future with you."

I swear my heart swells. "Fuck."

"Exactly. *Fuck*. This is all super new and strange to me, and it's caught me off guard, but when I think about losing you, it makes me panic. Like this gross feeling clawing up into my throat and making it hard to breathe."

"Fuck …"

"Can you say something else?"

"I really don't know." Robbie saying all these things is beyond anything I could have expected from him, and yet … it's everything I need. Everything I want.

"Great. And now I'm panicking again."

The sheer level of insecurity that takes over his face actually makes me laugh. I tackle him back onto the bed, and he groans at the movement, but I don't back off. "Promise you won't puke on me."

"Ah …"

I capture his mouth with mine. And goddamn he feels so good. Too good. It still catches me off guard every time how desperately my body reacts to his. He moans, and my cock perks up in interest when his moan morphs into a half sob.

"I can't believe I'm gonna say this, but I think I'm too sick for sex stuff."

I mock gasp. "Who are you, and what have you done with my boyfriend?"

"B-*boy*friend? Not brofriend?"

"No. We can stop kidding ourselves that this is nothing, because I think it might be everything."

"I like the way you think." He attacks me with a kiss, and even morning breath isn't enough to tear me away from him. He makes my heart full and my cock ache.

The next kiss I give him is softer. "I have one condition."

"Anything."

"Can you … do you think for the last few months you could calm things down a little? Small pranks and whatever is fine, but we've got finals coming up, and I need to be able to focus on those and not what you and Chad are getting up to, or if you're going to try and fly again at the next party we have. You said you were scared, but … I care about you, dude, and that scared me."

"Fuck, I'm sorry." His arms tighten around my waist. "I promise. No more pulling shit."

"That kind of sounds gross and like I'm trying to change you, but I swear it isn't that."

"I get it."

"Do you?" I brush his nose with mine. "Because I've gotta say, Rob-dog, I really like the you that you are."

"Cargo pants and all?"

"Right down to your fanny pack."

His troublemaker look appears. "I'm a big fan of your fanny too."

"Dude, call it an ass."

"My *boyfriend's* ass."

I like how that sounds. "You're going to get way too much enjoyment out of that, aren't you?"

"You don't even know the half of it."

"Wow," I say, suddenly realizing something. "You're in a relationship."

"Crazy, huh?"

"With me."

"Yep."

"So … that means I am basically the greatest person alive."

His brow bunches up. "How's that?"

"I've done what no one in the last three and a half years has managed. I've tamed the beast."

His laugh cuts off with a groan. "Ouch. Stop making me laugh, I'm tender."

"Poor baby."

There's a knock at the door, and we exchange a look.

"Brandon, you in there?"

It's Chad.

I only have a split second to make up my mind, but fuck it. I climb off Robbie, don't bother putting on clothes, and walk over to answer the door in my boxer briefs.

"Hey," Chad says. "Have you ..." His attention shifts from me to where Robbie is lying shirtless in bed.

"What's up?" I ask.

"Well, I was going to ask if you'd seen Robbie because I went to check on him, but it looks like you've seen a *whole* lot more of him than I meant."

"Was that all?"

"Nope." He leans around me. "Finally got some D, brother?"

"Yep. I got me some D and some A and some H, B, and J."

"Gross," I say.

They both ignore me.

"So, was this like a one-time thing?" Chad asks.

"Nope," I answer. "We're, umm, dating." And fuck if that isn't weird to say.

Chad stares from me to Robbie like we've grown balls on our heads. It's a mixture of shock and amusement, and I've gotta say, I'm not a fan.

"That all?"

"Nope. One last thing. When you tell the rest of the house, please make sure I'm there. The reactions will be priceless."

I close the door on him. "Goddamn Chad."

"Love you too," he calls through the door.

Silence falls, and when I glance back at Robbie, he's grinning wide, even though he still looks one foot in the grave. "We just told someone."

"We did."

"And you're not freaking out."

"I figure if we're dating, people are going to know."

"This is true."

I make my way back over to sit beside him on the bed. "You know what their reactions will be though, right?"

"Laughter?"

"We'll literally be the butt of all jokes—"

"Butt, heh."

"Shut up. You know what I mean. They're going to think this is ridiculous. Ten bucks says they take bets on how long we'll last."

He frowns. "I don't like that."

"Neither do I. But we're going to have to deal with it again, and again. All the dumbass questions and …" I take his hand. "I'm sorta protective of this. Being with you is the happiest I've maybe ever been."

"Me too."

"Wow. That's a big claim coming from Mr. Funsies over here."

He squeezes my hand as he thinks. "Give me a few days, and I'll handle it."

"You'll handle it?"

"Yep."

"Should I be worried?"

He cracks a smile. "Always. It's me you're talking to."

"That doesn't fill me with confidence."

"Will you trust me?"

"Fine, but don't forget your promise."

"I won't." He mimes drawing a halo around his head. "It'll be completely and totally safe."

29

ROBBIE

IT TAKES ME EXACTLY A DAY TO FIGURE OUT WHAT I WANNA do. I promised Brandon I'd play it safe, but I meant in the literal sense of the word, not the actual execution. All my man wants is fun, so he's going to get it in a big way.

Bro big or bro home has always been my motto, and I'm about to put that fucker to the test. When people find out about Brandon and me, they're *all* going to find out. Every one of them.

At once.

I tap softly on Chad's door, and I've barely finished my knock when it swings open and Bailey is standing there.

"He's still asleep."

"All good." I step around Bailey on his way out. "I'll wake him."

"If you touch his dick, you'll want to run," he sings back at me.

I laugh and close the door, then grab one of Chad's pillows and whack him with it.

"Fucking fuckstains," he grunts.

"Morning, sweetheart."

"Should have known it was you."

I drop lengthways across his bed. "I need your help."

"No, I won't hide a body with you, but I'm good for an alibi."

"Again with the body. Should I be worried you're the one who's going to need help there?"

"Hey, your bet was on Brandon, but with the two of you together, I'm waiting for the day one of you snaps."

"Fuck you, man. I'll protect that tight ass with my life."

"Don't need to know about his ass," Chad mutters.

"And you never will. That booty is mine." Because goddamn does he have a fine ass. "But Brandon is part of the favor I have."

"No I will not have a threesome with you guys, or a four-some, or a whatever-some."

"Shit, well, I guess that's that, then."

He jerks upright. "*That's* what you wanted?"

Naive little fucker. "No. As if I'd let you touch him. Are you insane?"

"And now you get why Bailey and I were a hard no on the rub and tug."

I'm also super grateful because if they'd whipped out their dicks and let me cop a feel, I never would have started this whole thing with Brandon in the first place. I never would have known how damn good being with someone could be. "Guess I owe you guys a thanks."

"I'm happy to take cash."

I shove him, and he shoves me right back. "I can't believe we only have a few months of this."

"Yeah, it's scary."

"Then you'll be in New York, right?"

"Looks like it."

I try to get a read on his face, but Chad looks as unbothered as ever. "You looking forward to it?"

"I felt weird at first. Like I was taking advantage, but I want to be with Bailey, you know? He's going to be in New York, and I can't afford an apartment myself, so staying with him makes sense."

"It does. And don't worry, brother, you're going places. You're too good of a guy not to be."

"Thanks, boo. Appreciate it."

"And I'm going places too, right?"

Chad grimaces. "Dude, after the other night, the only place you're going is to the hospital or AA."

"Urg. Yeah, it was a bit far. It's why I've decided I'm going dry for the rest of the year."

"Bullshit."

And I get why he doesn't believe me—we've all said at one point or another that we're giving up alcohol, and then there we are eating—or drinking—our words the very next weekend.

His amusement dies. "You're serious."

"Sure am."

"That's … going to be unsettling."

"Good thing I don't need alcohol to have fun. Speaking of …"

I fill Chad in on my plans, watching his eyes grow wider with every word. "You want to—"

"Yep."

"To—"

"Uh-huh."

He shakes his head. "If it was anyone else, I'd think they were nuts. But … well, this might actually be the most you thing you've ever done."

"We need to get the mayhem team together. I'll show them it isn't only about pranks."

"And score you some much-needed points."

That hadn't even occurred to me when I planned this; it's just an added bonus. "I like where your head's at."

Chad glances around. From his desk to the wall and back to his desk again.

"Where's my chair?"

I look as well. "Ah …"

"Fuck." He jumps out of bed and even checks under his desk as though it could be hiding there. His eyes widen. "*Bailey.*"

"I saw him leave. He didn't have it."

"He's King of Thieves-ed me!" Chad flies to his window, pushes it open, and sticks his head out. "You little shit," he calls.

I join him, hanging out of the side of the house to see where Bailey is out on the street. He salutes us both, sits in the chair, and wheels it backward, whistling as he goes.

Chad sighs. "I'm so in love."

I snort and pull him back inside, closing the window against the cold. "I have to say, I wasn't sold on him to begin with, but your boy is pretty cool."

"Pretty cool? *Pretty* cool? You wish your boyfriend was as cool as mine."

"Fuck off. Brandon has more cool points in one nut than the three of us put together."

"Bailey could kick Brando's ass with his eyes closed."

"His eyes *would* be closed, because Brandon would knock him the fuck out."

"Oooh, you underestimating my princess?"

I scoff. "You call the guy *princess.*"

"Yeah, because he's so damn gorgeous. Unlike that ugly butt-face you're fucking."

"What the hell are you talking about? He should be a damn movie star, unlike the skinny twig bitch you're sticking it in."

Chad shrugs. "Hey, sometimes he sticks it in me."

"He does? Damn …" My head drops back. "How good does it feel, am I right?"

Chad laughs, and we high-five. "Frat as fuck, my man." He turns pensive. "So you figured yourself out? How do you feel about it all?"

"Good. My head is still spinning, but that's less about the dick and more that I'm willingly entering into a relationship for the first time ever."

He reaches out to squeeze my shoulder. "Wanna know a secret?"

"Always."

"This brotherhood you love so much? The idea that we've all got each other's backs through thick and thin, no matter what. *That's* what a relationship is. If you do this thing right, you and Brando will be each other's number ones. Your main bro. Even though it's only new, the minute I met Bailey, I knew he was special, and I can count on him always to be there for me. Physically, mentally, emotionally. He's it. Hopefully forever. If I have my way, I'm never gonna have to worry about doing life solo."

"Wow. To think I've always been so scared of relationships."

"Maybe you weren't scared. Maybe you just knew none of the others were right. Because from where I'm standing, you and Brandon knew each other was special right from the start too. Maybe it wasn't attraction or something you recognized right away, but when I saw you guys together the other day, I wasn't even surprised."

"You'd be the only one."

He shakes his head. "Nah, anyone paying attention will get it. And those who aren't … well, once this plan of yours is done, everyone's gonna know about you guys anyway."

"Now to plan it without him knowing."

Chad holds out his arms. "Look at who you're talking to. We've got this."

I'M STILL NOT COMPLETELY SURE WE'VE "GOT THIS," BUT HEY, we're giving it our all. We get Raymond, Shifley, Dean, and Lance to catch up with us at an on-campus cafe. None of us ever come here when we could go to Deja Brew where Chad works, but because none of us come here, it's the perfect spot for this meeting.

Chad pretends to smack a gavel. "Shut up, you animals." He waits for the others to fall quiet. "Mastering mayhem is an age-old tradition passed from one Sigma Beta Psi brother to the next. I'm known as the lord of the pranks, but mayhem isn't only about pranking. It's a mindset. A lifestyle. It's not something that can be taught to anyone, which is why it's only the four of you here with us. Some people get it and some don't, and as you're about to see, Robbie gets it. This guy knows how to throw a party like no one else, his prank meter is a ten, and he's fun personified."

I grin, because while I'm always low-key worried that my brothers think I'm a pain in the ass, it's nice to know Chad at least sees me that way.

"He gets people talking, and that's power that you either have, or you don't."

"And I'm about to do it again," I say. "One last hit at the big time. Something to go down in Sigma history, and I need all of your guys' help."

Chad agrees. "It's going to be frat as fuck."

And hopefully romantic as fuck. Over-the-top and uncontrolled—exactly my style—and with any luck, Brandon will get a laugh out of it too. Because after what Chad said about not doing life solo, it made me realize I want that. My bro with me for life. With Brandon around, I'll never have to say goodbye to what we have right now.

Sure, we'll grow up, and priorities will change, but at heart, I'm determined to love my life, and how can I do that if the one guy I've always turned to since we met isn't there with me?

So while proposing and shit is Future Rob-dog's problem, I know my one focus, from now until eternity, is to make Brandon happy.

Because he's mine now.

And I'm making it my responsibility.

I email the pledges an individual list each.

"These are the things I need you to come up with."

Raymond reads through the list. "The school marching band? I dunno, Robbie …"

"*Part* of the marching band." I roll my eyes at Chad. I mean, come on. I'm not unreasonable. "You want my forgiveness for trying to cover up what happened with that Kappa prank? You'll do every point on that list, and you won't ask dumb questions about it. That goes for all of you."

They hurry to nod, and the obedience of pledges always amuses me because I was exactly the same back in the day. It's something that could definitely be taken advantage of, and that's why it's important that we don't. They do what we say, no questions asked, and we've gotta make sure we earn the trust for them to respond that way. It's what forms the strong brotherhood we have.

As a pledge, you bitch and whine about being bottom rung, about having to share rickety bunk beds all stuffed into one room, barely enough privacy to take a dump, and big brothers who could need you at a minute's notice, but looking back at it all, I wouldn't change it for the world.

Chad, Zeke, Brandon, and I are all as close as we are because of those years.

Hopefully it's enough for our friendships to last beyond graduation.

"What song are you thinking?" Chad asks.

"Crazy Little Thing Called Love."

"By Queen?" Raymond asks.

"It was Elvis first, you fool," Shifley says.

"No it wasn't." Dean sighs like he's too smart for the rest of us. "It was a tribute to Elvis by Freddie Mercury."

"Either way, isn't it about not being able to commit?" Chad asks.

"Basically my whole MO, brother."

"Yeah, but this is supposed to be some big romantic gesture …"

"Which is why I'm changing the words at the end. Where it says about not being ready, I'm changing it to 'I'm fucking ready' because there's nothing like throwing an f-bomb into a

Queen song. Besides, Mercury was bi as fuck, so I'm basically singing the song of my people."

Chad and I high-five.

Raymond glances up at me, then away again. "So, umm, you and Brandon—"

"What part of 'don't ask questions' did you miss?"

"Sorry, Robbie."

"Better. Now, obviously this a top-secret assignment, and if any of you squeal, you'll be super soaked for a month. Sleeping, pissing, in class? I don't care. I'll be there to drench you from head to toe."

They all hurry to swear silence, and as I think about what I'm trying to pull off, excitement hits me square in the gut.

Brandon jokes about taming me, and while I might not be tamed, I am focused. On him. Only him. For as long as that idiot will have me.

30

BRANDON

"HE'S UP TO SOMETHING."

Zeke's gaze moves from his laptop to me. "Who?"

"Robbie."

"Why do you sound surprised?" Zeke eyes me, clearly amused. "He's *always* up to something."

I almost tell him because my goddamn boyfriend promised to cut the shit, but Robbie said he'd take care of letting people know about us. Telling people is not something I want to do, especially not solo, because I don't want to deal with the smack talk. Robbie is mine, and hearing people talk shit about him makes me ragey.

Only I'm allowed to do that.

Raymond goes racing past, that same slightly unhinged look on his face that I've noticed some of the other pledges wearing. "Did you see that?" I ask Zeke.

"You're being paranoid."

"I'm not."

"When has Robbie ever kept you in the dark? If anything, he's the first one to tell you his plans just to see how you'll react."

Zeke is right, but what he doesn't know is it's different now. Robbie promised to calm down. No more pranks. No more giving me shit to worry about. Maybe I should be worried about how naive it makes me that I believe him, but I'm determined to take him at his word. Until he actually breaks his promise, I've made the conscious decision to trust him.

Consciously.

Trust.

Something I'm doing.

Then Shifley races into the room, looks around in a daze, and runs out again.

I exchange a look with Zeke. "Still think I'm being paranoid?"

"Okay, I'll give you that one. That was odd."

"I should probably check on him." My words come out on a groan because I'm *trying* to study. Being risk manager is a twenty-four seven job, but occasionally I'd like to be able to focus on something else.

"Leave it," Zeke says.

And while I might be risk manager, Zeke is president. Everything that happens in this house is on his head, so a fuckup might affect the whole fraternity, but he's the one to take full impact. "You want me to leave it?"

"Yes."

"A stressed pledge who looks like he doesn't know where he is?"

He's clearly unsure. "You have studying to do."

"Okay, dude, but remember I asked."

Zeke's phone vibrates, and he stares at it for a moment.

"Bad message?"

"Just Chuck."

"So yes, then?" I couldn't imagine anything worse. "I think that guy has a hard-on for you. He never leaves you alone."

Zeke lifts the eyebrow with the line shaved through the middle. "Maybe if my brothers weren't always causing him headaches he wouldn't need to blow up my phone all the time."

"It's totally an excuse. He's got the hots for you. A little presidential hanky-pank? A VIP spank and wank?"

"You've been hanging out with Robbie too much."

He's not wrong. The more time we spend together, the more like my old self I feel. The pressure of making sure the house runs safely is still there, but I'm remembering to let go now and then, and I fucking like it.

I have no idea if Charles is queer or not—he's about as private with his sex life as Zeke is—but in an objective way, Zeke is good-looking. He's got a hint of baby face that he tries to combat with his tattoos and hairstyle—always shaved around the sides and longer on top. He's got a laid-back, confident vibe about him, and even I can spot blow job lips when I see them. But … I'm not attracted to him at all. Not him, or Chad, or Bailey. Charles is a button-up preacher-boy-looking guy, and that doesn't do it for me either.

I've looked up a few different definitions for what I could be, and even though Robbie seems to be the only guy who does it for me, apparently that still falls under the bi umbrella. There are other terms like pansexual and demisexual, and if I'm honest, I fit into a few different definitions while also fitting into none. Other than Robbie, I'm straight, but being with him shows I'm capable of falling for another guy. I could be pan because it was his personality I was drawn to first. Or demi, because while Jenny was cool at first, the more annoyed she made me, the less I *wanted* to be physical with her, but it's not like I couldn't get it up when the time came.

For right now, labeling myself is the last thing I'm interested in. I only want to be with Robbie, and the rest I'm not going to lose sleep over.

Whereas he's embraced the bi label like he's making up for lost time.

"Hmm … Chuck said to go outside," Zeke mutters.

"Nope. Total trap." My phone lights up, and a message from Robbie fills the screen. "Actually, Robbie just said the same."

Zeke rubs his smooth jaw. "Think the Kappas stole his phone?"

"No idea."

We watch each other, thinking.

"Maybe we can look out the front window first?" Zeke suggests.

"Good plan."

Only, when we reach the front window and look outside, all we can see is Robbie standing in the middle of the street.

"What the …"

Zeke shrugs. "No idea. Let's see what the fuck is going on."

31

ROBBIE

MY GUT'S IN KNOTS AS I WAIT FOR BRANDON TO COME outside. This is either gonna be the moment I cement our relationship as the most epic romance in history … or he realizes exactly what he signed up for and suddenly remembers he's straight again.

If that's the case, it's probably better I find out now.

Then I have months to put my heart back together.

The thing is, if we're doing this, what he's signed on for is me. And what I am is a gigantic idiot who's always causing a scene.

My life partner can't scare easily, and if this scares him off, it wasn't meant to be.

As much as that makes me want to put a stop to this whole thing, I also know Brandon better than that.

I think.

I guess I'm about to find out.

My breath is caught in my chest, and I don't move as I

watch the door open and Brandon and Zeke walk outside. Brandon stands there for a moment, hands in his pockets, before he slowly makes his way toward me. He's wearing the scarf I made him, the green bringing out his eyes, and seeing him helps me breathe properly again.

"What are you doing?"

I crook my finger for him to keep coming closer.

He's clearly confused, and the look on his face is making me second-guess every decision that brought me to this moment.

He glances back at Zeke, then at me, then at where the entrance to the street is blocked off.

I have no idea what's going through his head.

But then a smile spreads over his face.

Thank fuck.

That one look tells me that whatever I have planned, Brandon is on board with it all.

He trusts me.

Completely.

He's perfect.

"What are you planning?" he asks.

I step forward and drop a quick kiss onto his nose. "Something for us to always remember." My voice is picked up by my mic and projected through the street.

Then the drums start.

Brandon

I can always tell when Robbie is up to something. There's this spark he gets in his eyes, this aura of over-whelming confidence—like he's trying not to be impressed with himself but can't help it.

In the past, it's a look that's always worried me. A look that has promised trouble is coming and I'm the one who will be left to clean it up.

But while Robbie has always put fun first, even without having to say the words, I know that things have changed.

I'm first.

And he knows all the things I worry about when it comes to big pranks and dangerous antics, so when he steps back and throws his arms out to the side, I don't even flinch.

I just trust.

That what I'm about to witness will be epic.

At the first roll of the drums, my heart surges into my throat and won't go back down again. I think there's a horn and then some other instruments I can't make out because my gaze is locked on Robbie as he opens his mouth and sings the first few lines to Queen's "Crazy Little Thing Called Love."

My man is good at a lot of things, but singing is not one of them, and yet …

And yet, there's something about the way he owns it. About how he pushes his voice and throws in his own words and doesn't shy away from the big notes that makes … that makes it work.

Dear frat fathers.

Robbie is making a complete fool of himself in the middle of Greek Row.

And I've never been more attracted to him in my life.

And as he sings about not being able to handle love, his voice is as off-key and gruff as it normally is, but his eyes are locked on mine, and that ever-present confidence is radiating from him.

Somehow, the way he's owning the song makes him *sound* better.

I can't look away.

I can't stop smiling.

He's dramatic and over-the-top, and when he throws in a kick and some ad-lib dance moves, a laugh slips out of me.

My reaction lights him the fuck up.

He winks, and I fall for him all over again.

Then the third verse starts, and all hell breaks loose.

As soon as Robbie sings, "*There goes my Brando ...*" a fucking marching band pours from the gaps between the houses.

They fill the street, marching in formation, a flood of WHU green and white behind Robbie in his goddamn cargo pants and shit-eating grin. He launches into the chorus, and my head spins at the uniformity as they turn and kick and move in the same direction.

Brothers from the other frat houses fill the street next, and it's a struggle to hold in my amusement. There're sparklers and air horns, signs with Robbie hearts Brandon. People every-fucking-where, and it hits me that this is the effect he has on people.

Robbie promises fun, and people show up.

He can barely be heard over the music, which is a good thing, but the energy all around us spurs him on.

His confidence amplifies.

And maybe this song was chosen on a whim, but Robbie *does* drive me crazy.

He throws in some extra *yeahs* and *oohs* and more hip thrusts than should be legal, and my head falls back on a laugh.

There's no being cool or relaxing when it comes to us.

I have no idea where to look. The band, the people filing out of the other houses to crowd around and dance on their lawns, or my boyfriend, who's pulling off none of the moves or the notes and yet killing his performance in every way.

The more I watch him, the more everyone else around us fades to nothing.

And maybe I should be feeling some kind of embarrassment or urge to hide, but all I can think is that this dude in front of me is all mine, and I'm never letting him get away.

Who else can say their boyfriend has done something like this for him?

The marching band? The dancers?

I jump at a loud bang and an explosion of color as confetti fills the air.

My frat brothers line the street, letting off more confetti cannons, while others fill the air with bubbles. I have one brief moment of worry about the cannons, and then ... I let go.

I'm low-key in shock at the sensory overload. Trying to hold in uncontrollable laughter.

Robbie grabs my hand. He steers me into a spin, then dips me back over his arm. I don't fight him, just fall into the moment, caught up in his orbit.

Until his eyes meet mine and he sings, *"I'm fucking ready, for this goddamn thing called love."*

Robbie

THE SONG COMES TO AN END, AND I DUNNO WHAT BRANDON'S thinking. Was it too much? Too soon?

Then the bastard laughs, grabs my face, and kisses me.

The band moves on to another song, and our brothers hoot and holler like the animals they are, but screw them all. I kiss Brandon with everything I'm worth. Zero chill, no holding back, I claim my man in front of the hundreds of people here, and I have no shame whatsoever about doing it.

"Did you mean it?" he asks when he pulls away.

"What?"

"The song." His face suddenly drops. "I'm reading too much into it, aren't I? Shit, I mean. That was awesome. Cool. I—"

"I love you. I'm crazy in love with you, Brando. And when I say crazy"—I indicate the chaos around us—"I mean it. I would do literally anything to see you smile."

"I'm gonna hold you to that."

"Yikes. That's what a guy wants to hear when he's spilling his heart."

Brandon looks so happy, his vamp teeth are on full display. "Of course I love you. I think I always have."

I scoop down and lift him, and he immediately wraps his legs around my waist. Then I kiss him again. His tongue spears into my mouth, strokes over mine, and I suck on it before he pulls back and bites down on my lip.

"Take me upstairs," he says. His tone is so fucking needy and perfect … and unfortunately caught by the mic and broadcast over the street.

Chad approaches and pats my back. "Sorry, Brando, you're going to have to wait."

He groans. "Why?"

"Because," Zeke says, joining us. "Your *boyfriend* has

started a street-wide party, and I won't be the one monitoring it."

"Beer's here," Bailey calls.

"Perfect." Chad grabs his boyfriend and kisses him.

Jesus fuck, is all this romance contagious?

Look at me setting a good example.

"Deal with it," Zeke says, leaving.

But as soon as his back is turned, I grab Brandon's hand and pull him toward the house. "If we're fast, I bet we can get off and get back here before he notices."

"You're on."

32

BRANDON

MY BOYFRIEND IS A GENIUS. WITH EVERYONE OUTSIDE AND the band still playing, we're once again alone in the house. I still can't wrap my head around what just went down, and as much as I might want to get out there and have fun with everyone, I also need this.

Him and me.

We stagger into my room, kissing hard and fast, unable to keep our hands off each other. I've never told someone I love them before, and I *know* Robbie's never said those words like he did to me. It's another first we get to have together, and with any luck, there will be so many more.

My hands run over his shoulders, down to grip his bulging arm muscles, and just the feel of them consumes me. I have this desperate need to be as close to him as possible, a need nothing can ever fill.

"Fuck, Brando," he says against my lips. "I need you inside me."

"No fair, that's my line."

"I'll flip you for it?"

"Or …" I push him back onto my bed. "We can *flip* for it, literally."

His eyes darken as his gaze sweeps over me. "You are one clever man."

I pull off my layers of shirts, and his stare locks onto my abs.

"And *so* pretty." Robbie grabs my waist and moves me so I'm between his thick thighs. He trails kisses along my muscles, running his tongue over my skin until he reaches my jeans. Somehow the cheeky idiot pops my button with his mouth and then slowly tugs down my fly with his teeth. He keeps eye contact with me the whole time, sending constant waves of lust rolling through me.

"Robbie …" I cup his scruffy jaw. "Fuck I love you."

He presses a kiss to my straining cock. "I love you too."

"Wait." I tilt my head. "Was that for me or my dick?"

"Why not both?"

I tackle him back onto the bed, kicking my jeans off, before starting on his clothes. The more of him I get naked, the hornier I get. He's fucking perfection. Masculine. Sexy. I still have no idea how he can drive me so far out of my mind, but I'm addicted to the feeling anyway.

I don't need reasons. I need him. Always.

"Can I tell you something?" I whisper once he's also down to his briefs.

"Always. Anything. Cum is thicker than water and all that."

"I think that's supposed to be blood."

"Yeah, but we're not just brothers anymore." He flashes me a cheeky grin.

"One day you're going to say that around the wrong person."

"Eh." He brushes his lips over mine. "I only do it because you look so cute exasperated. Now, what were you saying?"

"You've killed the mood."

He pouts, then runs his fingers lightly down my back before creeping them under my briefs, inching toward my hole.

I shiver.

"You sure about that?" he asks.

I swallow, fighting the effect his gravelly voice has on me. But then I meet his blue eyes, and everything around us ... stops. "I want to keep you."

He clears his throat, but his voice still comes out on a rasp. "I'm not going anywhere."

We meet in a searing kiss, and I pour all the emotion I have into it. My tongue tangles with his, and his legs wrap around mine as he takes my hands and pins them to the mattress. He gives a slow, hard thrust, rutting our cocks together through our briefs, and the only thing stopping me from begging for more is his tongue halfway down my throat.

We've come a long way from two inexperienced idiots trying to find out what they like. And what I like is everything. So long as it's with Robbie.

He finally pulls back, and I'm able to suck in a deep breath.

"You first," he says, grabbing my lube and making his way down my body. "Also, now that people know about us, we better pick up a lot more of this. No more holding back."

If he's been holding back up until this point, I'm in trouble.

I groan as he pushes his first thick finger inside me. There's nothing like that initial stretch. Like forcing my body to relax when it instinctively wants to tense up. Like

Robbie's murmured encouragement as he works me open, dropping sweet kisses on my thighs and ignoring my throbbing cock.

It's torture.

Sweet, sweet torture.

Thankfully, it doesn't take anywhere near as long as the first time to get me ready for him.

"I don't know which is better," he says. "Fucking you, or being fucked by you."

"Tough call." Gun to my head, I know which way I'd lean. "But there's nothing like the feeling of your cock tearing me apart."

He chuckles and slips his fingers free, then gives me a sweet, slow kiss as he rolls his condom on. "I want you on top. Stretch me while I fuck you."

I hurry to nod, and Robbie moves to sit back against the bedhead. He plants his legs wide, and I grip his knees as I turn and straddle his waist. He presses his cock against my hole, and I almost wish I was facing him to see the way his eyes go all unfocused when he's turned on.

This.

As I sink down onto him, that's the only word echoing around my brain. This is what I need, and he's the only one in the whole goddamn world who can give it to me.

I bottom out, feeling stuffed to the brim. His big hands roam from my hips around to my chest, and he pulls me back against him to kiss his way along my shoulder to my neck.

He might have told me he loves me, but right now, he's making me feel it. He's showing me with the soft touches, reverent kisses, and low moans of my name.

"You're so beautiful," he says on a breath. "But I'm going to need you to grab the lube and get to work."

I chuckle as I do exactly that. I lean forward between his legs, one hand planted on the bed as I open him with the other.

Robbie holds my hips tight, pounding up into me and bringing my body alive. On every thrust, his ass tightens around my fingers, and damn I wish we could fuck each other at the same time. To fill each other completely. I'm a mess of want for him, and it only gets worse as he works over that spot inside my ass that drives me out of my mind.

His grunting grows loud, more desperate, and his fingers are biting into my hips in a way that makes me think he's getting close. I remove my fingers and sit back against him, burying him so deep I almost go cross-eyed.

Robbie hugs me to him, lips connecting with every inch of skin they can reach. "You have no idea how sexy you look taking me," he says. "I'd spend the night inside you if I could."

"You don't have to stop, you know."

"Yeah, I do, because I'm ready to come, and I want you inside me when I go off."

A chuckle slips out, but it cuts off when Robbie tears open a condom and rolls it down my sensitive shaft. He strokes me with lube, rolling his hips softly, and it's almost enough to make me forget what I'm doing. To just be lost in the sensations.

"If you want me in your ass, you better stop."

He's never shoved me off his cock so quickly.

We swap positions, but when Robbie straddles my hips, he's facing me.

"I feel so empty," I complain. My ass is trying to clench around *something*, and it's frustrating me not to be full. I whine, and he strokes my face.

"We'll go shopping and get you some toys. As soon as we're done."

Thank fuck.

We kiss as he lowers himself down on my dick, and I breathe deeper as the tight heat surrounds me. He's right. The sight is fucking beautiful.

His body towers over mine from this angle, powerful thighs lifting him up and down. I watch the way his bicep strains from the grip he has on the bedhead, and all I want is to run my tongue over it. To bury my face in his chest and inhale his sweat.

So. Fucking. Hot.

His cock bobs between us, precum pooling in the condom, and I reach up to remove it. He shudders at my touch, and his responsiveness is something I want to explore every day we're together. I want to learn all the things that drive him crazy, maybe strap him to the bed one day and take total control of him.

I lick his nipple, and his free hand immediately twists through my hair. It's not painful, but it lets me know he's in charge. He always will be. I fucking love it.

And as he presses my face closer to his chest, I give him what he wants. I sink my teeth into his pec, and my cock throbs at the hoarse gasp he lets out.

"Yes," he pants. "Yeah, Brando. Like that."

I grip the other nipple and pinch it as tight as I can, loving the sounds it draws out of him. When I pull back, I find my teeth have left a purplish-red splotchy bruise behind. "You're going to feel that tomorrow."

"Good. I need more." He's riding me hard, gaze hooded and unfocused, giving me the Robbie I go wild over.

We flip around so I can drive into him, and then he rolls us again so he's back on top. I lie back and watch the way his big body works over me, that giant cock of his so hard it's bobbing between us. It draws my attention like nothing else, focuses me. I lick my lips at the sight of the shiny head, and I think … I think I can maybe reach it.

I lift my torso, duck my head, and … my lips close around the tip.

"Holy goddamn fucking shit," Robbie gasps. Both hands close in my hair this time, and he thrusts into my mouth and back onto my cock. Curses are tumbling from his mouth, and feeling him let go like this ramps up the tingling racing along my spine.

My cock is drawing tight, my balls pulling up close to my body, and I'm so close. So dangerously close to the edge, if he doesn't come soon, it's going to be all over.

So I bring in the big guns.

And slide my teeth along his staff.

Robbie cries out, and a spurt of cum hits my mouth. His cock throbs as he shoots, over and over, and when he's done, I pull off, flip us again, and pound into his ass. My eyes are locked where our bodies are joined as I chase the high, and I swear I'm holding my breath because I'm so … fucking … close …

My orgasm hits in a wave of immediate release, and I fuck him through it, milking my balls for all they have.

When I collapse against him, I'm struggling to catch my breath. My lungs are burning with the need to cough.

"You okay?" he asks.

I pat my head as I cough, but before I can move, Robbie rolls me off him, grabs my inhaler from my desk, and hands it to me.

I take a long hit, and when I release my breath again, I smile. He smiles back.

"You didn't panic that time."

He pulls me close. "What good will I be to you if I panic every time you have a little coughing fit?"

I tuck my face into his neck. "You're finally getting it."

"Yep." He slaps my ass. "Now I've taken care of you, you can take care of me. Get me something to clean up with, would you?"

"But I don't want to move," I complain.

"Fair enough." Then he pulls my leg between his and rubs his lube-covered ass over it.

"Hey!" I slap him. "Gross, dude."

He laughs. "What, so I can be covered in it, but when I share it's gross?"

Urg. Okay. He has a point. "Fine, I'll get the damn wipes."

33

ROBBIE

THE DAYS AFTER MY OTT DISPLAY PASS IN A BLUR OF Harmony Week celebrations. No one gives Brandon and me shit, no one comments or says anything. We get a few joking comments about getting a room, but otherwise, everything is the same as it's ever been.

But a thousand times better because I get to do it all with him.

We might have lost King of Thieves to those Kappas, but there's no way I'm losing Master of Mayhem to Chad. Sure, he's the prank go-to around here, but after being distracted by Bailey for the last few months, my chances are good.

I'm getting ready to head down for the vote when my phone lights up on my desk. I grin at the name and answer.

"*Marshmallow.*"

"Robert. How the fuck didn't you tell me you're with Brandon?"

I frown. "Ah … what?"

"You're all over social media. I don't think I've ever been more embarrassed for you."

What the shit is he talking about? "Huh. Someone filmed it."

"No need to sound so smug."

"Well, you're all the way across the country. How did you see it?"

"Are you kidding? I'm surprised you haven't. It's all anyone at school is talking about."

I'd be lying if I said I didn't puff up at that. "Guess I should probably tell Mom and Dad I'm bi, then, huh?"

"Or just show up home with Brandon like it's no big deal. Only, if you go that option, I want to be there to see the family's reaction."

Now there's an idea. "Deal."

"You know, I'm sort of hurt you didn't tell me."

My amusement drains away. "I'm sorry. Really. Shit's been crazy here, not that it's any excuse."

"It's not." He hums. "But I'm happy for you anyway."

"I *do* have a secret I can tell you that no one else knows."

"Oh, yeah?"

"I'm going to marry him one day."

"*What?*"

"I already know." I shrug even though he can't see me. "I'd propose to him now if we wouldn't have to deal with everyone thinking we're batshit crazy."

He makes a choking noise. "You're serious."

"Yup."

"Wow. Well … in that case, I can't wait to meet my future brother-in-law."

"Argh." I shake out the happiness that thought floods me with. "I'll drag him back there with me this summer."

"See you then. Love you."

"Right back at you."

We hang up, a mix of excitement and contentment flooding me. I almost want to search and see if I can find this video, but I'm already running late to meet my brothers, so I fire off a text to Brandon about it—only gloating a little bit—and head down to the war room.

Only, when I walk in, everyone is already there, and applause breaks out.

I bow because why not? But I have no damn clue what's going on.

"We got here half an hour early," Chad says. "The vote was unanimous."

"Wait, what?" I look from one brother to the next, waiting for one of them to point out that they're joking. "Unanimous, but …"

"I voted for you too," Chad says like it's no big deal.

"*Why?*"

Zeke taps something on his laptop, bringing the projector screen alive, and there I am, singing my heart out and dancing like an idiot.

"Yeah, I'm going to need the link to that," I say.

"Why?" Zeke asks. "You guys going to fuck while you watch yourself on-screen?"

"How narcissistic do you think I am?"

No one answers, not even my own boyfriend.

I point at him. "Tell them you're on my side."

"Look, I would, but I'm worried that's exactly where you were going with this."

My gaze strays back to the screen. "I do look *really* good."

Zeke hurries to close his laptop again as Chad bursts with laughter.

"Let's do this before Robbie gets his dick out."

Probably a fair call.

I stand at the front of the room while Zeke wraps the sacred Sigma cape around my shoulders. It's dark red with a fur trim, and every Master of Mayhem before me has signed it. Zeke brings me the book, and next to the year, I write my name, and then, because I'm a top-notch, totally mature human being, I draw a heart and Brando's name after it.

Zeke smirks and pats me on the back. "You good now?"

"Almost."

I walk over to Brandon, and like I'm claiming a prize, I pull him into my arms and kiss him.

His eyes have darkened when he pulls back and runs his hands over the trim on the cape. "Think you can bring this to bed?"

"Damn straight."

The others groan, and I shoot a quick wink at Brando before turning to Zeke.

"But I'm gonna need that link first."

EPILOGUE

BRANDON

Ten Years Later

A DECADE LATER, AND IT FEELS LIKE NOTHING HAS CHANGED. Robbie and Chad are smack talking, and Bailey is stuck to Chad's side.

The reunion is full of familiar faces and some not-so-familiar ones, and being back here on campus makes me grateful for everything I went through in college … and thankful we never have to go through that again.

Even if Robbie will never outgrow his Master of Mayhem title. But now, instead of frat brothers to wreak havoc with, he's got our five- and two-year-olds for backup. I'll never tell him, but seeing the three of them plot against me might be the most adorable thing I've ever witnessed.

But trying to convince the three of them that we need to eat actual people-sized food is a losing battle.

"Hey, sexy butt."

I yelp as my feet leave the floor and Robbie lifts me for a kiss. "You could have just bent down, idiot. You'll throw your back out again."

"I didn't throw it out the other time. I just … *pulled* something."

"Which is why you made me rub Icy Hot into your ass for a week."

His evil grin gives him away.

"You were *faking* it?"

"No. Well, not at first. But what did you expect me to do?" He pouts. "You were taking care of me."

I roll my eyes, and he sets me back on my feet. "Is Chad coming?"

"As soon as he sneaks away from Bailey."

We turn to look at where the two of them are dancing. And sure, it's sweet and whatever, but we're planning to TP the Kappa house for old times, and I'm sure as hell not missing out on that.

It's not until an hour later that Chad sneaks away, and Robbie waves Zeke over.

"Ready, fuckers?" Robbie asks.

I whack his head, and he knocks me into Chad.

"Come on," Chad says. "Before I get into trouble."

We rib him the whole way to our car to grab the stashed rolls of toilet paper, Zeke watching us like the proud dad he's always been.

"Admit it," I say, nudging him. "You love us."

He slings an arm around my shoulders. "I do. Sometimes I

wonder if I should have taken it easier in college. Had more fun like you idiots."

Chad snorts. "No one has fun like we do."

"I dunno," Robbie says, rubbing his chin. "Brando and I definitely get our fair share of fun in."

Of course he went there.

"Even with the kids?" Zeke asks.

"Early bedtime."

He hums, and something in it catches my attention. Out of all of us, he's the only one not married.

"You thinking of kids?"

"Maybe one. My career is starting to slow down. Seems like a good next step."

"Wow. Happy for you." And apparently, now Chad is the only one out of us not interested in kids. Selfishly, I'm glad. He and Bailey are amazing uncles to our two. Well, except for the time Bailey introduced Chad to the term *guncle* and Chad tried to make us call him *buncle*.

I shudder at the memory.

"So you guys are settling down, then?" I ask Zeke.

"We'll see." He smirks. "Not like you two, but definitely less travel."

I'd pretend to be offended, but I'm living the life I always planned to. Robbie falls back into step with me, and I let go of Zeke to snuggle into his side. He had an amazing career starting as a political advisor, and he gave it all up to stay home with our kids. We have our little property in Kilborough, I'm running my own business through Hartford and spend half the week in the office and the other half at home, and I can honestly say I've never been happier.

I used to worry Robbie would get bored of the quiet life,

but while he might not be employed, he's always busy. Either updating the house, or learning about irrigation systems, or tending to the vegetable garden, he's always got some project on the go. Plus, he has his own little dad group on the street, and seeing them together throws me back to our frat days in a way that's scary.

Zeke and Chad pull ahead of us, and I grin up at my husband. "Love you."

"I mean, you say that." He waves a hand as we turn onto Greek Row. "But yet you still haven't done a musical number for me."

"And I never will," I promise him.

"Well, you're lucky I love you too, faults and all."

And when we reach Kappa house and look down to where Sigma house is sitting at the opposite corner, he squeezes me tighter.

"You miss it?" I ask.

"Yeah. And no."

"No?"

"Well, I lived for those days, for the brotherhood, but … that isn't a home." He nods to Zeke and Chad. "It's us. Right here. And we've never lost that."

He's right. No matter how busy we've gotten or where in the world we are, the four of us have never lost touch. Instead, our friendship circles have grown. Robbie and I have thrived. And all of us are living our best lives.

"With any luck," I say, "we never will."

THANKS FOR READING FRAT WARS: MASTER OF MAYHEM!

To keep up to date with future releases, come join Saxon's Sweethearts.

www.facebook.com/groups/saxonssweethearts/

Or read on to find out which frat guys are coming next!

MY FREEBIES

Do you love friends to lovers?
Second chances or fake relationships?
I have two bonus freebies available!

Friends with Benefits
Total Fabrication

This short story is only available to my reader list so click
below and join the gang!
https://www.subscribepage.com/saxonjames

OTHER BOOKS BY SAXON JAMES

FRAT WARS SERIES:

Frat Wars: King of Thieves

Frat Wars: Master of Mayhem

Frat Wars: Presidential Chaos

DIVORCED MEN'S CLUB SERIES:

Roommate Arrangement

Platonic Rulebook

NEVER JUST FRIENDS SERIES:

Just Friends

Fake Friends

Getting Friendly

Friendly Fire

Bonus Short: Friends with Benefits

LOVE'S A GAMBLE SERIES:

Good Times & Tan Lines

Bet on Me

Calling Your Bluff

CU HOCKEY SERIES WITH EDEN FINLEY:

Power Plays & Straight A's

Face Offs & Cheap Shots

Goal Lines & First Times

Line Mates & Study Dates

Puck Drills & Quick Thrills

PUCKBOYS SERIES WITH EDEN FINLEY:

Egotistical Puckboy

Irresponsible Puckboy

And if you're after something a little sweeter, don't forget my YA pen name

S. M. James.

These books are chock full of adorable, flawed characters with big hearts.

https://geni.us/smjames

WANT MORE FROM ME?

Follow Saxon James on any of the platforms below.
www.saxonjamesauthor.com
www.facebook.com/thesaxonjames/
www.amazon.com/Saxon-James/e/B082TP7BR7
www.bookbub.com/profile/saxon-james
www.instagram.com/saxonjameswrites/

ACKNOWLEDGMENTS

As with any book, this one took a hell of a lot of people to make happen.

First, my cover designer Story Styling Cover Designs did a fantastic job on making this smoking hot cover.

Thanks to Sandra at One Love Editing for my amazing edits.

Lori Parks, you were a gem as always with my proof read and I always appreciate how timely you are with your work.

Thanks to my wonderful PA, Charity VanHuss for wrangling my scattered self on a daily basis.

Eden Finley, your notes and ongoing commentary were fucking incredible, and thank you for letting me pick your brain while talking absolute smack at each other. You're the bestest bestie I could ever ask for. Also, thank you for letting me borrow Chet when I needed him.

All of my fantastic beta readers, thank you so much for taking the time to read. Your support is incredible and I really appreciate it!

And of course, thanks to my fam bam. To my husband who constantly frees up time for me to write, and to my kids whose neediness reminds me the real word exists.

CPSIA information can be obtained
at www.ICGtesting.com
Printed in the USA
LVHW041332160322
713506LV00006B/440

9 781922 741035